THE THREEFOLD CORD

THE DARK HARVEST TRILOGY

The Dark Faith
The Scarlet Bishop
The Threefold Cord

THE THREEFOLD CORD

JEREMIAH W. MONTGOMERY

P&R
PUBLISHING
P.O. BOX 817 • PHILLIPSBURG • NEW JERSEY 08865-0817

ISBN: 978-1-59638-189-6 (pbk)
ISBN: 978-1-62995-131-7 (ePub)
ISBN: 978-1-62995-132-4 (Mobi)

Printed in the United States of America

Library of Congress Control Number: 2014937876

To Elizabeth, Rhiannon, and Sherry

And if one prevail against him,
Two will withstand him;
And a threefold cord is not quickly torn.
(Ecclesiastes 4:12)

CONTENTS

N
Grenmaur
GRENDANNATH
URRAS
Dunross
NORNINDAAL
Grindangled
Teru Bridge
LOTHAIR
Deasmor
Toberstan
TRATHARAN
TYN
Marfesbury
Noppenham
Laucura
Ring of Stars
MERSEX
DYFANN
Hoccaster
Mereclestour
Banr Cluidan
Narrow Channel
Naud
CAELDORA
Versaden
Dericus
Agnorum
Lorudin
Aevor
Tumulan
Hills

PART I

KINDLED FLAMES

PROLOGUE

It is a rule worth remembering as long as one lives: syncretism is worse than sorcery, the blending of faiths far deadlier than any witch's brew. The crooked heart will always rail against exclusive claims; the twisted spirit ever strives to unmake the truth of Holy Writ. The enemy incessantly calls man to be his own god, to make his own heaven, to pick his own piety. These whispered urgings are a serpent's promise. For doubt it not: there yet lives a dragon more frightening than most can imagine, and the passage of ages has not sated his ancient craving—to devour both reason and revelation.

It was the morning after the Feast of the Sacred Tree, and sunlight turned scarlet as it streamed through the red glass of the nave's high windows. It permeated the dark interior with ruddy iridescence and soaked the floor of the sanctuary with long, bloody stains. No flames flickered in the tree-shaped candelabras flanking the altar, and no lamps burned in the sconces dangling on chains from the ceiling. No worshipers knelt before the image that overshadowed the apse: a great carving of the Mother tree cradling a baby in two of its lower boughs, while two other boughs made the sign of the cross over the crèche.

The Feast was over.

Yet in the bishop's study above the apse, all was far from finished. Here sunlight fell unadulterated through clear, leaded windows. On the chamber's far wall, a small fire smiled from its neat hearth at the burgeoning daylight. In the space between these greater and lesser lights, two figures faced each other across a table. Both felt plenty of heat—but neither smiled.

"It is all here, Somnadh." The woman stabbed a finger at the volume lying open on the table. "Every filthy article of faith, every murderous ritual." Urien riffled through its leaves. "Every last odious cantillation." She stopped turning pages and stepped back. "It's all right here."

Somnadh turned the Bone Codex so that it faced him. For a moment he looked down, running a long finger over the open pages. Then his gaze lifted to Urien. "You got this book from the monk?"

"From Morumus, yes."

Somnadh flinched at the name. "Where would an Aesusian monk get such a book?"

"What does it matter to you?"

"Very little, I confess. But perhaps he did not tell you? I'm not surprised. Ignorance makes manipulation easier."

Urien bristled. "You wouldn't know anything about that, would you, Somnadh? Or should I call you *Simnor*? Or maybe *Archbishop*?" She gestured at his fine Mersian vestments. "Morumus is nothing like you."

"Then where did he get the book?"

Urien hesitated. Morumus had told her all about how he had first found the Bone Codex in Bishop Anathadus's library, and how Oethur escaped with it on the night the red monks murdered the bishop. He even told her how Anathadus found it in the great library at Tayaturim while Umaddians still ruled Hispona. But none of that was important now.

"Where he got the book is not the issue, brother. What matters is what it says."

Somnadh's all-black eyes bore into her. "And what do you think it says, sister?"

Here at last they had come to it: the reason for Urien's flight from Urras Monastery, the purpose in her pursuit of Somnadh across leagues of land and sea. Everything that had driven her journey from Marfesbury through Cyrdol, up to the very steps of the altar here in Banr Cluidan, came down to this.

Here they were at last. Urien met her brother's gaze without flinching and took a deep breath. "It says that the faith of our ancestors is evil, Somnadh."

"Evil, Urien?"

"Yes, evil! The Old Faith is nothing but a detailed scheme of lies and depredation—a perverse system of *inhuman* devotion to a *subhuman* idol!" Urien's eyes burned as she unleashed her torrent. "It is nothing but an elaborate justification for the strong to butcher the weak! And for what? For what, Somnadh!? An illusory power that terrifies many but saves none!"

A lump rose in her throat. This was her history: shadow, slaughter, and terror. But she was not finished. "It says that both of us—you and I, Somnadh!—have devoted our lives to darkness. What we have practiced is not the 'Old Faith,' but the Dark Faith."

A heaving sob interrupted the flow of her words, and Somnadh raised a hand to cut her off. But, seeing his gesture, Urien growled with such ferocity that he took a step back.

"But worst of all, brother," she forced the words out, stabbing her finger like a pike thrust at his chest, "worst of all, it says that you knew. Father did not know, and I did what I was told. But you were different, Somnadh! You weren't led into the lies. You embraced the darkness with open eyes—every vile, murderous bit!"

For a long moment after she finished, Somnadh said nothing. Then he stepped back to the table, put a trembling hand to the Bone Codex, and slammed it shut. His fingers lingered on the leather cover until they steadied.

"This is not a book for any but the Mordruui," he said at last.

Urien was surprised at the calm tone, but when he looked up she saw fire behind the void of his eyes.

"Not even for the Mother's Heart." He scooped up the book, carried it to the hearth, and tossed it into the flames.

Urien made no move to stop him. What need was there? "I'm the Mother's Heart no longer, Somnadh. And you can burn the book. But you cannot deny what it says."

"I do not deny the *facts*, sister. What I dispute is your *interpretation.*" His eyes showed something almost like pity. "I am convinced now of what I suspected before: that this monk has poisoned your mind. Your words reek with the most narrow-minded Aesusian invective: *Lies! Depredations! Subhuman idol!* You have always been too dramatic for your own good, Urien, but this is beyond you. *Dark Faith!* Really? Do you hear yourself? This isn't you, dear one—not the real you. You have been infected with Aesusian lies. That is why you burned the Mother's seedling. And that is why the Mother will receive you back."

Urien gaped. She had not thought it possible that anything could make her angrier than the contents of the Bone Codex. After unleashing her accusation, she felt certain that her anger had been spent. But as she stood here now, drinking in the full measure of her brother's condescension, she felt the flames within leap back to full strength—and beyond.

"Don't you 'dear one' me, Somnadh!" She forced the words through clenched teeth, her voice rising. "Don't you *dare* call me that!" Urien was seeing red now. "Do you want to know who forced me to burn the Mother's seedling? Nobody! *I* caught Morumus and his friend prowling around the Muthadannach, and *I* led them to the Mother! *I* threw my lamp at the Mother's roots! *They* did not lift a finger! *I* did it! *Me*, Somnadh! And do you know what? I'm *glad* I did it! I renounced the Mother then, and I renounce her again! She is no powerful goddess, just an *impersonal*, *impotent*, *unthinking* tree!"

Urien was screaming now, but she did not care. "And as for *Aesusian lies*, you are wrong again! I am *no* Aesusian, Somnadh—though I wish I could be! It is a far better faith!"

What Somnadh did next surprised Urien even more than his horrible words . . .

He struck her.

It was a hard blow, and she hit the floor almost before she knew what had happened. Pain blossomed on the side of her face, and dark spots replaced the red in her vision. But worse than the physical impact was the emotional shock.

He hurt me—my own brother!

Looking up, she saw Somnadh standing over her, his chest heaving. "How dare you speak thus?" he snarled. "How dare you?"

"You *hit* me," she sobbed, the words sounding incredible to her ears. "You *hurt* me, Somnadh!"

But if there was any remorse or pity left in those black pits from which her brother looked out on the world, Urien did not see it.

"And what about the hurt you would cause our Father, Urien?" he raged. "In his old age, as he lies moldering in his bed, what would Father say if he heard your words? To this day, I have concealed from him your treachery to the Mother. Must I tell him now that his beloved daughter has renounced the faith of our ancestors?"

Somnadh's thin attempt to justify his actions only provoked Urien further. She pushed herself up and glowered at him. "I will tell him myself!"

"You will do no such thing!"

"Oh, I will, brother. And I will tell him that his son is a coward—a coward who struck his own sister, and then tried to blame her for it!"

Somnadh's face took on the ugliest expression Urien had ever seen, but whatever he was going to say—or do—next was interrupted by a sudden knock at the door.

"Your Grace?" The muffled, Vilguran call came through the heavy door.

Somnadh's face changed even as his hands smoothed his vestments, and he turned away from Urien toward the door. "Come!"

The door swung inward to admit a catechumen. He wore the scarlet robe of the Red Order, but his cowl was down and his head shaved. He touched his forehead to Somnadh, then bowed.

"What is it, my son?"

"Your Grace, Duke Stonoric sends his compliments and requests an audience at your earliest convenience . . ." He noticed Urien, then averted his eyes as he realized she was not a monk. Looking back to Somnadh, he hesitated. "Shall I tell him you are . . . *indisposed*, Your Grace?"

"By no means," said Somnadh in a firm tone. "Tell the Duke that Archbishop Simnor sends his compliments, and will be pleased to come to him presently."

When the servant had gone, Somnadh turned back to Urien. "You will come to see your error, sister. The Mother has guaranteed it."

"It is you who are in error, brother. The Mother is just a tree. Trees do not speak."

Somnadh raised his hand again, but then shook his head. "No. No, you will see for yourself. Llanubys promised that you would."

"Llanubys?" Urien had never heard the name before, but it sent an inexplicable shiver down her spine. "Who is Llanubys?"

"Llanubys, sister, is the Heart of Genna and Keeper of the Last Secret. For years untold she had tended the Mother. Unlike you, she has never found her service too burdensome." Somnadh sighed. "But only the Mother lives forever, and very soon even Llanubys must return to her."

"So she's dying?" Urien shook her head. Her suspicion turned to pity. Only too well could she imagine a whole lifetime of serving the Mother. "I am sorry for her."

For the first time that morning, Somnadh smiled.

It made Urien's skin crawl.

"No, dear one. One Llanubys may pass, but another will take her place. *You* will take her place, Urien. Llanubys is the past and the present—and she is *your* future."

In all his life, Oethur had never felt such joy as he did this evening.

Just a few hours earlier, he had stood alone at the front of Dunross Great Kirk, his shoulders heavy with the weight of his future. He had survived the destruction and pillage of Lorudin Abbey. He had escaped torture and execution at the hands of the Red Order. Finally, he had denounced his brother as a heathen, a murderer, and a usurper. With the backing of the kingdom of Lothair, he had claimed the crown of Nornindaal for his own.

But steel was thicker than parchment. Oethur knew that swords would ring and blood would flow before the future of Nornindaal was secure. And there was no guarantee that it would be secured for him. His brother Aeldred was a cunning foe, and he had allies, armies, and a castle of his own.

Oethur had realized then just how tenuous the situation truly was.

But then the doors at the back of the Great Kirk had swung open, and he saw . . . *her.*

Princess Rhianwyn.

Resplendent as a ray of celestial light, the princess had caught his eye down the long distance of the nave. And then she had smiled.

Rhianwyn knew the precarious position of their cause. She was the only daughter of King Heclaid of Lothair. Though she was delicate, she was not frail. She understood as well as any that by cancelling her engagement to Aeldred and marrying Oethur, she had signed her own death warrant if their cause should fail. Yet as her father escorted her down the aisle, neither eye nor smile wavered from Oethur.

Rhianwyn.

He had loved her for a long time. But all the while she was engaged to his elder brothers—first Alfered and then Aeldred—and so Oethur had never dared allow himself to see her as more than a sister.

All that had changed now.

The remainder of the wedding ceremony had passed like a dream. It *was* a dream in which he was conscious of participating, but like a dream it seemed to pass with preternatural speed. Before he knew it, he was awake again.

Happily, though, Rhianwyn was no dream. She had not vanished when Bishop Ciolbail concluded the service. Instead her smile had only grown wider, and the warmth of her hands in his filled him with new life and resolve.

Against every hope of a long-guarded heart, Rhianwyn was now his wife.

His brother might have powerful allies and a strong position. But Oethur had more.

Queen Rhianwyn.

He had a bride to protect. He had a cause to vindicate. He had a kingdom to win.

Aesus help me, I will do it!

That was his determination as he escorted Rhianwyn from the Great Kirk. That was his pledge as they stepped out of the church to meet the waiting cheers of Dunross.

Now, as he stood at the center of the high table, Oethur silently repeated the prayer before speaking aloud. "My lords and ladies," he began in a voice calculated to rise above the festive din filling the great hall. "Friends and guests, may I have your attention!"

The effect was more or less immediate, if not quite complete. Though the evening was young, already eager servants had ensured that the guests were well supplied with food and well plied with wine. Even at the high table, several of the attendants seemed to waver on the border between a gladdened heart and outright dissipation. In particular, the Lady Isowene—one of his wife's attendants—seemed quite beyond it. Her expression was glazed, her laughs careless, and she seemed quite oblivious to his call for attention.

As he stood from his chair, she continued chatting in Rhianwyn's ear.

Oethur gave Rhianwyn an imploring look, and his bride turned to hush her friend.

"My lords and ladies," he began anew, turning back to his guests. "It is time for the First Toast. If you will fill your glasses, please—the royal goblets will be brought!"

There was a flurry of livery and silver as servants scurried to fill every glass in the hall. A moment later, a servant girl carried a gold tray toward the high table. On the tray were two large, ornate goblets.

The royal goblets were as traditional as the First Toast itself. Cast in gold and carved with the symbol of the Threefold Cord, the ancient vessels had been used at royal weddings in Dunross since the days of Lothair the Wise. According to tradition, Oethur and Rhianwyn would each take a goblet. Oethur would praise his bride to the assembled guests, and then offer her the first drink from his goblet. She would then return the courtesy.

As the tray approached, all the guests stood—including those at the high table. The servant girl's eyes glittered as she proffered the goblets to the beaming bride and groom. Oethur reached for his goblet—

—but it was snatched away!

More than one guest gasped as Isowene grabbed the king's goblet and held it aloft before the assembled guests.

"To the new king and queen!" she declaimed in a loud, slurring voice. She gave both Oethur and Rhianwyn a disheveled smile and lifted the goblet to her lips.

"No!" hissed the servant girl.

But it was too late.

Isowene drained the glass in a single gulp.

The entire hall fell silent. Festivity notwithstanding, the breach of protocol was appalling. Rhianwyn gaped. Oethur just stared.

But almost immediately, he saw that something was wrong.

For several long moments, Isowene seemed frozen in place—unnaturally transfixed, with her head tossed back and the goblet tipped to her mouth. Then her face twitched, a shudder convulsed her body, and the goblet fell.

Its clattering echo vanished in the wake of her scream.

Isowene's shriek pierced the silence of the hall, sending panic into most of the ladies and not a few of the men. The cords of her neck stood out with taut rigidity, and she clawed at her throat with a desperate ferocity—leaving rivulets of scarlet streaming down her pale skin. She bent over double, then jerked back upright as her back arched and stuck. Her eyes rolled back into her skull, her face turned blue, and she frothed at the mouth. Then, with terrible suddenness, it was over.

Her screaming stopped, and Isowene collapsed into Rhianwyn's arms.

Oethur kneeled beside his wife and put a hand to her friend's neck.

Dead.

Though he was as stunned as anybody in the hall, Oethur's mind had never stopped working. Even before Isowene collapsed, he knew what had killed her.

Poison.

As all other eyes remained on the fallen lady, Oethur's went to the servant girl who had carried the tray. His glance confirmed his instinct.

There was emotion in the girl's face, but it was not shock or surprise.

It was anger.

"You there, girl!" He rose to his feet. "Stay where you are!"

The girl's eyes turned toward him, and there was such malevolence in her expression that Oethur paused in mid-step.

"Who are you?"

"*Muthadis!*" she hissed. She flung the heavy tray at him edge-on, then turned and fled.

Morumus and King Heclaid had been conversing on the balcony outside the hall when the sudden scream shattered the evening air.

"What was that?" Morumus stared at the king. But both he and Heclaid knew full well what they heard.

Without another word, both turned and raced back into the hall . . .

. . . just in time to see a lady collapse near the center of the high table!

"Rhianwyn!" shouted Heclaid, terror rising in his tone. He shoved into the panicking guests like a crazed bear fighting toward its cub.

At the same moment, Morumus heard Oethur shouting. He saw a golden tray flying at his friend, and watched as a servant girl fled toward the entrance of the hall. Without a second thought, he veered away from the churning mass of guests at the center of the hall to the empty space behind its flanking colonnades. He could see the servant girl holding up her long skirts as she sprinted toward the far doors.

"Oethur!" he shouted as he gave chase, "I'll catch the girl! See to the queen!"

But the servant—whoever she was—had no intention of being caught. She reached the doors several seconds before he did, and by the time he crossed their threshold she was almost to the stairs at the far end of the corridor. Several servants stood in that corridor, looking alarmed and confused.

"There's been an attack on the queen!" Morumus shouted at them as he ran past, not daring to pause in his pursuit. "Call for guards, and send them after me!"

A moment later he hit the stairs at full tilt and clutched the hem of his robe to avoid tripping as he ran up the winding flight. He could hear the girl's steps above him, and he growled.

She's outpacing me!

Praying for strength, he forced his feet to move faster. He could not sustain such a pace for long, but he dared not let the servant escape.

As he ran, his mind turned over the sudden events. He did not know exactly what had happened in the hall, but even the limited sounds and sights told him all he needed to know at present. This servant had attacked the queen. Whether Rhianwyn survived or not he could not tell . . .

Lord Aesus, let her live!

Morumus could not bear to think what Rhianwyn's death would do to his friend. Oethur was strong as oak, but some storms might fell even the sternest timber.

Morumus's mind churned almost as fast as his burning legs as he pounded up the steps.

The servant must have acted at the behest of a patron.

Mersian? Nornish? Does it make a difference?

He shook his head.

No. What's important is whether she has associates here in Dunross.

There was only one way to find out.

Oh God, help me catch this girl!

Morumus tumbled out of the stairs into a corridor running the length of the upper level of Dunross Castle. The servant girl had made it halfway to the far end when she paused. At first, Morumus could not tell why she had stopped. Then he saw what she had already heard.

A tall figure crested the stairs at the corridor's far end. In his hand he bore a heavy saber. He had fair hair and wore a festal garment, but even from this distance Morumus could see wrath in his expression.

Oethur!

The Norn saw him at the same instant, but directed his words at the girl.

"You are trapped, girl! Surrender to us now, and you will receive a merciful death. Resist, and you will drink the same cup you gave the Lady Isowene!"

Lady Isowene.

The name did not register with Morumus except by negation.

Lady Isowene—not Queen Rhianwyn. God be praised.

It seemed a strange thing to praise the Almighty for sparing one in place of another. Was such a prayer even appropriate? But Morumus did not have long to dwell upon the question, for in the next instant, the servant girl wheeled toward him.

In her hand appeared a knife. It had a long, wide blade that curved back at the tip. Morumus became suddenly conscious of the fact that he bore no weapon.

"Morumus!"

"I see it!"

"Let her pass! There are guards on the lower level."

"We cannot take the chance." But what would he do to stop her?

With Oethur approaching from behind, the girl took half a dozen steps toward Morumus. The blade of her knife reflected torchlight like a dull, cruel fang.

Torchlight! The torches!

"Do not risk yourself," Oethur insisted. "She will not escape!"

"Let's make certain." Morumus took a torch from the wall sconce next to him and brandished it before him. How much defense would it provide?

Seeing the torch, the servant hissed, pulled back her knife as if she were about to lunge . . .

. . . then turned sideways, yanked open a small door, and vanished!

Morumus reached the door before Oethur and saw that it opened onto a much narrower servant's corridor. A dozen paces ahead of him, their quarry was shoving at side doors, trying to force entry. But none of them would budge.

Seeing Morumus, she gave up on the attempt and resumed her heedless flight. The servant's passage ended at another door, through which the three of them spilled in quick succession. The chase continued down a second passage, up another flight of steps, and then down a third corridor. This last hallway had only one exit.

Always several steps ahead, the girl reached the doors at its end well before her pursuers. As she flung them open, Morumus caught the smell of fresh air and feared she would escape. But he need not have worried.

The doors opened onto a high, open balcony.

Morumus and Oethur stepped through the doors side by side. The cornered assassin, seeing her only hope of escape blocked, backed away from them until she stood against the stone rail.

"It's over, girl." Oethur leveled his saber at her chest. Morumus had never heard such authority—or doom—in his voice.

"My name is Muthadis," she spat, her eyes defiant as she raised her knife. "Come and kill me, if you can."

Oethur looked ready to oblige, but Morumus put a hand on his arm.

"Wait. We need to know who sent her."

Morumus took a step toward the girl. "Your name—Muthadis—it means 'Mother's Maiden' in Dyfanni. But your accent is northern. For whom are you working?"

Muthadis glared at him. "I serve the Mother."

Morumus looked at Muthadis. He could see that she was young.

Has she had seen even a score of years?

And yet here she was, about to sacrifice her life . . . for what?

"The Mother does not order assassinations. She is just a tree." He took another step toward her. "Don't die in the service of an idol. Put down the knife. Cooperate with us, and we will give you a chance to repent. There is more at stake here than your life in this world."

The words seemed to have some effect. The tension in Muthadis slackened. For a moment she lowered both her eyes and the knife.

"You will promise?"

"We will." Morumus turned toward Oethur. "Won't we, sire—"

"Morumus, watch out!" Oethur raised his sword and lunged forward.

Morumus turned just in time to see Muthadis's face jerk up.

"I do not want your promises!" Her eyes were wide and her face twisted with hatred. "Nor do I wish to repent!" With the suddenness of an uncoiling serpent, she sprang at him.

Morumus saw the knife flash in the sunset and knew he was too close. There was no way he could avoid its keen edge . . .

But just when he was sure the blade must slice open his throat, Oethur's saber blade struck downward.

The curved knife fell to the balcony stones—still clutched in a pale hand.

Muthadis howled, blood spurting from the severed stump of her wrist.

But the failed assassin was not finished yet. With the fluid nimbleness of a cat, she pounced at her severed hand, retrieved the knife with her remaining hand, and sliced at Oethur's outstretched arm.

Oethur tried to pull back, but he was not fast enough. His blade had stuck in the balcony stones, and the instant required to pull it free was all Muthadis required. Her knife sliced into the meat of his forearm.

A look of feral glee sprouted on the girl's face. "You will never be king now!"

Oethur gasped, but now he had his saber free again. This time he swung it straight at her middle.

Muthadis saw his stroke and jumped back—too far.

Morumus saw her legs hit the balcony rail, saw her momentum carry her balance over the edge. For a moment, the girl seemed suspended in midair as she flailed her arms.

"No!" Morumus dove toward her.

He reached the rail just in time to watch her fall.

And to see her smile up at him.

"Aeldred has triumphed!" she shrieked, mere moments before she slammed into the courtyard below. "The knife was poisoned!"

Satticus frowned as he walked through the corridors of Malduorn's Keep.

For a long time he had enjoyed his role as private secretary to Prince Aeldred. These days, he was worried.

For many years Satticus had played the eager assistant in his master's underhanded rise to power. He facilitated the meeting at which Aeldred pledged his soul to the Mother. He penned the correspondence coordinating the joint murders in Lothair and Nornindaal. The hoped-for war had not materialized, yet both Raudorn of Lothair and Alfered of Nornindaal—Aeldred's own elder brother—had died.

Another obstacle to power cleared.

Satticus took a special pleasure in assassinations. Any man could stick another with a sword in open battle. Success there was a simple matter of brute strength and raw luck. But to strike with cunning and surprise required keen foresight and careful preparation.

In the last two years, he had arranged three assassinations at the behest of his prince. The first had been the double murder of Luca Wolfbane, the late king of Mersex, and his brother Deorcad—the last archbishop of Mereclestour.

Not within our borders, but to our advantage.

The murders had been necessary to clear the way for the accession of Somnadh. Satticus smiled. *The very Hand of the Mother, now Archbishop of Mereclestour!*

The murders had also brought about Wodic's succession to the throne of Mersex. But that thought made the private secretary frown. The second assassination attempt had failed.

The intent had never been to murder Wodic and Caileamach. That was all a ruse. The real target had been the Duke of Hoccaster—a close advisor to the Mersian king and a known skeptic of the merger with Dyfann. The hope of both Somnadh and Aeldred had been to eliminate Stonoric and implicate Lothair.

At least we succeeded in the latter . . .

Most recently, Satticus assisted his prince in the slow poisoning of his own father, the late King Ulfered. Here they had met unqualified success, and it seemed that at last they had scaled the final barrier to their triumph . . .

Then Oethur and the two bishops had escaped.

Satticus remembered his conversation with Aeldred on the evening that grim news had arrived. With surprising clairvoyance, the Crown Prince had predicted what would happen next: Oethur would denounce him, and the king of Lothair would cancel the arranged marriage between Aeldred and his daughter. Instead, Oethur would marry the Princess Rhianwyn.

At least, he would try.

But Aeldred had been prepared. He had an agent in Dunross. She would prevent his brother—or any other man—from marrying the princess.

Prince Aeldred had put great confidence in his agent, a young woman he referred to as Muthadis . . .

"She is very devoted, Satticus. She will not fail."

Today the private secretary had received word that his master's confidence had been misplaced.

Muthadis had failed.

At least she had the courtesy to die!

Details from Dunross were scant. The palace was keeping a tight lid on the alarming events and their aftermath. But one thing was certain. Princess Rhianwyn had married Oethur, *and* she had survived the attempt on her life.

Aeldred would be incensed.

The closer Satticus drew to the Prince Regent's chambers, the greater the number of liveried servants he saw passing in the opposite direction. All of them kept their heads down and their feet moving. None wanted to meet his eyes. Apparently his master was not having a good day.

He grimaced. *And I am about to make it worse.*

But how much worse? That was the question. Satticus had never been one to walk into an unknown situation.

Not if I can help it.

"You there!" he called to a footman. The young man, who had been doing his best to blend into the corridor's far wall, jumped at the secretary's address.

"Me, sir?" he asked, his eyes wide.

"Yes, you. Come here, boy!"

Every servant in Malduorn's Keep knew better than to cross the Prince Regent's private secretary. So it was no surprise that, though his face betrayed keen apprehension, the footman complied. His fellow servants, clearly grateful to be spared, hurried past, eyes averted.

"Sir?"

"Have you seen the Prince Regent today?"

"Yes, sir."

"Is he well?"

"Begging your pardon, sir." The young man licked his lips and looked away. "I don't think it's my place to say."

Satticus knew the footman was trying to show respect. Under normal circumstances, he might even reward such a response. But deference had its time and place, and right now what he needed was information.

"Listen, boy. I know the Prince Regent has been . . . unwell. What I want to know is how affected he is today. You don't have to pretend you have not noticed—"

"Private Secretary," said a clear voice close at hand. "Did I hear you asking after the Prince Regent's health?"

Satticus looked up. When he saw who addressed him, he dismissed the footman with a wave. "Doctor Lildas." He smiled. "Just the man I hoped to meet."

In truth, Satticus was never sure how he felt about meeting Lildas. The old physician, grey with age but still steady on his feet, had served the royal household for decades. An expert healer, the man was also a model of discretion. When King Ulfered lay dying, Lildas had somehow managed to ensure that the king's deteriorating condition remained a matter of strictest confidence among the household staff. That was no mean feat, and Satticus had never quite learned how he pulled it off. Nowadays the physician was maintaining a similar shroud of privacy concerning Aeldred's . . . discomfiture.

Nevertheless, Satticus couldn't bring himself fully to trust Lildas.

The private secretary's problem with the old man was not his discretion, but his integrity. Abstemious in habit and scrupulously honest, the physician appeared to have no weak spot—no seam in which to work a hook, no vice that could be exploited. Satticus had made inquiries, but the man appeared to be above corruption—to serve out of mere loyalty.

Satticus admired such integrity, but he also feared it. Men like Lildas could not be controlled, and this made Satticus nervous.

But for now, he smiled. The day might come when he would have to deal shrewdly with the good doctor. But today, the physician's honesty could serve to his advantage. "I am on my way to see the Prince Regent, doctor. Tell me, how is he?"

The grey face scowled, and the voice lowered. "He is not well today. Not well."

"What do you mean?"

"It's a strange condition." Lildas shook his head. "I can find no diminution of physical strength. As far as I can tell, there should be nothing wrong with the Prince Regent. Yet something is sapping his vitality. I know that certain present circumstances—of which you are better informed than I—have put him under a lot of stress. But I fear it may be more than this."

"Is he still having the nightmares?"

Lildas arched an eyebrow. "Has he spoken of them to you, then?"

"He has."

"Has he told you of their contents?"

"No," Satticus lied.

"Nor me, despite my several requests." The physician shook his head. "But I fear therein lies our culprit."

"Has he asked you to increase his sleeping draught?"

"As a matter of fact, he has." Lildas gave Satticus a penetrating look. "Was that your suggestion?"

Satticus saw no reason to hide the truth. "It was."

"I see."

"And how did you answer his Highness?"

"I told him that I am loath to do it. He is already taking a great deal—so much so that my considerable stores have depleted. However . . ." For a moment, the doctor looked away.

"However?" Satticus pressed.

The doctor looked back, and the private secretary resisted the urge to flinch under his sharp gaze.

"However, I fear there is no alternative. The prince is unwell in his spirit. He needs deep, unperturbed sleep. So I have agreed to increase the dose—for now."

"Very good." Satticus nodded. This was good news. "I must see the Prince Regent as soon as possible. Is he awake now?"

"Yes, but he is agitated. I hope your tidings will cheer him?"

"I am afraid not, doctor."

Lildas sighed. "Well then, I'm off to the apothecary's shop now."

With this, the two men parted and Satticus walked on.

Though he was now better informed, the private secretary's mood was unimproved.

As if all the external enemies were insufficient, a new threat had arisen—from within Prince Aeldred's unconscious mind. There was good reason why the Prince Regent dared not tell Lildas about the contents of his nightmares. Of late, Aeldred's sleep had become haunted by the ghosts of his past. The faces of those he had sent to their graves stalked him in his sleep: The red-haired Lothairin lord. His elder brother. The last Mersian king and the former Archbishop of Mereclestour. His own father. What did it all signify?

Was it burgeoning conscience or incipient madness?

And which—if either—could be more easily suppressed?

Whatever the cause, Satticus knew no good could come of it. The sooner Lildas could drown Aeldred's sleep in dreamless physic, the better.

But what if that did not work?

After all these years, he and Aeldred stood at the cusp of total victory. At long last, they finally drew near the summit of their treacherous climb. But everything might yet fail if Aeldred lost his mind.

Satticus had long since sold his soul to the oldest, most pagan god of all—power. Power was older even than Aeldred's Mother. Or maybe they were the same, as Aeldred ever insisted. Satticus did not care. He knew they were alike in at least one respect: just as Aeldred's tree flourished only on fresh blood, so his power survived only to the extent that Aeldred's sanity remained intact.

What would become of him if Aeldred fell?

It must not happen. I will not let it happen!

Satticus found the Prince Regent scowling at his dinner. "You look grieved, sire."

Aeldred looked up. His brown hair was drawn back taut to the nape of his neck, making more pronounced the thin lines of an increasingly gaunt face. Sleeplessness etched the Prince Regent's chiseled features, and there were dark patches under his grey eyes. Yet for all the apparent fatigue, Aeldred did not look tired.

He looked angry.

"Have you seen these?" he growled, picking up three sheets of parchment and shoving them toward his secretary.

Satticus scanned the documents.

"The Lords Aberun, Corised, and Geraan send their duty, and will be honored to attend your coronation three days hence." He looked up. "Sire, this is excellent news."

"Where are the other four?" Aeldred leapt to his feet with such violence that he overturned the silver tray, along with all its steaming contents. "Aberun, Corised, and Geraan!" He ignored the spilled dinner and stomped toward his windows. "That's only three, Satticus. Three of seven! Where are the pledges from Halbir and Jugeim? Where are the promises of fealty from Meporu and Yorth?"

Satticus groaned. So. That explained Aeldred's anger.

Nornindaal was a land ruled by inviolable customs. Led across the sea to Aeld Gowan by Malduorn, grandson of Nuorn the Valiant, they had brought nothing with them except their longships, their swords, and their traditions. In the centuries since then, as seafaring faded into legend and swords were forged into plowshares, the ancient traditions had acquired an ever-increasing significance as the last remaining link between Nornindaal and the Old Home. The keeping of the customs was what made one Nornish, and only Holy Writ was esteemed higher.

One of the inviolable customs stipulated that no king could be crowned without the consent of the majority of the Nornish lords. Of the seven lords of Nornindaal, only three had sworn to the Prince Regent. Without the support of at least one other . . .

Aeldred could not be king.

Satticus bit his lip. "Sire, might we not delay the coronation?"

The Prince Regent wheeled around, his visage mottled with rage. "*Delay!* No, Satticus, there will be no delay."

"But sire, surely if we had but another week, we might persuade—"

"Persuade? Persuade *whom?*" The prince waved his arms as he paced back and forth across his chamber.

"One of the remaining four lords, sire."

Aeldred stopped pacing and glared at his secretary. "If you could find them."

"Sire?"

"They've gone missing, Satticus."

"Missing, sire?"

"All four of them, along with their men-at-arms."

"I see." Satticus's stomach lurched, and for the first time in many years, he contemplated a horrifying prospect . . .

Defeat.

He shuddered. *Could it really happen? What would I do?*

"But I suppose it doesn't matter." Aeldred slowed his pace and lowered his voice.

"What?" The question escaped before Satticus caught himself. His heart was still racing, and his master's sudden calm alarmed him. "I mean, it doesn't, sire?"

"No." Aeldred walked back toward his chair. "If I do not receive their pledges by tomorrow, I will declare Halbir, Jugeim,

Meporu, and Yorth traitors. That will vacate their titles, leaving only three reigning lords—the three who have sworn to me!"

Satticus gave a low whistle. It was a bold stroke. "That will be unprecedented, sire. The people may not accept it."

"They may not like it, Satticus," conceded the Prince Regent. "But once I have crushed Oethur, they will have no choice but to accept it."

"Crushing your brother may take some time, if the four lords have gone over to him."

"Our three can match those four. And you forget our Mersian allies, Satticus. Very soon their campaign in Dyfann will end. When it does, Wodic has promised us soldiers."

"So long as he continues to believe that Lothair was behind the attempt on his life. But what if our escapees send word?"

"What difference would that make?"

"If Wodic learns that Bishop Ciolbail has been your prisoner, he may come to doubt that the bishop really sent those assassins."

Aeldred laughed. "Archbishop Simnor will intercept any communication of that sort. He's got Wodic surrounded by his own people."

Satticus's pulse slowed. Perhaps defeat was not imminent. "Very good, sire."

"Come." Aeldred frowned at the mess on the carpets. "Let's have some dinner."

So saying, the Prince Regent called for servants, and a few minutes later his spoiled dinner was cleared and replaced. An extra chair was brought, and the two of them sat.

"What word from Dunross?" Aeldred took a glass of wine in his hand.

Satticus winced. "Perhaps now is not the time, sire . . ."

The glass shattered in Aeldred's hand.

"That's a large order, doctor."

The apothecary frowned over the counter at Lildas. "I can give you what I have at hand now, but it might take me some days to prepare the rest."

"That will do nicely, Nebbs." Lildas understood all too well what was involved in preparing *valerisaan* extract. "But send the rest along as soon as you are able, please."

"Somebody in the Keep having trouble sleeping, eh?"

"You know I never discuss my patients, Nebbs."

"Of course, doctor. Of course." The apothecary, a good-natured man about the same age as Lildas, smiled. "I'll send my current stock to the Keep within the hour, and when the rest is ready, I'll fetch it up immediately."

"Very good, Nebbs. I think that will be all." Lildas turned to go.

"You wouldn't happen to be needing any more nightshade, would you, doctor?"

Lildas looked back.

"*More* nightshade, Nebbs?"

"What with your regular orders over the last year, I took the liberty of stocking up some additional supply."

Nightshade?

An inexplicable tingle crept up the doctor's spine.

Seeing the blank look on Lildas's face, the apothecary reddened. "Never mind, doctor. I know you don't like to discuss these things."

"No, it's fine, Nebbs. Remind me, when did you last receive such an order?"

The apothecary scratched his balding pate. "Oh, been more than a month, I suspect. Maybe two. But I can check my receipts, if you would like."

"Please do."

As Nebbs rooted around behind his counter, Lildas's mind raced . . .

As a medicinal herb, nightshade did have a few esoteric uses. In small doses prepared with care, it could help alleviate several inconvenient conditions—situations involving over-reliance upon a chamber pot. It was this that Nebbs probably had in mind, and it explained his embarrassed reticence.

But I've seen nothing of that sort for quite some time!

But there was another, far more common use for the potent herb . . .

Poison.

In strong doses, nightshade was a fast, efficient killer. But Lildas remembered a case from his training days at the Physicians Guild in Mereclestour. There too nightshade had been used, but in a much-diluted form over a period of several months. In that case, the victim had experienced a precipitous decline . . .

. . . and the poison had remained undetected until the apothecary came calling!

"Here we go, doctor." Nebbs called Lildas back to reality and proffered him a stack of parchment slips. "These are the receipts from your orders. Like I suspected. Been two months since the last."

Lildas took the stack and looked at the receipt on top. Sure enough, it was an order for nightshade. It was written in his name, but it was not written in his hand. He looked through the others.

The same.

A sudden, terrifying suspicion came over Lildas.

What if King Ulfered had *not* died of natural illness?

The late king's remarkable decline had troubled Lildas from start to finish. When young Prince Oethur left for Caeldora after midsummer, the king had been hale as a bull. Yet by the time of Oethur's brief return just a little over a month ago, Ulfered was on his deathbed. From the picture of health to the pall of the grave in less than half a year. Lildas had never understood it.

Until now.

But who?

Again, a terrible suspicion filled his mind as a memory struck him . . .

Did not Aeldred frequently insist on tending his father personally? What was haunting the Prince Regent's sleep?

There was one way to find out.

"Two months." He nodded to Nebbs. "Yes, it's coming back to me now. Although there's no immediate need now, I am willing to buy the remainder of your stock—on two conditions."

"Name it, doctor. I've got scarce use for the stuff otherwise."

Lildas arched an eyebrow at him. "The first is that these receipts come with me, and you mention this purchase to *nobody*. It's an awkward herb to need, you understand?"

Nebbs bobbed his head, trying to hide his smile. "Of course, doctor."

"Secondly, I need you to throw in a few extra items—off the record."

When Lildas left the apothecary's shop, three additional herbs were tucked in his pouch along with the remainder of Nebbs's nightshade . . .

Nerwunaan would detach a man's control over his limbs, rendering him immobile.

Passiferaal would loosen the mind and numb the inhibitions, rendering even the most secretive person as honest and open as a child.

And then there was *foorsbaan* . . .

Used to mix the memory-erasing tincture of *droelum*.

It was almost three weeks to the day since the Feast of the Sacred Tree in Banr Cluidan. A strong breeze blew amid the broken hills of southwest Dyfann, carrying on its gusts the signs of fading battle: the haunting cries of horses and men, the iron smell of blood, and the stench of opened bowels.

Astride one of the many hills overlooking the field of victory, two men stood beside the stirrup of a Mersian commander. The Mersian was grim-faced, and blood smeared his armor. One of the men, a tall Dyfanni warrior, had half of his face painted green. The other half bore an irregular pattern of crimson spatters. Beside the warrior stood a shorter man, wrapped head to foot in a hood whose ruddy hue made it impossible to tell whether he had tasted combat.

The warrior was speaking to the mounted Mersian in Dyfanni, and the red monk was translating his words into Vilguran.

"My lord, Chief Garallodh says that the last of the rebels have surrendered."

From atop his horse, Stonoric, Duke of Hoccaster, nodded. *A bloody bit of work, but it was finished.* The duke dismounted his horse and extended his hand toward the Dyfanni.

"My compliments to *Lord* Garallodh. He and his men fought well."

By proclamation of Wodic, King of Mersex and High Chieftain of Dyfann, all Dyfanni clan chiefs who fought for the pacification of Dyfann were to be awarded Mersian peerages.

Garallodh nodded as the monk translated the honorific, then grasped Stonoric's forearm.

"He says your men also fought well, my lord." The monk paused as Garallodh added a further stream of speech. "And he says you yourself fought like Tarwu."

"Like who?"

"Tarwu is the Dyfanni name for the battle god who appears as a three-horned bull. It is a great compliment among my people, my lord."

Stonoric bowed, then looked out over the killing ground.

The two armies had drawn up their lines at dawn, but it was an uncertain morning. The sun had lumbered out of the east into a vague, leaden sky, and it had remained out of sight for the duration of the fight, skulking behind the thick clouds as though unwilling to condone what would presently transpire. The dullness of the morning at first muted the bright greens of the rolling swath beneath the soldiers' feet, but that reversed soon enough as the grass began to shine with ruddy iridescence.

Stonoric had been in the thick of it. He had never been the sort of commander who led from behind, for he could not abide the thought of sending other men to their deaths while he maintained a safe distance. And so at the very beginning—at the moment when the Dyfanni rebels raised their ghoulish cry and raced forward—he lowered his sword, spurred his horse, and charged into the center.

At first it had been easy. The enemy was poorly trained, and the initial row of pikes were lowered too far. His mount leapt them easily, and thus he smashed into the Dyfanni line with terrifying force. His heavy cavalry saber sang as it sheared through wooden spears and sliced through soft flesh—half a dozen died almost before they knew what hit them.

But then a Dyfanni arrow caught Stonoric's horse in the neck. The mount tumbled beneath him, and the duke would have been crushed if he had not leapt free at the last moment. Yet no sooner had he regained stable ground underfoot than he realized the peril of his situation.

He was surrounded. He had ridden too far ahead of his men, and leapt over the pikes, which infantry could not vault. By all ordinary accounts, he should have died.

But Stonoric had not died. Morhwen, his weapons master back in Hoccaster, knew all about his duke's heedless gallantry. Consequently, he had insisted for years that Stonoric practice melee fighting in addition to single combat. Today, that training had told. In those first critical moments on foot, another half-dozen died beneath Stonoric's blade. Moreover, the duke's ferocity caused the Dyfanni—most of whom were conscripted tribesmen rather than regular warriors—to hesitate. And before they had regained their nerve to try another encircling attack, the duke's reinforcements arrived.

Stonoric smiled now at the recollection. It had been hammer and tongs until the very end, yet from that point forward, he never lacked men at his back. And despite his adjutants' insistence, he refused to return to his hillock command post until he broke the enemy's back.

A bloody bit of work, indeed.

Stonoric patted his new horse before turning back to his translator. "Ask Lord Garallodh if he would like to ride with me as I visit the men."

The monk turned to the Dyfanni. Garallodh shook his head and smiled, then he made a traveling motion with two of his fingers.

"He would prefer not to ride, my lord, but he is happy to walk with you."

"Tell him we shall walk together, then."

While the monk translated, Stonoric turned to his adjutants and bannerman. "Lord Garallodh and I are going to visit the army. We shall walk. Bring my mount, and ride behind us."

As he descended the hill toward the carnage below, Stonoric reflected on both the brevity and ferocity of this campaign . . .

Brief, because most Dyfanni had embraced the new order. During the Feast of the Sacred Tree, Archbishop Simnor managed to convince most of the worshipers that they had witnessed a miracle. What really happened Stonoric could not say, for he had not attended the cathedral service. But many Dyfanni insisted they saw "the Miracle," and so embraced the New Faith.

Yet Stonoric *had* been present a week later, when the Archbishop issued the proclamation that Caileamach, Queen of Mersex and High Princess of Dyfann, was with child. For many Dyfanni, this was an even greater miracle than the first, for they understood as well as Stonoric what it meant.

Their own flesh and blood would one day rule Aeld Gowan from east to west.

For most, such a prospect eased the acceptance of the present Mersian hegemony.

But not all Dyfanni exulted at the news. A few chiefs refused to accept either Wodic as their sovereign or the New Faith as their religion. These retreated into the southwest of Dyfann, hoping in the rugged hill country of their ancestors to make their stand for the Old Faith and the old ways.

It was Archbishop Simnor who ordered their destruction. For all his former talk of liberality and spiritual balance, the archbishop's tone shifted now that he had established his foothold. Simnor would brook no pockets of dissent, however few or remote, to his new golden age. Stonoric's former assessment of the archbishop's zeal had proven true . . .

Just as narrow as the men of the North . . . different, but just as dangerous.

The duke himself cared nothing for the New Faith, and little enough for the Old. But his loyalty was to king and country. And Wodic's orders had been clear. Those who resisted the new order were to be compelled . . .

With persuasion, if possible . . .

. . . and with steel, if necessary.

The campaign lasted but two weeks. The rebel chieftains made a credible showing, and for the first week they possessed the upper hand. During that time, the enemy avoided any large-scale combat, contenting themselves instead to minor ambushes and night raids. These inflicted heavy losses, and proved a surprising counterbalance to the rebels' radical disadvantage in numbers, equipment, and training.

But it did not last. Stonoric had the troops to sweep the countryside in long lines, and Garallodh and the other allied chieftains had the scouts to inform their maneuvers. Thus it came to pass today that the combined forces loyal to Wodic had forced the rebels to present proper battle. The enemy fought like wild demons, but in the end, superior numbers and discipline overcame desperate ferocity.

And now they were broken.

The evidence lay strewn about them as Stonoric walked with Garallodh amidst the human wreckage. Many Mersian soldiers milled about among the slain and wounded, but there were far fewer Dyfanni—and none who did not bear the green face-paint of Mersex.

Stonoric turned a blind eye to those who appeared to be plundering the dead. However distasteful the practice, it was long-established and accepted in warfare. And it seemed small enough reward for those poor soldiers who had risked their lives for lands and power they would never inherit.

Let them have their few coins and trophies.

But then Stonoric saw something that made even his world-weary eyes bulge.

He had to look twice to make certain. And when he was sure of what he saw, he wanted to retch. But anger mastered apprehension, and instead he turned to Garallodh.

"My lord, do you see what some of your men there are doing?" He stopped walking and pointed to a clutch of Dyfanni kneeling over a body not a dozen paces away.

Garallodh followed his companion's gesture, but his face remained impassive and his tone was casual.

"He says they are plundering the fallen, same as your men, my lord."

Stonoric's look made his translator take a step back. "They are cannibalizing the dead—and even some who look as though they yet live!"

Garallodh shrugged, then began to walk on.

"He says they will be dead soon enough either way, my lord."

Stonoric did not move. "Tell him that I will not abide it."

As the monk translated the words, Garallodh turned. He walked back to Stonoric and put a hand on the duke's shoulder. The two men were about the same height, and so the Dyfanni chief faced Stonoric eye to eye.

"Even Tarwu cannot turn bulls into sheep, my lord," translated the monk. "The men of Dyfann say nothing as you Mersians strip the dead of the goods they will need to journey through the underworld on their return to the Mother. What is unthinkable to us is common among you." The monk paused as Garallodh continued, then went on with the translation. "It is the same in this. The men of Mersex may find it unthinkable to consume the life of their foes, but among the Dyfanni it is common. If our peoples are truly to become one, each must be willing to abide the . . ."

Here the monk trailed off, apparently lost for the appropriate word.

"Idiosyncrasies?" suggested the duke.

The red monk nodded. "Ah, yes. That is the word I wanted, my lord. Lord Garallodh suggests that if our peoples are truly to become one, each must be willing to abide the *idiosyncrasies* of the other."

Stonoric hesitated. Was there really no difference? He had to admit that the Dyfanni's words carried a certain logic. Yet he sensed there was a flaw. How could looting coins truly be equivalent to eating a man alive? Surely they were not . . .

Surely? On what basis do I make that distinction? He frowned. It was a fair question, but did it not come down to mere common sense?

But is common sense anything more than personal preference?

Of this he was not sure.

If so, then what is it? But if not, then who says my preference is better than his?

Garallodh took Stonoric by the arm and gestured that they should continue.

"He suggests that you come along now, my lord. There are others we must visit."

Stonoric allowed himself to be led away from the disturbing scene. He could have forced his will upon the Dyfanni, but to what end?

The king had ordered Stonoric to conquer the land, not to convert the people. And he had achieved his objective.

His victory was complete.

And yet, as he continued walking alongside his Dyfanni counterpart, the savage images he witnessed continued to haunt him.

Stonoric's creed was discretion in all things—in faith as much as in food and drink. Discretion was one of the chief virtues of Mersex. The region's climate was mild, its Church moderate, and most of its people content to live quiet, sensible lives.

For all of Stonoric's life, discretion had seemed a simple and sufficient creed. But the spectacle of one man cannibalizing another, and Garallodh's defense of the practice, had brought him up short. He sensed it was wrong . . .

. . . but by what standard?

The question had not vanished by the time Stonoric remounted his horse several hours later. But it had grown quieter. Other thoughts now dominated his mind.

The enemy was vanquished, his task in Dyfann was complete, and at last he could lead his army east—back across the Gwyllinor Mountains to Mersex.

Back to Hoccaster.

War was brewing in the North, but for now, he could go home.

Home . . . but for how long?

"Morumus is waiting to see you, my love."

Rhianwyn leaned over the bed and placed a light kiss on Oethur's forehead.

He opened his eyes at the soft voice and delicate touch of his wife. In truth, he had been awake for the better part of an hour. But he knew that if he stirred immediately upon waking, Rhianwyn would rouse the servants and summon his breakfast without delay. From that point forward, their privacy would vanish. Though a man of action, in marrying Rhianwyn Oethur had come to a new appreciation of delay—and privacy.

He had been married now for two weeks . . .

. . . though his wedding day had almost been his last.

"Very good." Oethur pushed himself upright and lumbered out of bed. He reached for his robe. "I'll be happy to breakfast with him. Will you stay, darling?"

Rhianwyn laughed. "That's kind of you, love, but I've already had my breakfast. I suspect the same is true of Morumus."

"What?"

"It's midmorning, Oethur."

"It is?"

Rhianwyn walked to the window of the bedchamber and drew back the heavy drapes. Sunlight streamed in, catching motes of dust in bright beams with angles far too high to be the first rays of dawn.

"I should have been up hours ago," Oethur grumbled as he dressed. "Why did you not wake me?"

"Doctor Halen says you are still recovering and should be allowed to sleep as much as you will." She gave him a modest smile. "Which is little enough."

Oethur returned her smile, but it vanished as he reached for his boots. They felt heavy, and dull pain coursed through his body as he straightened.

"Doctor Halen is correct. I still feel weaker than I should."

"I am just thankful you are alive." Rhianwyn turned her face to the window.

The poison on Muthadis's knife was of a different sort than the kind she had mixed in his wine goblet. The latter was intended to produce excruciating pain and quick death—and had indeed killed Lady Isowene within minutes. But the former was a more subtle toxin—a true assassin's herb. It paralyzed the victim slowly, beginning with the extremities. The idea was to render them unable to move, but still capable of answering interrogation, for several hours—until the poison stopped the heart.

"I am thankful *we're* alive." Oethur sat down and pulled on his shoes. "It was a near thing for both of us."

"Poor Isowene." Rhianwyn sniffed, still looking through the glass.

Oethur nodded and closed his eyes. "The Lord's providence is inscrutable," he said at last, lacing up his last boot. "None of us is guaranteed another day."

Rhianwyn turned to look at him, determination on her reddened face. "All the more reason to make every day we have together count, Oethur."

He stood. "Agreed, my love."

"Will you not let me come east with you, then?" A tear trickled down the left side of her face.

Oethur shook his head. "I will not—and you know why."

She stiffened. "I know why, my love, and I will obey. I promised as much at our wedding, did I not?" She turned from the window, paused to place a brief kiss on his cheek, and then proceeded past him toward the door of the chamber. "But I do not agree."

"Rhianwyn . . ."

"It will not do to keep your friend waiting."

Morumus stood as Oethur entered the sitting room.

"Sit down, brother." The Norn waved Morumus back into his seat, and then joined him. "I've asked the servants to bring me breakfast. Will you take something?"

Morumus shook his head. "No, thank you."

"But you don't mind if I do?"

"Of course not."

"Good"—Oethur grinned.—"because I was going to whether you minded or not!"

As the door opened and servants brought in a steaming tray, Morumus smiled. The return of Oethur's constitutional humor was a strong indicator of recovery. "How are you feeling?"

"A bit better every day," Oethur said as he sliced into a loaf of dark bread. "But still not as strong as I should like."

"Doctor Halen said that's to be expected. That *laedhoth* was old and withered."

"But it worked."

"It did, thank God."

Doctor Halen, the court physician to King Heclaid, had spared little hope for Oethur at first. Retrieving the knife from Muthadis's broken body, he had identified the poison by taste. That was the good news. But it was also bad news, for the poison was an obscure sort whose only remedy required an obscure herb.

Laedhoth root.

At that point, Oethur could not move the arm that had suffered the wound.

And there had been no laedhoth to be had in Dunross. A frantic search of every apothecary's shop in the city over the next two hours had yielded the same reply: laedhoth was not only out of season, it was out of country. It only grew in Dyfann.

By then, Oethur was immobilized.

Yet it was at precisely this point, as Morumus sat watching his friend fade, feeling angry and helpless and praying for mercy, that a sudden memory shook him . . .

What had Nerias said to him years ago, on the morning after his father's murder?

"During the winter that your mother was pregnant with you, she fell ill and things looked grim. The midwife told her you would probably die, and that even she might not survive. The sickness was only treatable with regular tonic made of laedhoth root. Though it was not a common herb of our country, your mother laid some back every year, just in case one of the households needed treatment."

Nerias had gone on to tell Morumus that in the year he was born, the entire supply had burned in a cellar fire. But surely his mother, who survived for a few years beyond that winter, would have resumed her former practice . . .

In that instant, Morumus had known where they could find laedhoth!

But would it be in time?

Taking spare mounts and riding through the night, Haedorn and Morumus had reached their ancestral home at Aban-Tur and found a much-aged, but still viable, quantity of the herb. In their absence, Doctor Halen had used all his skill—and a panoply of intermediate herbs—to preserve Oethur's life. It was a desperate night on all fronts . . .

But Oethur had survived.

This same Oethur now paused halfway through buttering his slice of bread and gave Morumus a sober look. "I do thank God. There is nothing like almost dying to make one appreciate life."

Morumus nodded. In the last year, he had learned the same lesson—more than once. "I thank him, too, for you, brother. You saved my life."

"And you saved mine in Versaden. Remember?"

"False grabber." Oethur chuckled. "I remember. Though I had some help with it."

"Donnach."

Donnach had stepped in front of a blade intended for Morumus. *One of the many murdered by the Red Order.*

"God rest his soul," said Oethur.

For the next several minutes, neither man spoke. Oethur devoured his breakfast, and Morumus—despite his earlier refusal—busied himself with a hunk of cheese and small heap of dried fruit. It was not until they were both finished that Oethur broke the silence.

"I have received a summons, brother."

"A summons? From whom?"

"Four of the seven lords of my country: Halbir, Jugeim, Meporu, and Yorth. They summon me to meet them at Teru Bridge a week from tomorrow. No doubt they will have their men-at-arms, but I am to bring no Lothairin army."

"Teru Bridge, the border between our countries. An interesting choice. Can you trust them?"

"All four loved my father, and none has sworn to Aeldred."

"Do they intend to support you?"

"That remains to be seen. The letter demands my presence, but makes no promise."

"Will you go alone?"

"No. Treowin will accompany me."

"Speaking of the bishop"—Morumus eyed the last chunk of cheese—"where is he? I haven't seen him for a few days."

"He is staying with family."

"Bishop Treowin has kin—here, in Dunross?"

"Apparently, yes. His nephew is a cobbler in the city." Oethur grinned. "Which should guarantee that he'll have a stout pair of boots for our journey."

"You're not planning to walk to Teru Bridge?"

"No. We will ride. In fact, your brother has promised to escort us."

"Good. Haedorn should be able to keep you out of trouble."

"I'm surprised he's not going with you, brother."

Morumus looked up. "King Heclaid has told you of our embassy?"

"Rhianwyn told me."

Morumus sighed. "It is a desperate throw to begin with, and Donnach's death makes it even more so. But your father-in-law hopes to persuade the Grendannathi to join with us against Aeldred and the Mersians."

"And he wants you to help?"

"Donnach taught me Grendannathi, so I will translate. And I was there when he was murdered by the Red Order."

"The same Red Order that now backs our enemies."

"Exactly."

"Will the Grendannathi believe you, you think?"

"That's the question. The king says the clans are coming to Aesus, but it's a touchy thing. They've agreed to meet with us, but that's no guarantee they'll agree to support us."

"Sounds like my situation."

"You've at least got Bishop Treowin to attest to your account."

"And do you not have Donnach's Volume?"

"No. I left it with Urien on Urras."

"So why not send for it?"

"We did, a week ago."

"But?"

"Urien has vanished."

"What?" Oethur sat upright. "What happened?"

"Nobody knows. They found her cell empty, and her translation of the Bone Codex in ashes."

"And Donnach's Volume?"

"Gone."

Oethur shook his head. "I'm sorry, brother. I know the book was important."

"Its loss will set our translation work back by years, but at present I am more concerned for Urien."

Oethur arched an eyebrow. "Really?"

"Yes. There is more to her story than you know, brother."

"I know that she was a prisoner of the Red Order, and I know that you and Donnach rescued her from their Muthadannach in Caeldora."

"Yes."

"So what else am I missing?"

"Everything you said is true, but the reality is more complicated than the bare facts."

"Oh?" Oethur arched an eyebrow. "Do tell."

"I cannot. I promised her I would keep it secret."

"Fine. But remember, Morumus, she is no Aesusian. I remember from our time on Urras that she was quite insistent on that point. Be careful."

"Holy Writ teaches us to keep our word, even to infidels."

Oethur gave Morumus a level look. "That's not what I mean, brother."

Morumus's face reddened. He knew what Oethur was implying, and he could not dispute either the danger or the warning. So instead he nodded, avoided his friend's eyes, and seized the small hunk of cheese. And as he chewed, he prayed . . .

For Urien.

Urien.

Somnadh could not get his sister out of his mind. Almost three weeks had passed since their heated confrontation. Almost three weeks since Urien denounced the Mother with shocking vehemence—and to his face. Almost three weeks since he lashed out and struck her.

The memory of it still upset him.

But why?

This was the question that dogged him as he climbed the hill to the Muthadannach. On this night the moon was new above the Mother Glen. A host of stars shone bright against the sky's obsidian dome, but their light did not descend to illuminate the grassy slope. Yet in this place Somnadh needed no lamp, and he did not stumble as he trod the ancient path.

Why was he upset?

Part of it was frustration with himself for losing his composure.

Always a mistake.

But that was not all. Part of him was also angry that he had struck Urien.

But why? Did she not deserve it?

This was the real question, and on this point he was of two minds. On the one hand, he felt a sense of indelible guilt. As a boy, his father taught Somnadh that no man ever struck a woman. Ever. Yet on the other hand, even his father had disciplined Urien when her misbehavior required it.

Is that not what I did? Was I not simply exercising discipline? Was it not necessary?

The memory of Urien's raving speech made him shudder. *So many blasphemies against the Mother . . .*

That his sister needed correction was beyond dispute. Had it not then been his responsibility, both as her brother and as a son of the Mother, to end her ranting? Had it not been his duty to silence her sacrilege—even if it required physical force?

Why, then, do I feel as though I've done wrong?

The tension was still with Somnadh as he reached the hill's summit. It still nagged at him as he passed through the circle of great standing stones. But once he came within the Ring of Stars, the sight at its center made him forget all other cares.

The axis of the universe . . .

The center of all worlds . . .

The one constant athwart past, present, and future . . .

The Mother.

A great serenity blossomed within Somnadh as he beheld the Goddess Tree. Despite the paucity of natural light under the new moon, the Mother seemed to pulse with maternal iridescence. Her boughs were an image of the ineffable, and the flow of her limbs filled him with a sense of sublime eternality. From root to branch, Genna represented unbroken perfection. Moreover her myriad scarlet leaves, each divided into five slender fingers, clutched small dark clusters of the nomergenna herb. That potent herb, more precious than ever since the fall of Cuuranyth, promised him the powers of the goddess herself.

It was a beatific vision, and it called him to communion with the Source of all things.

"Genna ma'guad . . ." *Genna, my goddess . . .*

"Genna ma'muthad . . ." *Genna my Mother . . .*

"Genna ma'rophed." Genna, my salvation.

Somnadh sighed.

So long as Genna endured, the world would continue to turn. The sun, moon, and stars would continue in their courses. The cycle of life and death would continue.

"And death is a natural part of life," he whispered, reciting the mantra of the Old Faith. "One feeds into the other, and the other back into the first."

"Life and death are but two sister paths," came a voice out of the darkness, "but both lead home to the Mother."

Llanubys.

The Heart of Genna emerged from the canopy of the Mother's branches. She had long white hair and pale, mottled skin. The former fell in sparse, wispy strands over her scarlet gown. The latter stretched taut over gnarled, knobbled hands. Eyes as black as midnight peered out from her gaunt face . . .

These dark eyes crinkled at their corners as she approached Somnadh.

"My dearest child," she said in a thin voice, taking his face in her hands. Somnadh could feel her hands shaking. "You have come just in time. Come and sit with me."

Taking him by the hand, she guided him to the raised stone lip that bound the Mother's earthen bed. Here they both sat.

"It is good to see you, Llanubys."

"And you, dear one. I had feared that I would return to the Mother before you returned to me. But now you are here, and I see you with these eyes. One last time."

Somnadh's breath caught in his throat. "Surely not! Surely not the last time!"

"Look at me, Somnadh. What do you see?"

Somnadh looked.

Llanubys was older than any living man. But the long years—even Somnadh did not know how many—had taken their toll. Her flesh was a thin covering over a skeletal frame. But most telling were her eyes. Like his own, they were entirely black—a result of long use of nomergenna. Llanubys's eyes had always burned with an inner fire that defied their lack of color . . .

But not anymore.

Tonight, those black orbs seemed dull—almost as if Llanubys had no eyes at all.

As though she is already moldering . . .

The horrid thought brought burning tears to Somnadh's eyes. *No! It cannot be! Not now! Not yet!*

"I see strength," he lied. "I see the woman who nurtured me in the ways of the Mother—the woman who is needed now more than ever. I see beauty and . . ."

But Somnadh could not finish. His words dissolved into sobs.

Llanubys patted him on the arm. "You have always been a good boy, Somnadh—but never a good liar." She withdrew her hand and wrapped it about herself. "Let us speak now of other things. Tell me, how is Urien? She has returned to you, has she not?"

"She has returned," Somnadh choked out the words, "but Aesusian poison courses through her, and she rails against our faith. That is what I came to ask you, Llanubys. Will you intercede for her to the Mother? I am sure that if the Mother would but speak to her—speak to her directly—then Urien would know once and for all that she is a true goddess."

Above them, a wind seemed to stir in the top branches of the white tree. For a long moment, Llanubys sat quite still—as if listening. When she spoke again, her voice seemed far away.

"The Mother approaches. Time is drawing short."

Somnadh looked up. "Will you ask her, Llanubys? Please ask her to speak to Urien!"

"No." Llanubys shook her head. "Nevertheless, Urien *will* be Llanubys."

Somnadh shook his head. "If the Mother does not speak to her, she will never believe. Please, Llanubys! Please, you must help her!"

"What you ask is impossible, Somnadh. The Mother never speaks directly."

"But she spoke to me!"

"It was not the Mother who spoke to you, Somnadh. It was I."

Somnadh leapt to his feet. "What?"

"It is true. Genna our goddess speaks only through those with special knowledge. Come back and sit."

Somnadh's heart lurched, but he obeyed. He sat down again. Hard. His head felt light, his mind dizzy. "Has it all been a lie?"

"Of course not, dear one." Llanubys put her hand on his arm. "Look around you! The Mother is real. Nomergenna is real. The Holy Seed that you planted in Caeldora was real. All of it is real. But the reality is different than you realize."

"I don't understand."

"No, dear one. That is why you must listen now." Again the Mother's leaves rustled above them, only this time the preternatural wind seemed lower . . .

"Listen!" hissed Llanubys, looking up. "She comes closer!"

Somnadh shivered as he felt the icy breeze graze the top of his scalp.

Llanubys returned her eyes to Somnadh. "Listen now, dear one. I must teach you the innermost secret of the Old Faith, the truth within the truth of the Mordruui. It has never before been known to any but the Heart of Genna, but I am fading, and you must keep it safe. When she is ready, you must commit this secret—the Last Secret—to Urien. Then, and only then, will she be Llanubys."

Despite his disorientation, a thrill surged up Somnadh's spine. "I am listening."

"The Last Secret is this: though the Mother is the *focus* of our devotion, she is not the *object* of our faith. The Mother is but a sacred image, a concentration of the divinity scattered in all things. In her form and in her fruit, Genna is but a focus of the Source that permeates all of us. The properties of nomergenna are but more potent forms of the power latent in all of us. The White Tree is but a tangible manifestation of the deeper truth of our own reality. That truth is this: that *we* are gods and goddesses, all of us!"

Llanubys's weak voice rose to a fever pitch, and something of the old fire returned to her eyes. "This is the knowledge that Yeho tried to keep from mankind in Adinnu! This is the truth that his jealousy tried to drown—by flooding the earth to murder the Mother! This is the secret that Tham's wife, first Llanubys, preserved by carrying the Holy Seed of Eolas, First Genna, on the Great Ark! All the mysteries of the ages come down to this: that in reverencing the Mother, we do but worship ourselves."

Llanubys finished with a sigh. "This is the Last Secret, Somnadh. Keep it well."

Somnadh was stunned. His mind churned with the force of Llanubys's words, his spirit struggling to process it all. It was overwhelming . . .

But it all fits.

"I have always wondered why Yeho wanted to destroy the Mother—what could fire his jealousy so hot that he would flood the world."

"Now you know, dear one."

"Now I know." But a sudden pang of doubt pierced him. "But how do we know it's all true, Llanubys?"

"I have lived for centuries, Somnadh—only the Mother is older than I. And what has preserved me these many generations?" She gestured to the branches above. "Our own divine power, Somnadh—concentrated in the Mother's precious herb. That is our proof."

"Nomergenna can extend life?"

"Yes, dear one. It will extend both your and Urien's life beyond count of years. The recipe for the Water of Life is etched on a white stone buried in this earth." She touched the soft earth behind their seat. "Bury me here, and you will find it."

Somnadh nodded, but then he frowned. "I believe everything you have revealed to me, Llanubys. But I fear Urien may not." Tears began to fill his eyes again. "I fear she is close to embracing the faith of Aesus. She told me she believes it is a far better faith."

Despite her weakness, Llanubys made a guttural noise. "Disabuse her of the notion, Somnadh."

"How?" He shook his head. "If only we had rescued her sooner from the island monastery."

"Destroy the place where she learned these lies. Capture its inhabitants and feed them to the Mother. But break them first! Do it slowly, Somnadh, and make Urien watch! Let her see them die renouncing Aesus—or even better, crying out for him without answer! When they die alone and miserable, Urien will see. The god of Holy Writ is a fraud, while the Mother can be seen and touched. She will cease dreaming about the god she would like, and she will return to serving the goddess that she has."

Somnadh nodded. "I will do as you say, Llanubys. And I pray it will work."

The wind blew again, and this time it was all around them. It seemed almost to lift Llanubys for from her seat, and she drew her knees up to her chest. Her white tresses floated on the moving air, and she looked at Somnadh.

"I have but moments, dear one, and there is one other thing you should know. There is another stone buried amidst the Mother's roots—a black stone covered in runes. It contains the recipe for the Elixir of Knowledge. Use it only if all else fails. It will make Urien obedient to your command . . ."

"What? I can use nomergenna to turn Urien back to the Mother?"

"Yes, but only as a last resort—for it will destroy her will."

The wind picked up, and Llanubys gasped. Her life was leaving . . .

"Yet if all else fails, you must use it. Urien *must* offer the blood of Morumus in atonement for her sin. She *must* embrace the Last Secret. And she *must* take my place . . . Whatever else may come, Somnadh, the Mother *must* be tended."

"She will be." Somnadh tried to shield Llanubys from the engulfing wind, but the task proved impossible. She shook with a final shiver . . . and then she was still.

Somnadh stood and turned. Cradling the withered frame of Genna's Heart, he lifted his eyes to the Mother's white branches. And there, alone in the dark, he worshipped.

"You are the goddess now, Llanubys! I believe the Last Secret!" He could not restrain his weeping. "And Urien will believe it, too—whatever it takes. This I swear!"

It could not have been a more perfect day for working in the gardens of Urras Monastery. The sun beamed down at her from its high, meridian perch, and the blue canopy of its kingdom bore only a light smattering of clouds. A warm breeze wafted in from the sea, carrying with it the pungent tang of salt. All around her, beds of flowers and rows of vegetables stood in full bloom, soaking up the daylight.

Abbess Nahenna smiled, soaking up the joy of the moment.

But she knew that she was dreaming.

The first clue to the abbess was the prodigious splendor surrounding her. The monastery gardens had progressed to the height of summer, but she knew that, in reality, spring had just arrived.

The second clue was Nahenna's company. Several paces away, stooping in the soft earth to thin a patch of carrots, she saw Urien . . . but she had vanished from Urras six weeks prior.

Nahenna sighed. For all its unreality, it was a happy dream and she would be glad to spend hours under its enchantment. But now that she recognized the spell, she knew she must awake.

But she did not. Instead, she saw Urien stand and walk toward her.

"Abbess." Urien frowned. "Can I ask you a question?"

"Certainly, dear. What is it?"

"You said to me before that faith—faith in Aesus, that is—is born when a person stops denying the whispers of conscience or the words of Holy Writ."

"That's right."

"Does such faith produce certainty?"

"Certainty of what?"

"Certainty of the truth of your faith."

"It does, dear."

"Do you think that it is possible for somebody who has such faith to renounce it?"

"That's a good question, Urien." Nahenna paused. "There are many who *profess* faith in Aesus, only to later renounce him. But I don't think that's possible for somebody who *possesses* true faith. Our Lord Aesus himself said, 'I give them eternal life, and they shall certainly never perish, and nobody shall pluck them from my hand.' "

"But could a person pluck himself?"

"What?"

"Could a person pluck *himself* out of the hands of Aesus?"

"Oh, I see what you are asking. I don't think that's possible, either. Holy Writ says faith comes from God giving us a new heart. It says, too, that, 'he who began in you a good work will accomplish it—even unto the day of Aesus.' "

"Then what of Feindir, Abbess?"

"What of him, dear?"

"When I first came here, he was so gentle and kind to me. I was sure that he really was a follower of Aesus. But they say he murdered that man I found in the old chapel, and even tried to kill Oethur. Then he took his own life. It doesn't seem to fit."

Nahenna frowned. "You're right. It doesn't fit."

"So then what do you say? That he only *professed* faith, but did not *possess* it?"

"Maybe." But Nahenna heard the lack of conviction in her voice. Feindir had lived on Urras for many years, with never a hint of duplicity in his devotion to Aesus. "Or maybe there is something we don't know about all of it."

"You mean maybe he didn't really kill those men—or himself?"

"Maybe not."

"That would mean that the real killer was still—"

But Abbess Nahenna held up a hand. "Do you smell that, dear?"

Urien sniffed. "Yes, it smells like . . ."

Smoke!

Nahenna opened her eyes, but the smell did not disappear. Instead, it grew stronger.

"Nerias!" She reached out and gave her husband a violent shove. "Nerias, wake up!"

Though by nature a heavy sleeper, Nerias opened his eyes. "What did you say?"

"Fire. Something is burning!"

"What?"

In an instant, both of them were out of bed. While Nahenna pulled on her robe, Nerias went to the window.

"Oh no."

Nahenna heard the doom in his voice. "What is it?"

"Sea-raiders, Nahenna."

"Oh no! No, Lord Aesus!"

"Saint Calum's Hall is in flames. We must raise the alarm!"

Nerias and Nahenna stepped from their shared chamber and paused. Each knew they must separate—just as each was well aware that this might be the last moment they shared together in this life.

Nerias took his wife's head in his hands and kissed her forehead.

"I love you, Nerias," Nahenna said through tears.

"And I you." Nerias stepped back. "I will go to the chapel tower and ring the bell. You must get the families to the escape tunnel."

"You will join us?"

"If I can." He squeezed her hand and turned away. "Now we must both go!"

What followed in the next quarter hour was a blur of confusion, smoke, and terror.

Nahenna moved as fast as she could through the corridor of the family dormitory, pounding on doors and shouting warnings. Many of the sleepers, oblivious to their danger, were slow to respond.

"Wake up, brothers and sisters!" she screamed until she was hoarse. "We are under attack! Sea-raiders are upon us!"

Meanwhile dense, choking smoke rose from the ground floor to fill the corridor. From the far side of the monastery grounds, she heard men and women shouting. The raiders had breached the dormitories.

O God, have mercy! Nahenna shuddered and renewed her pounding.

But now at last, as the fires spread and more screams pierced the night, Urras Monastery woke to its danger. Doors unbolted and families emerged. Children cried as parents wrested them from slumber, but there was no time to soothe their piteous wails.

"There is an escape tunnel!" Nahenna shouted. "Down the steps at the end of the dormitory, then south through the lower hall to the scriptorium. In the basement there you will find a trapdoor hidden beneath four large barrels. The barrels are filled with water, but there are two axes hanging on the wall. Brothers Cuthral and Daagen!" She motioned to two of the larger monks among those filling the hall. "Take the axes and break the barrels. Clear them away and open the door, then stand guard while the others descend the stairs. Do you understand?"

The two monks nodded.

"Keep the way open for as long as you can, but if you see sea-raiders you are to get into the tunnel yourselves. There is an iron latch and bar on the inside. Seal the door behind you. Protect our people!"

"What about you, Abbess?"

"Abbot Nerias and I will follow if we can. Now go!"

While the others moved toward the stairs at the south end of the corridor, Nahenna raced toward the stairs at the north. She needed to get to the ground floor to direct any who managed to escape the far dormitories.

But Nahenna was not optimistic. She had heard the screams . . .

And the chapel bell had never rung.

What had happened to Nerias?

Lord, protect my husband!

The monastery's main corridor was on the first floor, and so Nahenna had no choice but to descend into the inferno. The air on the steps was thick with choking ash, and it only got worse as she reached the lower level.

Everywhere she looked, there was fire.

Nahenna had no time to weep. All her thought was bent on saving as many brothers and sisters as she could. She staggered forward to where the dormitory passage joined to the main hallway . . .

. . . and collided with a fleeing monk!

"Abbess Nahenna!" The monk helped her back to her feet. Soot smeared his dark features.

"Landu! Thank God you are alive!" She peered down the main corridor. "Have any others escaped?"

Tears filled Landu's clear blue eyes. "No, Abbess. The others have been taken."

"Taken? You mean they've been killed?"

Landu shook his head. "Slavers."

More screams echoed down the hallway from the western dormitories, followed by loud shouts and sounds of struggle. Nahenna's stomach heaved. "Have no others escaped?"

"None, Abbess. I only made it out because I was working late in the kitchens. When I realized what was happening, I thought to get to the chapel and raise the alarm . . ."

"Abbot Nerias had the same idea. But there has been no bell."

Landu shook his head again, this time closing his eyes. "We were too late. These barbarians are clever. They must have anticipated us, because they were waiting. Abbot Nerias was just ahead of me. When he realized our danger, he stood his ground so that I could flee . . ." He opened his eyes. "Abbess, there was nothing I could do."

Oh, Nerias! Oh, my dear husband . . . O Lord Aesus, why? "They killed him?" Nahenna's heart gave a violent lurch.

"I don't know, ma'am. I saw him go down . . . but they may have taken him alive."

"You must flee, Landu." She forced the words to form through her sobs. "You must escape with the others."

"Escape, Abbess?" Landu's eyes widened. "How can any escape?"

Nahenna pointed a shaking hand south. "There is a secret tunnel . . . in the basement of the scriptorium . . . a tunnel . . . hurry!" She collapsed to the floor, shaking.

"We'll go together." Landu knelt beside her. "Here, let me help you up."

Nahenna let him help her to her feet. But when he tried to turn her south, she shook her head. "I'm going to the chapel."

"Abbess, no!" Landu tried to pull her south.

"No." She shook her hand free and waved him on. "If there's even a chance that Nerias yet lives, my place is with him."

"Please, ma'am . . ." The young monk's voice shook, and his eyes pleaded. "There is no hope that way. Please, come with me!"

"Go with God, Landu." Nahenna stepped away from him. "Go now, that's an order!"

Abbess Nahenna watched until the young monk disappeared into the gloom before turning north toward the long passage that led to the chapel. *I've done what I could, Nerias. But I will not leave you.*

Nahenna faced the dim corridor with determination. Its far terminus was shrouded in thick smoke, but flashes of light punctuated the darkness. As she moved toward its end, words from long ago drifted up out the recesses of her memory.

"To have and to hold, from this day hence . . ."

A burning rafter crashed down from the ceiling just ahead of her, sending a cloud of sparks in every direction. A few of these landed on the hem of Nahenna's robe, but she ignored them and stepped over it.

"For better and for worse, in riches or rags . . ."

". . . in freedom and in slavery . . ."

"In sickness and health . . ."

A shout sounded behind her. It was a harsh cry in a foreign tongue, and it came from the junction of the corridors where she had met Landu.

A sea-raider.

Nahenna did not look back. Instead, she quickened her pace. *"To love and to cherish . . ."*

The corridor before her was a tunnel of fire. The flames engulfed the hanging tapestries, causing them to heave and billow from their moorings like great sails of fire.

Years of embroidery, centuries of history . . . gone in minutes.

A second shout came from the direction of the first, and through the roar of the flames Nahenna heard heavy footsteps pounding after her. Yet she still refused to look.

What difference does it make?

Gathering up the hem of her robe, she began to run. "To help and obey, till death us do part . . ." *I'm coming, Nerias!*

Nahenna reached the chapel before her pursuers, only to find that the hall of worship had become a picture of Belneol. Fire engulfed the wooden pews and raced along the vaulted beams of the roof. As she stepped across the threshold, the cords that held the tall cross-in-crown banner behind the pulpit snapped—their thick strands consumed by the bright jaws of fire devouring everything in sight. Outlined in flame, the great tapestry descended like a shroud over the front of the ruined chapel . . .

Urras Monastery had fallen.

But where was Nerias?

As if in answer, a great gong reverberated through the burning chapel.

Once . . .

Twice . . .

A third time the warning tolled out into the surrounding night.

But Nahenna had no thought to flee. Not now!

The bell! He made it to the bell tower!

Somehow Nerias had escaped his captors and managed to sound the alarm.

Too late . . . but did we ever have much chance?

The sea-raiders had struck with the speed of lightning . . .

Yet some have escaped. A few of the families, along with Landu . . . a remnant of Urras will endure, despite the horrors of this night. O Lord, let us be among them!

Feeling a new strength, Nahenna almost flew down the aisle and across the front of the chapel. Reaching the stone-framed archway at its northwest corner, she raced up the stairs beyond.

Hope filled Nahenna as she burst through the door onto the belfry platform.

"Nerias!"

A moment later, her hopes died.

It had not been Nerias who sounded the alarm. The figure staring at her from the belfry was not her husband. It was a monk robed all in scarlet.

The bell had not pealed a warning.

It had tolled out the Red Order's victory!

But Nahenna had little time to digest this, for in that instant she saw Nerias. Her husband hung suspended in a noose, dangling from the great bell's clapper.

The Abbot of Urras was dead.

"No . . ." She moaned, shaking her head. "My husband! No, no, *no*!"

Rough hands seized Nahenna from behind.

"Let me go, you fiends!" She kicked out, trying to pull free as the slavers took her. "Let me cut him down!"

Then something blunt struck her on the back of the head, and everything began to go black. Just before the darkness took her, she heard a voice speaking in Vilguran. It was the red monk.

"This is his wife. Put her with the rest of the archbishop's prisoners."

PART II

SHIFTING ALLEGIANCE

The men of the North had several names for the high mountains forming the border between Lothair and Grendannath. Some called them the *Firaith*, the Grey Men, for above the tree line the fog-shrouded summits resembled a host of village elders. For others, the mountains were known as *Tudbara*, Tuddreal's Barrow. A more imaginative name alluding to the legend that Tuddreal, the ancient king who raised the Threefold Cord, had fallen and was buried somewhere among them. For the more pragmatic, the mountains were simply the *Ballaith*, the Strong Walls.

"For generations, these mountains have kept Grendannathi warriors out of Lothair." The deep voice paused. "Yet now we cross these mountains in the hope of persuading them to take just such a course. Does it not seem strange?"

Morumus turned. Wrapped in a heavy fur cloak, Heclaid rode his horse like a great brooding raven. Though grey had long since laced his brown beard, the king's dark eyes had lost none of their sharp luster.

"We live in strange days, sire."

"Indeed!" The king snorted, then his voice grew quiet. "Indeed we do."

Despite his own thick cloak, Morumus shivered. It was more than a day now since they had crossed the barren summits of the high passes, yet still the icy winds raked the mounted company. Even now, the horses stamped and the men hunkered down in their saddles as another frigid gust gathered force. Morumus tried to tighten his collar.

"Did your father ever tell you of our adventure in these mountains?"

Morumus turned to see a glint of humor in Heclaid's eyes. Was the king jesting? "You and my father? Here, sire?"

"Well, not here exactly." The king smiled. "We didn't make it quite so far as here. But Raudorn and I did make a grand foray into these mountains."

"Whatever for?" Morumus forgot himself in his surprise. "I mean, why, sire?"

Heclaid chuckled. "We were looking for the *Tudbara*, of course! You know the legend, Morumus?"

"Only a bit, sire. I know these mountains sometimes go by that name."

"Right. But we were looking for *the* Barrow—we wanted to find the very tomb of Tuddreal. You see, we wanted the Sword."

Morumus could hear the way the king emphasized the last word, and he almost shivered again.

The Sword?

"I don't know that part of the legend, sire."

"Your father never told you?"

Morumus shook his head. "Perhaps he didn't want my brother and me to go looking for it?"

Heclaid laughed again. "No doubt! We ourselves were nearly killed."

Morumus leaned forward in the saddle. His father had not spoken often of his childhood. "Please, sire, tell me about it."

The king nodded. "It happened when both of us were lads. We were accompanying our fathers on a hunting expedition on the Southern skirts of these mountains. The hunt had been successful, and one afternoon while the servants were preparing dinner, Raudorn and I slipped away. We had heard the stories from childhood, you see, but this was the first time that either of us came close enough to the mountains to seek the Sword in earnest."

"What is this Sword, sire?"

"Ah, that's right. You don't know about the Sword." The king blew out his whiskers. "According to the legend, Tuddreal lost his first sword in his duel against Yustaan. Have you heard of Yustaan?"

Morumus shook his head.

"Legend describes Yustaan as a giant of man, born in the icy wastes of the far north. It says he led a band of *olmhori*—giant men like himself." Heclaid gave Morumus a significant look. "It says, too, he was backed by a dark power."

"The Dark Faith?"

"It would fit, for Yustaan was a ruthless marauder who offered human sacrifices to the old gods. But the spread of Tuddreal's Aesusian kingdom threatened his power. So the olmhori attacked Tuddreal's knights, and in the subsequent fight Tuddreal faced Yustaan in single combat. The giant wielded a massive war hammer, and with it he shattered Tuddreal's sword. But the king leapt upon the hammer's shaft and plunged what was left of his weapon into Yustaan's eye."

"And so he won?"

"Yustaan died immediately. It was a great victory for Tuddreal, but his sword was beyond repair. That's when the Sword comes into the story. As Tuddreal returned from battle, he met two strange monks bearing a long chest. From this chest the monks drew a long sword, which they then presented to the king. It was covered in strange symbols which neither Tuddreal nor his knights recognized."

" 'What sword is this?' Tuddreal asked. 'And what are these writings?' "

" 'This is *Melechur*,' said the monks, 'The Sword of the King. It belonged to Dathidd, who took it from the giant that he himself slew, as recorded in Holy Writ. These symbols are Semric characters.' "

" 'What do they say?' asked Tuddreal."

" 'Their sword shall pierce their own heart,' was the reply. 'So long as you wield it in this spirit, O King, Melechur will never fail.' "

"A verse from the Psalms." Morumus knew the passage well. "It speaks of what happens to the wicked." He frowned. "But Holy Writ never speaks of Dathidd's sword having any extraordinary powers."

"Nor does the legend," Heclaid said. "It says only that the blade was unbreakable and never lost its edge. But this was because it was forged in the ancient days, by skill now lost in the world—not from any intrinsic power in the blade itself. Even the verse inscribed on the blade was meant not as an incantation, but as a reminder to the bearer."

Morumus nodded. "All the same, to possess Tuddreal's sword would be a potent symbol."

Heclaid chuckled. "You begin to see the appeal, I think."

"Yes, sire. But you said that you and Father were nearly killed. What happened?"

"We found a cave, and were foolish enough to enter. We thought we had found Tuddreal's grave. But in reality, we found the home of a bear."

"How did you escape?"

"We fled. The bear was not fully awake, and that gave us a head start. Still, we would have died had it not been for Toercanth."

Morumus inhaled sharply. "Donnach's father?"

"Yes. He was not much older than we at the time, and had himself wandered far south through the mountains from his own country. I never did learn the reason why . . ." Heclaid frowned as if trying to remember, then shook his head. "In any event, he saw us fleeing and saved our lives."

"He killed the bear—single-handedly?"

"No, but he managed to give it a fright with his sling and stave. The beast was still groggy and eventually gave up. Still, it was the bravest thing I have ever seen—and the beginning of a friendship that lasted to this day."

The mention of Donnach's father brought Morumus back to the present.

"Do you think he will believe us, sire?"

Heclaid looked north over the wide lands of Grendannath. "Toercanth will believe us. Of that I have no doubt. The real question is whether he can persuade the other chiefs to believe us. Our missionaries have witnessed great success among the Grendannathi. But spiritual transformation is a different thing from cultural assimilation, and our present embassy aims at the latter."

"I don't understand, sire. I thought we were seeking a military alliance."

"The Grendannathi will never agree to a mere military alliance, Morumus. It is an inviolable custom among them that they fight for none but themselves."

"If that be so, sire, then what hope do we have?"

A bright light flared in Heclaid's eyes as he turned his gaze on Morumus. "Our hope is in a grander design, my boy. The Grendannathi will not fight for any but their own, so we must persuade them that we are their own. By and large, they have embraced our faith. Now we must persuade them to embrace our race—to become one people with us."

Morumus gaped. "Is that possible, sire?"

"The Mersians have united with the Dyfanni. The High Princess of the Dyfanni, now the Queen of Mersex, is with child. That child will rule both peoples. The only way we will ever stand against such a united South is if we unite the North. On this Oethur and I are in full concord. He and Rhianwyn bring together Lothair and Nornindaal. But alone this is insufficient. Yet if we can persuade the Grendannathi to join with us, we may yet protect all three of our peoples against Mersian hegemony and the depredations of the Dark Faith."

"It's Tuddreal against Yustaan all over again," Morumus whispered.

"What's that?"

Morumus repeated his words for the king to hear, and Heclaid nodded.

"Let us pray for the same outcome, then."

Morumus nodded.

It wouldn't hurt to have the Sword, either . . .

"Sire!" One of the men-at-arms, who had gone ahead as a scout, now came charging back up the trail. "Sire, a Grendannathi party approaches!"

Heclaid raised his hand, then turned to his companion. "Your hour approaches, Morumus. Take great care to listen and translate exactly what you hear. You know now how much depends on our endeavor."

Morumus took a deep breath. "Yes, sire."

It was not long before the Grendannathi came into view. There were seven men in all, exactly half the number of the Lothairin party. Six of them were warriors on foot. These carried halberds, and long-bladed knives hung from their kilt belts. The seventh, riding at the center, bore no weapon beyond his obvious authority. It was he who spoke first when the two parties met.

Morumus translated the man's words. "Hail, King Heclaid! The sons of Lothair are ever welcome in the land of the

Grendannathi. My name is Anguth. I am *brenilad* to Clan Glachmor."

Heclaid smiled. "Toercanth's clan, Morumus. Return his hail, and tell him we are honored by his welcome."

"Hail, Anguth, King's Echo!" Morumus said, acknowledging the meaning and import of *brenilad*. "You do us honor with your welcome."

Anguth smiled, and Morumus guessed the brenilad was not much older than himself.

"And what is your name?"

"I am called Morumus."

"Prince of Roots?" Anguth gave a low whistle. "A fine name."

The translation of his name caught Morumus off guard.

"Finish the translation, Morumus. Bring the good news to my people, Prince of Roots. I will wait for you in Everlight."

Donnach's last words brought a sudden lump to Morumus's throat. He swallowed hard.

Anguth's smile vanished. "Have I offended, Morumus?"

"No, Anguth." Morumus shook his head. "No, all is well."

The smile returned, though less sure. "You are *brenilad* to King Heclaid?"

"Something like that. I am his translator."

"Very good. Would His Majesty prefer I speak Vilguran?"

"*Can* you speak Vilguran?"

"A little. One of your missionaries teaches me. I understand it better than I speak it."

"No need to trouble yourself, then—so long as you do not mind my faltering Grendannathi."

"Thank you, Morumus—and I might add that you speak my people's language well. But now, please tell His Majesty that we are sent to escort your embassy to the *ceilheath*—the meeting of our clans—at Grenmaur."

Morumus relayed the message, and Heclaid nodded.

"Tell him we welcome their company and ask him if he would do us the honor of riding with us at the head of the company."

Anguth agreed, and the combined company set out north. At first Morumus had wondered if they might lose Anguth's horseless escort, but the warriors showed no sign of difficulty in keeping up with the mounted men. King Heclaid had offered them the use of the Lothairins' spare mounts, but Anguth declined.

"My lord is most kind," he said, "but except at great need, regular warriors are forbidden to ride. There are two days yet until the ceilheath begins. We have plenty of time."

"Tell me, Anguth," Heclaid said through Morumus as their march commenced, "what news of my friend, Toercanth mac Creiddor?"

A pained look flashed on Anguth's features. "My lord Toercanth has fallen asleep in Aesus."

"What?" The king closed his eyes for a long moment. "When did this happen?"

Morumus relayed the question—and its reply.

"Six weeks ago, sire. He was thrown from his horse and struck his head on a rock."

Heclaid frowned. "It was an accident?"

"Yes, sire."

The king sighed, and it was at least a minute before he spoke again. "I suppose Mannoch is chief now?"

Anguth nodded.

Heclaid glanced at Morumus. "This is not good news for us."

"Is Mannoch Donnach's brother, sire?"

"Yes. He is an honest man, but he is less enthusiastic about our Lord than Donnach—and less friendly to Lothair than his father." The king frowned. "And he was very much attached to his brother. He will not take his death well."

Though Anguth spoke no Tuasraeth, he was evidently a careful listener for he caught the mention of Donnach's name. He looked at Morumus. "Did I hear His Majesty speak of Donnach, brother to my chief?"

"Yes."

"May I ask, how is he?"

Morumus relayed the question.

"Ask him if he knows Donnach."

"Oh yes," Anguth's smile was instant and unfeigned. "It was my lord Donnach who taught me to believe the good news of Aesus!"

Heclaid sighed as Morumus translated. "Tell him."

"How much should I tell him, sire?"

"All of it, Morumus, but ask him to be discrete. I must give the news to Lord Mannoch myself."

Morumus turned to Anguth. "I will give you news of Donnach, if you promise not to share it with your master. His Majesty is anxious to convey the news personally."

Anguth considered for a moment, then nodded.

"I spent a considerable amount of time with Donnach in Caeldora. I tutored him in Vilguran, and he taught me to read and write your language."

"Ah. I wondered how you, who are no native, could speak our language so well. But I am not surprised! Donnach is a good teacher!"

"He *was* a good teacher."

Anguth caught the emphasis in Morumus's words, and he frowned. "I do not understand."

Morumus looked at the Grendannathi. "Donnach has also fallen asleep in Aesus."

If the news of Toercanth's death had hit Heclaid hard, the news of Donnach's death seemed to wound Anguth. His smile crumpled, and his countenance dropped.

"Oh no. No, Lord!" The brenilad shook his head—as if thereby he might undo what he had heard. When he looked up again, there were tears running down his cheeks. "How did this happen?"

"He saved my life." Morumus struggled to keep his own emotions from bursting forth to join Anguth's. "But in saving my life, he himself was murdered."

"Murdered?" Anger blossomed in the other man's cheeks. "By whom?"

"By wicked men masquerading as Aesusian monks. They wear robes of scarlet, and call themselves—"

"The Order of the Saving Blood?"

Morumus stared at Anguth. "You know of them?"

"I know of them."

"How?"

The *brenilad* ignored the question. "Can you prove these things?"

"I was there, if that's what you mean."

"Were there other witnesses?"

"Yes. The red monk who murdered him, and one other person from our abbey."

"And where are they now?"

"The red monk is dead. I killed him myself."

"And the other?"

"He fled—to where, I have no idea."

Anguth pursed his lips. "This is very bad, Morumus. Please tell His Highness that he must take great care in relaying this news to my chief."

Morumus relayed the words. Heclaid, who could not understand their words but who had been watching the exchange, narrowed his gaze. "There's something he is not telling us, Morumus."

"I think you're right, sire. He knew the name of the Red Order before I gave it. But when I asked him how, he did not answer."

"Ask him again—from me."

When Morumus did so, the brenilad looked from Morumus to Heclaid, then back again. "You must not say that I gave you this information, for it is not the place of a brenilad to speak beyond his master's commands. We may trust each other, yes?"

"We will be as discrete with your news as we ask you to be with our own."

"Very well." Anguth looked grim. "You are not the only ones to have sent an embassy to the ceilheath. The Red Order has also come."

On its own, the small stream would not have justified the construction of such a large bridge. But the men of the North had not constructed Teru Bridge to cross a meager water. Rather, they had built the bridge to span the wide lip of the brook's deep ravine.

The abrupt canyon itself was most peculiar. Formed by some great earthquake beyond the memory of living men, the fissure opened without warning amidst the central moorlands of the North. It was not particularly deep—no more than a hundred feet at most points—but its cliffs were precipitous and its length notable. For generations it had formed a natural border, the undisputed frontier between Lothair to the west and Nornindaal to the east. Where the main road from Dunross to Grindangled crossed its path, the two nations had cooperated to construct the Teru Bridge. The bridge was not garrisoned on either side, and in the long years of peace between the two nations no force of men had ever crossed the bridge in arms.

But that would all change soon.

The thought struck Oethur as he crested the last small rise west of the bridge.

"Look well upon the bridge this afternoon, Your Grace." He spoke to Bishop Treowin, who rode at his ride hand. "This may well be the last time we cross it in peace."

"I pray you are mistaken, sire."

An armed camp covered the ground on the bridge's eastern side, swaddling the earth with smoking campfires and canvas tents. The host belonged to the four lords of Nornindaal who had not sworn to Aeldred—Halbir, Jugeim, Meporu, and Yorth.

Will they swear to me?

Oethur wished he knew the answer.

"Whatever happens today, Your Grace, armies will cross this bridge. If things go well, they will be our armies marching east against my brother. But if things go ill, his armies will march west on Dunross. Either way, the days of peace are behind us."

"But not forever, sire. May we not hope to see such days return?"

"We may hope."

A few minutes later, Oethur and Treowin drew up beside the bridge's western end. Behind them, a dozen Lothairin men-at-arms, commanded by Morumus's brother Haedorn, also drew rein. The latter rode forward.

"What terms shall I ask, my lord?"

Oethur looked at Morumus's red-haired brother. The man's green eyes were grim. "I ask only for safe conduct—for Bishop Treowin and myself."

"Very good, my lord."

As Haedorn nudged his horse out onto the bridge, Oethur saw a rider from the Nornish camp step out to meet them. The two riders converged at the bridge's center.

Oethur never took his eyes from the conference. But as he waited, he prayed. *Lord, give me wisdom this day. How can I persuade these men?*

That the four lords needed persuasion seemed obvious. He knew that all of them had loved his father. He knew, too, that they must harbor significant doubts about Aeldred.

Otherwise why risk his wrath by refusing to attend his coronation?

Yet their letter of summons had given no assurance to Oethur, either. *Even after reading my letter they have not backed me.*

Oethur's letter—sent before his wedding to Rhianwyn—had denounced his brother Aeldred as a heathen, a murderer, and a usurper. Besides his own signature, that letter had borne the attesting seals of bishops Ciolbail and Treowin. It had laid out his own claim to the crown, including Treowin's testimony that King Ulfered had intended to change the succession. If the lords were not convinced by Oethur's letter, what additional evidence could he offer? What further persuasions could he produce?

O Lord, give light!

No sooner had he finished the prayer than Oethur saw Haedorn turn his mount. He watched the Lothairin return, trying to read some sense of the conversation from the man's expression. What he saw was not encouraging.

"They will grant safe conduct to Bishop Treowin"—Haedorn's face flushed with irritation—"but not for you, my lord."

Treowin scowled. "That makes no sense."

"Oh, it makes sense, Your Grace," Haedorn growled. "It makes sense if they intend to take Oethur prisoner. How much favor could they curry with Aeldred by presenting his brother's head?"

"Did they speak thus?" asked the bishop.

"The man with whom I spoke would not deny the possibility."

Treowin sighed. "It was a long ride from Dunross. I had hoped it would be more profitable."

"Indeed." Haedorn nudged his horse to move past Oethur toward the men. "I'll prepare the men to move out."

"Wait." Oethur laid his hand on Haedorn's arm.

"My lord?"

"We're not leaving."

"What?" Treowin and Haedorn spoke together.

"I'm going across."

"My lord, you cannot be serious."

"But I am, Haedorn."

"Sire." Treowin gave him a stern look. "It would be madness to surrender to those men without safe conduct."

"And what choice do I have?" Oethur met the bishop's gaze without flinching. "Retreat to Dunross?"

"*Return* to Dunross, yes," interjected Haedorn. "But as a stratagem, not a retreat. Think about it, my lord. These four lords have already refused your brother's summons. That makes them outlaws in Grindangled. They have only two ways to return thither: with your head, or at your back. My counsel is that you refuse them the former, and so force them to choose the latter. Return with me to Dunross, and invite them to follow. Promise them the safe conduct they refused to grant you."

Treowin nodded. "Haedorn speaks sense, sire."

Oethur shook his head. "I appreciate your counsel, Haedorn—and yours, Treowin. But no Norn would follow a king who trusts foreigners over his own people. I myself would not!"

Treowin frowned. "You think it is a test?"

"I think that's exactly what it is." The pieces seemed to fall into place as Oethur spoke. "So far my crown rests on Lothairin arms. An insistence upon safe conduct is an insistence to be able to return to those arms. But if I surrender without any promises provided, I demonstrate that I am willing to rest my claim to the crown solely in the hands of those I seek to rule."

"You have a point." Haedorn frowned. "It's not implausible. But you may be overthinking the matter. What if you're wrong?"

"It's possible," Oethur conceded. "And I remember telling your brother that he thinks too much." He smiled at the memory of those simpler days. "But the facts are simple. I cannot depose my brother without the support of these men. And if I cannot depose my brother, what is my life but a liability to those who protect me?"

Haedorn said nothing, but Treowin nodded.

"You have the right of it, sire. Shall we go?"

Oethur nodded.

As the two Norns nudged their mounts forward, Oethur looked back.

"We will return, Lord Haedorn. Depend upon it!"

Green eyes bored into him. "My lord, *everything* depends upon it!"

As their horses clopped across the bridge, Oethur's thoughts returned to their previous question: how could he persuade the lords to side with him against Aeldred? What evidence did he possess, beyond his own testimony and that of Bishop Treowin—

The bishop!

A sudden memory rose—a fragment of a conversation he'd almost forgotten. It had occurred just after his father's funeral, while he and Aeldred were alone . . .

"A very moving service," said Aeldred. "Erworn did well."

"Yes, though I confess I was surprised that Bishop Treowin did not speak."

"He could not, brother."

"What do you mean, Aeldred?"

"The man can no longer speak."

Oethur tripped, and only just caught himself from falling. "What?"

"It happened on his return voyage from Midgaddan last year. For some misguided reason, he took passage on a Trathastudy ship. A Tratharan ship, brother! Something happened, and they cut out his tongue before casting him off on the wharf at Toberstan."

It had been a lie, of course—as Oethur had learned soon enough. But had Aeldred lied to anybody else? Surely others who attended the funeral would have noticed the bishop's silence?

Perhaps one of these four lords?

Perhaps one of them had asked Aeldred the same question?

And if so . . .

Perhaps he received the same lie in reply?

Oethur knew it was a slim hope. But it was something.

Without stopping his horse or turning his head, Oethur spoke sideways in a low voice. "Treowin, don't turn your head. But do you remember what my brother said—about the Trathari cutting out your tongue?"

The bishop snorted. "Yes. A foolish lie."

"But a necessary one, if he was to explain why you did not speak at Father's funeral."

"He threatened to kill both you and Ciolbail if I so much as opened my mouth!"

"Peace, Treowin!" Oethur made a small placatory gesture. "I'm not accusing you. I'm asking if you remember, because it may be our only chance. Others besides me must have marked your silence—perhaps even one or more of these four lords. If Aeldred told them the same lie . . ."

"It would be further proof of your brother's duplicity."

"Exactly."

"Should be easy enough to find out. As soon as I speak, they'll know—"

"No. Don't speak at all until I give you the signal."

"Sire, I don't see how perpetuating such a deception—"

"We're perpetuating no deception." Oethur shook his head. "For any who have not heard the lie, your silence will be interpreted as appropriate deference to me. But if any have heard it, your silence will remind them."

"As you wish, sire. But I still don't see how this ruse will help."

"These lords are honest men, Treowin, but they are also proud. Suppose only one of them heard Aeldred's lie. Do you think he would volunteer the fact that he was deceived? But if one of them speaks it, then you must speak—thus offering undeniable evidence."

"Clever." Treowin grunted. "It might work."

"Let us pray that it does."

Reaching the eastern end of the bridge, Oethur and Treowin were greeted by a mounted captain. His bearing told of easy competence, and he greeted them with neutral courtesy.

"My lords bid you both welcome." He offered a seated bow to both men in turn.

Treowin nodded a mute acknowledgment.

"You are well met, captain. Please take us to their lordships."

The captain nodded, then turned his mount.

As they rode through the camp toward its center, Oethur saw the men-at-arms pause in their labors to look at him. He could see the question in their eyes, and suspected it was the same one he asked himself:

Would he be their king?

The captain led them to a large pavilion tent at the center of the camp, and all three men dismounted. Four soldiers stood waiting by the entrance. One pair took their mounts, while the others held the tent flaps open.

"Their lordships await my lords," said the captain.

"Thank you. I do not believe I know your name, captain."

"Marrow, my lord."

"Thank you, Captain Marrow." Oethur inclined his head.

Inside the tent, Oethur and Treowin found the four lords of Nornindaal seated around a circular table within a wider circle of pole-mounted braziers. None moved to rise as the newcomers entered, yet one of them—Oethur recognized Lord Halbir—gestured that they should take the two remaining empty seats.

Coming to the table, Oethur gestured that Treowin should seat himself first. Then he drew his sword. "My lord Halbir, my lord Jugeim." He eyed each of the older men in turn as he spoke their names. "My lord Meporu, my lord Yorth. Loyal servants of King Aesus and faithful thanes to my father Ulfered, king under the King . . ." He paused to draw deep breath.

This is it.

Then he laid his sword broadside on the table.

"To you, true lords of Nornindaal, I surrender."

Over the years, Yens had undertaken many unsavory assignments.

He was a Lumana, a Hand of the Moon.

As the name implied, it was not a job full of sunshine and sugar lumps. To the contrary, the world of the Lumanae was a realm of secrecy and shadow. Shadows were dark, messy places. Most people could never guess just how much mess they concealed.

But somebody had to know. That was the purpose of the Lumanae. Just as the moon guarded the earth in the name of the sun, so the Hands of the Moon watched over the Vilguran Empire in behalf of its emperor.

Only now, the Lumanae were not watching over the empire.

This time, Yens and his fellows were operating in Aeld Gowan.

The Lunumbir had brought them to this island in pursuit of answers. Why had the Red Order brutally sacked Lorudin Abbey in Caeldora? It was thought that two monks who escaped that slaughter and returned to Aeld Gowan—Morumus and Oethur—would provide the answers. But upon landing, the Lumanae found much larger questions to occupy their attention:

Why was the Red Order working hand-in-glove with the Mersian king? Why was the Order of the Saving Blood, which had played the loyal handmaiden to the emperor's ambitions on the continent of Midgaddan, now working to strengthen the only nation on earth that could threaten the empire?

To penetrate these machinations, the Lumanae had intercepted one of the Red Order's dispatch riders. The rider himself they had killed. Then the Lunumbir sent Yens to Mereclestour in the rider's place, to learn what he could by masquerading as a red monk.

"Until we meet again, your name is Gwurn. You know what to do."

In the weeks since undertaking the disguise, Yens had learned much. So had the Lunumbir. The information gathered established a clear picture.

The Red Order intended to subvert the world order.

They would start with the Church, where they had gained a foothold already. From within the Church, they were seeking to conquer Aeld Gowan—and to eradicate the men of the North who opposed them. Once Aeld Gowan was firmly in hand, they would reactivate their activities on the continent of Midgaddan. To this point, the Red Order had feigned to serve the emperor within the Church. But once they had a secure foothold independent of his patronage, that well-placed service would become widespread treachery.

His investigation complete, the Lunumbir had returned to Versaden to report to the emperor. But he had left Yens behind—still disguised in the role of the red monk Gwurn—in order to sabotage the efforts of the Red Order.

"Don't waste your talents on something piddling, Yens. Wait for a significant opportunity. When it comes, take it—and then escape. Deal them a crippling blow, then return to Versaden."

Thus the Lunumbir had instructed at their secret meeting a fortnight prior. Yens had immediately suggested assassinating the Archbishop of Mereclestour . . .

"He's already betrayed the emperor, sir. Why not eliminate him? They've got me stationed in the Tower of Luca. It would be a simple task . . ."

"No, Yens. Nothing that overt. Just last year Mersex lost both her king and archbishop to assassination, and there has already been one attempt on the life of their new king. I don't want you throwing any more fuel on that fire. Hurt the Red Order, but do it without further enflaming the political situation. We are the Hands of the Moon, not the dogs of war."

So Yens had resigned himself to wait.

Wait, and continue to pretend he was an enthusiastic tree worshiper.

Had this been the most he had to endure, he thought he could bear it indefinitely. But today, the archbishop intended to stoop to a new level of depravity. And he expected his loyal red monks to participate.

Over the years, Yens had received many unsavory assignments.

But nothing like this.

Simnor's agents had sacked the Aesusian monastery on Urras in the north.

Today he would begin torturing his prisoners.

Urien steeled herself as the door to her cell swung open.

"The Mother's Hand requires your presence, my lady."

The red monks' courtesy infuriated Urien. If they had shown it out of respect for her gender, she might not have minded. But the Red Order cared nothing for women; they murdered little girls! The monks called her "my lady" for one reason only . . .

Her brother had ordered them to give proper honor to the Queen's Heart.

"I'm not your lady," she said to the two monks who escorted her down the hall of the Tower of Luca. "*Your lady* is a senseless wooden idol."

The monks made no reply.

"You know what the Aesusians say about that?" Urien continued in a conversational tone. "They say we become like what we worship. Do you *like* being senseless?"

"To become like the Mother—to return to her someday—will be an honor."

Urien looked sideways at the monk who had spoken. The raised hood made identification impossible, of course, but she thought he must be new. By now, most of the monks simply ignored her.

"Why wait for someday? If it's such an honor, why not throw yourself from the walls of this castle and return to the Mother today?"

Before the new monk could reply, his fellow interjected. "Do not argue with her ladyship, brother. She is suffering from a strong delusion. But we take her to the cure."

"You take me to my brother, you mean." Urien snorted. "Has he now taken to calling himself the Cure? Were his previous titles insufficient?"

"We're taking you to the dungeons!" snapped the new monk. "And you'll see soon enough what these Aesusians say when their faith is put to the test! You'll see how shallow—"

"Enough, brother!" said the other monk. "No more!"

After this, Urien knew that no amount of goading would provoke either monk to speak. But she no longer cared. Now she was worried about the words of the new monk. She had visited one dungeon of the Red Order in Marfesbury. And she remembered all too well the lower levels of the Muthadannach in Caeldora . . .

The Well of Souls.

Urien shuddered at the recollection, shivered at the memory of falling into that frigid cistern of human blood . . .

What would Somnadh have waiting in these dungeons?

Buried in the subbasement of the Tower of Luca, the Hall of Inquisition was a large, square chamber. Arched colonnades along two of its walls had been divided and barred to form facing rows of small cells. Through the bars of these cells, doomed prisoners could see and hear those on the three expandable frames at the room's center being put to the question.

The far wall contained extensive racks of cruel implements. Some of these looked wickedly peculiar, and Urien forced herself *not* to envision their many uses. The racks flanked a pair of small ovens recessed into the wall itself. It was at these ovens—each of which glowed like a livid dragon's eye—that she saw the two questioners heating their specialized tools to a dull, sinister red.

This was worse than she imagined. Urien had heard the moans and screams of the current victim almost as soon as they began descending the lower flight of steps. But it was not until they passed through the doors that she recognized her.

It was indeed a *her.*

"Abbess Nahenna!"

The former abbess of Urras Monastery was stretched upon the chamber's middle frame. A pair of heavy chains bound her wrists to its top corners, while another pair bound her ankles to the bottom. Geared mechanisms had pulled the chains taut, and the abbess's face—which Urien remembered as being ever lined with kindness—was now etched with agony.

Nevertheless, Nahenna stirred at Urien's cry.

"Urien?" she called, and lifted her head.

What Urien saw next made both her heart and stomach lurch.

Her eyes!

The questioners had removed Nahenna's eyes. The unseeing face turned this way and that, trying to locate Urien by sound.

"Urien?"

"Abbess!"

She tried to rush to Nahenna's side, but she had not taken three steps before a third figure stepped out from behind one of the other torture frames to intercept her. Seeing him, she reel backed with an angry hiss.

"Somnadh!"

"Dearest Urien." Whatever the affectionate terms, his tone was ice. "I see you know our guest. I wonder if you know these others?" He waved a hand toward the cells on either wall.

Urien followed his gesture, and gasped. The cells were filled with familiar faces . . .

The monks and monkesses of Urras Monastery . . . but how?

And then she knew.

Fallen.

Somehow, Urras Monastery . . .

"Release them." She wheeled back toward her brother. "Release them, Somnadh!"

The tilt of his head reminded Urien of a raven. His black eyes flashed. "I will release all of them alive, if you will return to the Mother."

So that's what this is really about . . .

Urien clenched her teeth, and turned away from him. She looked at the frightened faces crammed into the small cells. Their eyes transfixed her.

"You don't have to love the Mother, Urien," Somnadh continued behind her. "Though she is lovely, I am willing to accept that you cannot see it. At least not yet. All I require is that you serve her."

She looked back. "If I agree to pour the blood, you will let these people go?"

"Yes."

"All of them?"

"Yes, dear one." Somnadh was studying her carefully. "It really is that simple."

"How?"

"What?"

"How will you free them? You've destroyed the monastery, haven't you?"

"Fair's fair, Urien. You destroyed the Muthadannach in Caeldora."

"Then where will you send them?"

"Wherever you say. I will place their lives entirely into your hands, if you end right now this foolish and senseless rebellion."

"And if I said you must put them all on a ship to Dunross, you would do it?"

"There are ships in the harbor."

"How do I know you will keep your word?"

Somnadh glowered. "You may not agree with what I've done, Urien. You may not even like who I've become. But have I ever lied to you directly?"

Urien considered. "Will you swear—on the Mother?"

Somnadh sighed. "If your brother's word is not enough for you, Urien, then yes. I will swear upon the Mother herself. There is no greater oath. But if I swear, then you too must swear."

"Swear what?"

"You must pledge the rest of your life to the Mother's service."

"You already said that."

"And you must renounce Aesus—once and for all."

To this point, Urien had been on the brink of capitulation. But now she stiffened. At the same moment, she heard a stir among the prisoners.

"Urien, *no*!" several of them whispered at the same time.

Somnadh ignored them. "The Queen's Heart cannot be divided in her loyalties."

"Loyalties?" Urien protested. "You said nothing of loyalties, Somnadh. In fact, you said I did *not* have to love the Mother. I only have to serve her."

"And if you serve her with a whole heart," Somnadh's face reddened and his voice grew vehement, "you will come, in time, to love her. But not so long as you cling to this false affection for the things of Aesus!"

Somnadh looked as if he would say more, but then he stopped. When he spoke again, his tone had returned to a reasonable pitch. "You've told me more than once, Urien, that you are no Aesusian. All I'm asking you to do is swear you won't become one."

"No, Somnadh. You are asking for more than that." Urien looked straight into the vacant darkness of his eyes. "You are asking me to become a little girl again—to forget all that I have learned about the Mother and the Mordruui, and return to being your pet sister." She shook her head. "But the little girl you swept away to Caeldora died. She died in the dark isolation of the Muthadannach—starved by the hollow promises of the Dark Faith."

Urien could feel the tears beginning, and knew that when they came she would not be able to speak for a long time. She turned to look at the prisoners.

"I wish more than anything that I could free all of you." She saw that she was not the only one with tears in her eyes. She turned back to face her brother. "But I can't do it, Somnadh." Her shoulders heaved. "I cannot go back to the Mother, and I cannot renounce Aesus."

As the flood of tears engulfed Urien, complete silence fell upon the Hall of Inquisition . . .

But only for a moment.

"You cannot?" Somnadh's quiet words quivered the tense air. Then the tension broke. "You *will*!" he roared, his face contorting with anger and turning an ugly, mottled color.

Urien tried to turn away, but he grabbed her by the chin and pointed to Nahenna. "You think her faith is better than mine? You think she has more certainty?"

Urien tried to pull free, but Somnadh's grip was like iron.

"You think she has more certainty in death than I?" he screamed into her face. "I will show you how wrong you are, sister!" He lifted his head. "Guards! Bring a chair, and bind her to it!"

As the guards took hold of Urien, Somnadh turned away. "Heat the knives! We will skin the abbess alive!"

"No!"

"Yes!" shouted Somnadh, wheeling on Urien. "Unless you swear this very instant!"

Before Urien could respond, Abbess Nahenna lifted her head . . .

And *looked* at Urien.

"You must not do it, Urien." Though her eyes were gone, there could be no mistake in the direction of her gaze. "You would injure me far more than he can, dear."

"But you will die!" Urien sobbed.

"'He that believes on me, even if he should die, he will live.' They've already murdered Nerias, Urien. When I die, I will see him with my Lord in Everlight. Do not fear those who can only kill the body. Rather fear him who can destroy both body and soul in Belneol!"

Transfixed by that eyeless gaze, Urien nodded. "I won't, Abbess."

As the red monks forced Urien into a chair, Somnadh looked from her to the abbess, then growled at his servants.

"Make it excruciating!" he said to the questioners, then turned to the men holding Urien. "Hold my sister's head so that she sees every detail . . . and if she tries to close her eyes, hold them open!"

Hours later, Urien fell through the door of her cell. Her mind would not run in straight lines, and she found she could not stand. So she crawled to her bed . . . where the only interruption to her wracking sobs were her shuddering screams.

But it all transpired in silence. Her tears were dry, and her voice was gone.

All spent watching the abbess die . . .

Hours.

Somnadh's minions had done their work with an eager, macabre delight. They had used nomergenna to make the abbess see and hear things too horrible to imagine. Nahenna had died in horrific agony—but only after they had used every trick possible to prolong her suffering.

Hours.

And yet at the end, something inexplicable . . .

At the very end, just as her life was slipping away, a change came over the abbess. Without warning, Nahenna's face shone with that motherly glow that had characterized her life at Urras Monastery. Urien could not believe her eyes.

At the last, Abbess Nahenna had died with a smile . . .

And she had not renounced Aesus.

All the power of the Dark Faith had failed to break the abbess . . .

But something *had* broken.

Inside Urien.

She could feel things changing inside her, like a thousand windows shattering all at once . . .

What is happening to me?

She did not know . . . but she was no longer afraid.

The ceilheath of the Grendannathi had just begun . . .

Already it was proving to be an overwhelming experience.

Riding toward the great roundhouse situated at the settlement's center, Morumus let his eyes soak in his surroundings. A city of tents stretched as far as he could see. Some of these were large, some small, and many bore colorful swaths of tartan decoration to signify clan affiliation.

There are so many!

The ceilheath had drawn representatives not just from all the major clans, but also from many of the minor septs.

Along with the sights, Morumus could hear the sound of pipes playing. It would begin with long, low droning. Then, without warning, the rumbling would burst into a stream of bold notes. The effect was like a storm breaking: powerful, startling, and yet sweet. Like waves of rain, the sounds moved up and down, back and forth. There were constant variations, sometimes quite subtle—but the pipers never repeated the exact note twice in a row. The peculiar music filled the wide valley with strange, haunting melodies.

Morumus turned his face back toward the roundhouse before them. Soon they would meet Donnach's brother, Mannoch mac Toercanth.

Soon I will have to tell him that his brother is dead. Anguth had warned them to take great care in relaying their news . . .

But how can such a blow be softened?

Morumus prayed for wisdom. So much was at stake. If their embassy failed, it would be more than Lothairin-Grendannathi relations that suffered. The North itself would fall to Mersex. And the old order of the Church would fall to the Red Order . . .

To the Dark Faith.

As these thoughts burned in his mind, Morumus lifted his eyes and saw—through the shimmering smoke escaping the peak of the roundhouse—the hulking mass of Carrad Gren. The steep hill reared up just beyond the eastern edge of the settlement. And though daylight was already beginning to wane, he could still see the crumbling stone circle squatting atop its summit. Most of the stone monoliths were missing. But a few still stood.

The pagan ruin reminded Morumus of the precariousness of their situation. *The Grendannathi are not far removed from the old ways . . .*

Would his ill tidings, combined with the presence of the Red Order, push them back?

He was about to find out.

Drawing up before the great roundhouse, the men dismounted.

Anguth turned to Morumus. "My men would be happy to care for your horses and feed your guards while you meet with the chiefs. May I give them the order?"

Morumus translated the question for Heclaid, who nodded. "Thank you, Anguth. That is most kind."

Morumus smiled as he watched the six Grendannathi warriors leading away their Lothairin escort. The men-at-arms were well-seasoned troops, but from their expressions he could tell that they had never experienced anything like a Grendannathi ceilheath.

At least I'm not the only one.

But his smile vanished as Anguth led them indoors.

There were no chambers within the great roundhouse. The great open space was interrupted only by the round pillars—thick evergreen trunks, stripped of bark and branch but now seasoned with years of smoke—supporting the thatched roof. Morumus had a clear view of the sunken fire pit as soon as he entered the hall.

What he saw chilled his blood.

Eleven great chairs formed a semicircle around the far side of the ring of fire. On these were seated the major clan chiefs of the Grendannathi. Behind the chairs were two rows of benches, also semicircular. The lesser chiefs, the heads of the minor septs, sat on these, and the farther bench was raised a foot above the nearer so that all could see the fire—and those who stood before it.

It was the latter sight that made Morumus's veins run cold.

Standing on the near side of the fire, facing the assembled chiefs, were red monks. There were two of them: one to speak, and the other to translate. They had just finished speaking as the Lothairins entered, and so Anguth stepped forward.

"Hail, my master!" He addressed his words to the tall chief at the center.

As the man stood, Morumus could see the resemblance. Though a few years older, he had the same red hair—only here it was allowed to grow long rather than cut in an abbey tonsure. And there was the same intelligent expression. There could be no doubt as to the man's identity.

Donnach's older brother.

"Hail, loyal Anguth." came the reply. "Whom bringest thou to this hall?" The formal question indicated that both Mannoch and the other chiefs knew the answer already.

"I bring the King of Lothair and his brenilad, my master."

"Let them share our fire," the chief intoned, and made a bidding gesture.

As the Lothairins came forward, the red monks shuffled off to the left. Morumus was surprised to see that the two men had lowered their cowls. But he was even more surprised when his eyes met those of the taller monk. There was no recognition evident in the man's face, but Morumus's heart lurched.

It cannot be!

Not only that . . . it was impossible!

Ulwilf?

The first man Morumus had ever killed. It had been a just killing, too. Not only had Ulwilf led the Mordruui who butchered and burned Lorudin Abbey, it was he who murdered Donnach.

Morumus had plunged a knife deep into the Dree's dark heart.

He had watched the villain die.

How then could he be standing here?

Morumus strained his eyes, squinting at the red monk through the smoky light. After a long moment, he let out a breath he had not realized he'd been holding.

The monk was not Ulwilf.

But the resemblance is eerie . . .

"Hail, Heclaid, King of Lothair!" Mannoch's booming declamation reclaimed Morumus's attention. At the name of the king, the other chiefs flanking Mannoch stood. "You are welcome to our fire, and to this ceilheath of our people."

Speaking through Morumus, King Heclaid addressed the gathering.

"Hail, chiefs of Grendannath!" He made a series of bows around the semicircle, then made a deeper bow to the man at its center. "Hail, Mannoch mac Toercanth!" Straightening, the Lothairin king spread out his arms, then bent them to touch his heart. "I greet you as my brother."

A wave of nods bobbed through the assembled chiefs. Though far senior to their newest chief, King Heclaid had shown him full honor according to protocol. A murmur of approval passed through the clan leadership.

Mannoch acknowledged the compliment with a bow of his head. "Bring a chair for my brother-chief!" he called into the shadows behind him. "And bring stools for these others."

Within moments, servants appeared. Two of them bore chairs like those of the eleven, which they placed behind the king. Two others bore stools: one for Morumus, two for the red monks. At Mannoch's gesture, the assembly sat.

Then the chief addressed himself to Heclaid. "Has my brenilad told you of my father's death?"

"He has, my lord. And I grieve for Toercanth." Heclaid's eyes moistened, and his words ran thick with emotion. "He was a great chief, a good friend, and a trusted ally. I look forward to meeting him again in Everlight."

"Doubtless." Mannoch sounded anything but certain. The chief turned his gaze upon Morumus. "And who is your brenilad?"

"I am Morumus, my lord." Morumus stood and bowed.

"You have a fine name, Morumus. Do you know what it means in my language?"

"I have been told, my lord, that it means 'Prince of Roots.'"

"And are you a prince?"

"No, my lord."

"Then how came you by this name?"

"In the language of Dyfann, my lord, it means 'Root Mouse.'"

"But you are Lothairin."

"Yes, my lord."

Mannoch leaned back in his chair. "There seems to be much mystery about you, Morumus. I do not believe we have ever met, yet you speak the language of my people well."

"Thank you, my lord."

"How came you to know our speech?"

Morumus paused.

Heclaid studied Morumus. "What is he asking?"

Morumus translated the question, and the king nodded. "You must tell him."

"Sire, that may lead to . . ."

"I know."

Morumus turned back to Mannoch. "I was taught the language of Grendannath by your brother, my lord."

"Ah!" Mannoch's stern face cracked into a smile. "There is no mystery here, then. My brother would make a natural teacher. He is very zealous, eh?"

"Very zealous, my lord," Morumus agreed.

Mannoch leaned forward, chuckling. "Has he become a bishop yet, my brother?"

"No, my lord." Morumus could not disguise the sudden pain in his voice. "Donnach is not a bishop."

The chuckling stopped. "Then where is he, Morumus?"

Morumus hesitated, then turned back to the king. "He wants to know where Donnach is, sire."

Heclaid looked grim. "Tell him, Morumus."

"Tell him *now*, sire?"

Though his head remained still, the king's eyes turned toward the red monks. "Tell him *who*, Morumus."

Morumus turned back to Mannoch. All eyes in the roundhouse—including those of the red monks—were now fixed on him. They might not have understood the words that had passed between Morumus and Heclaid, but everybody had sensed the tension.

Morumus took a deep breath. His eyes burned, and his heart was in his throat. *How do I say this?* "I regret to inform you, my lord, that your brother is with your father."

Mannoch's smile vanished. "Donnach is . . ." The chief's words faltered. "Donnach is dead?"

"Yes, my lord."

A gasp rippled through the assembled chieftains, and many eyes went wide.

"How, Morumus?"

"Murdered, my lord."

Mannoch's face darkened. "Murdered? My brother, murdered?"

"Yes, my lord."

"By whom?"

Morumus raised his arm, and extended a single finger toward the red monks. "By the Order of the Saving Blood, my lord!"

"What!" Mannoch was on his feet in an instant, his eyes flashing like a bull's at the red robes. "You!"

"It is a lie, my lord!"

The red monks had leapt from their stools. The taller one was speaking in hushed tones, the sentences tumbling over one another in rapid succession. His translator was struggling to keep pace.

"The men of Lothair tell lies, my lord!" The monk shook his fist at Morumus. "It is as I warned my lord before they arrived! This king was no friend to your father, and he is no friend to you, my lord. It was to Lothairin missionaries that your father entrusted your brother's life—and it is the Lothairin king who bears the responsibility for his death!"

The red monk wagged his finger at Mannoch. "Your brother's death is an omen of doom. The men of Lothair covet the land of Grendannath. They seek to swallow up your people, to spend the lives of your warriors in fighting their battles. Then, when you are all dead and they yet live, they will claim your women, kill your children, and take your lands. Mark my words, my lord—they will speak to you of alliance and friendship, of a shared faith and future. But what they really seek is charnel for their wars. Ask them for yourself."

At these words, half the hall was on its feet. Some of the minor chieftains on the back benches were shouting. But Mannoch, his face as red as the fire before him, silenced them.

"Enough!"

There was such authority in his word that the hall immediately fell silent.

The chief turned to Heclaid. "What have you to say to these things, brother-chief?"

Heclaid rose from his chair.

" 'The first seems just in his case, until another comes and investigates him.' "

Morumus translated the proverb with some difficulty.

"The long friendship between our peoples, let alone between your father and me, should be sufficient to dispel this accusation outright."

A few of the older chiefs in the front row nodded.

"And where was that friendship when my brother died?"

This time the approval sounded from the back benches.

Heclaid continued. "Is the land of Lothair too narrow for its people?" The king's eyes flashed. "Are our women less fair than those of Grendannath? Have we ever asked a single thing in return for our friendship? Have we ever asked compensation for our many missionaries martyred in these lands during the darker times?" He shook his head. "No, my lord, we have not. And yet would you now receive an accusation against us—an accusation from foreigners who themselves stand accused?"

"I receive no accusation until it is proven." Mannoch's face was hard. "But I demand an accounting for my brother's blood."

"And you shall have it. For my brenilad, Morumus, witnessed your brother's murder. He has told you already who is responsible. He can tell you how it happened, if you will hear him."

The Grendannathi looked at Morumus again. "You were there, Morumus?"

"Yes, my lord."

"Then speak, brenilad—but be warned!" Still standing, Mannoch drew a heavy sword and plunged its point into the planks before him. The blade struck and quivered, and the bright steel flashed in the firelight. Mannoch's eyes reflected fire as they moved from the sword, to the red monks, then back to rest on Morumus.

"There is but one fate awaiting those who tell lies around the fire of a ceilheath."

"You show great courage in coming to us."

Yorth, the eldest of the four lords of Nornindaal at Teru Bridge, arched one eyebrow as he looked across the table. "You are your father's son."

Oethur inclined his head. "Thank you, my lord."

"But you are not the eldest son."

The second speaker was Halbir. He was neither eldest nor youngest among the four lords. But he was the wealthiest. Of the four, his holdings were the closest to Grindangled.

He has the most to lose. It is no wonder he is the most hesitant.

"No, my lord," Oethur agreed. "But neither is Aeldred. My father's eldest son was Alfered, whom Aeldred murdered."

"So you said in your letter."

"You think Aeldred incapable of it, Halbir?" This question came from Jugeim, a burly lord with a straw beard and a strong brogue. "For myself, I doubt it not. I've known Ulfered's sons since they were bairns, and Aeldred was ever the schemer. Once, when they came with their father to my keep, I caught him stealing eggs from the servants' hennery. Can you imagine such disgraceful behavior? The son of a king, robbing servants!"

"There is far more at stake here than eggs, Jugeim." Meporu's cool tone matched his dark, reflective features. "We are talking about insurrection."

"Character is evidenced in the small things!" insisted Jugeim. "That is my point."

"It is a point well-taken, my lord." Yorth leaned back in his chair, and motioned for a servant to refill his wine goblet. "And I think all of us at least have *reservations* about the prospect of Aeldred as king." He nodded toward Oethur. "Especially in light of your letter."

"But we also have responsibilities," continued Halbir, "both to God and to our people. Reservations alone do not justify rebellion."

"Nor do unproven accusations," added Meporu.

Yorth lifted a sheet of parchment from the table before him and held it before the light. "You have denounced your brother as 'a heathen, a murderer, and a usurper.' You claim Aeldred has sworn allegiance to the pagan religion of Dyfann, which you further claim is now masquerading as the Red Order of the Mersian Church. You allege that he both orchestrated your eldest brother's murder *and* poisoned your father. Lastly, you aver that your father intended to change the succession to make you his heir."

Yorth set the paper down. "Given the seriousness of these accusations, and your own position to profit from them, surely you can see why we require some evidence—or at the very least, a great deal more explaining?"

"Of course, my lords." It was a perfectly reasonable demand. "Where would you like me to begin?"

"I have always found it most profitable to begin at the beginning." Lord Yorth took a sip from his renewed goblet. "Why don't you start by explaining to us how you know that the Red Order is connected to the Dark Faith?"

Oethur nodded, and for the next hour he explained to the lords what had happened in Caeldora—beginning with Versaden and ending with the flight from Lorudin Abbey. He then told them what he and Morumus had encountered in Dorslaan upon their return to Aeld Gowan—and what the latter had discovered in the Deasmor. He concluded with Aeldred's confession—and his own imprisonment with Ciolbail and Treowin—in the dungeons of Grindangled.

"My brother told me himself that he poisoned our father. In order to avoid detection, he used small quantities administered over a period of months."

"And your eldest brother?" asked Meporu. "Did he admit to killing him as well?"

"Yes. It was part of a coordinated effort by the followers of the Dark Faith to start a war with Lothair. According to the bishop"—Oethur gestured at Treowin, seated to his left—"that is why father intended to change the succession. Somehow he, too, had learned the truth of Aeldred's treachery."

"Is that so, Your Grace?" asked Jugeim.

Treowin nodded.

"It's a persuasive story," said Yorth, his face pensive and his glass again empty.

"One of them," said Halbir.

"My lord?"

"I agree with Lord Yorth that your account is sensible." Halbir frowned at Oethur. "But doubtless your brother could also present a compelling version of events."

Oethur stiffened. "Do you accuse me of deception, my lord?"

"I accuse no one. I observe simply that so far, all we have heard is a story that seems to fit the facts. You tell us that Aeldred is a heathen and a murderer. After what I've heard, I do not discount the possibility. But that is just it, Oethur. You ask us to join an insurrection on the basis of a possibility. You ask us to risk much on little."

"And you've got much to risk, is that it, Halbir?" Jugeim's eyes flashed. "Do you think you risk more than the rest of us—more than Oethur, for that matter? If Aeldred triumphs, all of us will hang. Or worse."

Halbir's face flushed. "Yet if war erupts, it will be my lands—my people!—who face the edge of the pillager's scythe. Am I to stand before my men—whose wives and children will be left to face Aeldred's wrath—and tell them that I lead them to war on a *possibility*? And when my life is spent, could I stand before God on such thin turf?"

"Halbir has a valid point." Meporu's calm voice came between the two men. "There are many paths between two points. Can you offer us even one solid piece of evidence, Oethur, that corroborates your account?"

"My lords"—Oethur spread his hands, "I have given you my surrender without promise of safe conduct. It is fully within your power to carry me back in chains to my brother. If that is not proof sufficient, Bishop Treowin himself sits beside here me. He can verify firsthand the most important portions of my explanation."

This seemed to satisfy Jugeim, Meporu, and even Yorth. But Halbir persisted.

"How do we know that Bishop Treowin has not been . . . *compromised*?"

"Now you question the man of God, Halbir?" Jugeim's astonishment was severe.

"Since all of this began, I have made certain investigations." Halbir's voice was careful as he picked up a piece of parchment. "Is it not true, Your Grace, that you have family in Dunross? A nephew employed as a cobbler?"

Treowin frowned, hesitated, and then nodded.

"You see, Jugeim?" Halbir turned. "My question is not so far-fetched. Even a man of hitherto impeccable character—a man who would not lie to save his own skin—might be coerced to do worse to save the life of his kin."

Treowin looked fierce. He shook his head in denial, and glared at Halbir.

"I do not allege it, Your Grace," Halbir insisted. "But what if—*if*, I say—what if all of this were orchestrated in Dunross, and our good bishop compelled to go along to save his family? What if they threatened to give his nephew to the Trathari—the same Trathari who cut out the bishop's own tongue? If the possibility even exists, are we not right back where we began—without sure evidence?"

"My lord," Oethur interjected. "If I may ask, how did you hear about the bishop's tongue? One of your investigations?"

"No. That unsavory piece of news I received from your brother." He looked at Treowin. "And I was most sorry to hear it, Your Grace."

Treowin looked at Oethur, who nodded.

"Don't be sorry, my lord," Treowin said. "My tongue is quite intact."

Halbir gaped at the bishop, and for a long moment he said nothing.

Oethur stood. "I regret, my lords, that my list of charges against Aeldred was incomplete. My brother is not just a heathen, a murderer, and a usurper. He is also a liar." He gestured at Treowin, but looked at Halbir. "Is this sufficient evidence for you, Lord Halbir?"

"Aeldred has lied to my face."

Halbir stood, and came around the table. He knelt before Oethur.

"I require no further proof . . . sire." He took Oethur's hand, and kissed it.

Meporu came next, and followed Halbir's example. "Your servant, sire."

Jugeim gave Oethur a bear hug before dropping to his knees.

Yorth was more reserved, but his smile was genuine. "Your father would be pleased, sire."

Treowin, who had hailed him as king in Dunross, bowed again. Then he handed Oethur his sword.

"May God's people find it strong," he said, "and may God's enemies feel its edge."

Morumus bowed to Mannoch.

"I met Donnach when he came to Lorudin Abbey. I helped him with Vilguran, and he taught me Grendannathi. We became friends, and were to work together to translate Holy Writ. It was Donnach's great hope to bring the Word of God to his own people in their own language."

He paused, and the chief nodded.

"So it was. Go on."

"We were making progress, but then the Red Order attacked Lorudin Abbey. They murdered the other monks and—"

"My lord!" One of the red monks rose.

Mannoch cut him off. "You will have your chance to speak—after he has finished."

He turned back to Morumus. "Why would the Red Order attack this abbey?"

"Because Lorudin Abbey stood for the True Faith of Aesus as revealed in Holy Writ. The Red Order does not believe Holy Writ—it follows the Dark Faith of Dyfann. It does not worship Aesus, who gave his blood; it serves a tree that grows on human blood."

"If this be so, then why does the Church harbor the Red Order?"

Morumus shook his head. "The Red Order deceived the Church, my lord. It persuaded the emperor to give it great power. Nobody suspected their true identity."

He paused, remembering a conversation he'd had with Abbot Grahem just days before Lorudin Abbey was destroyed . . .

"Sir, what if they are connected?"

"The Dark Faith and the Red Order?"

"Yes."

"The thought has crossed my mind more than once, but it doesn't fit."

"It doesn't?"

"No. We were tracking Dree long before there was any Red Order. Further, from what you've just told me of Ulwilf's story, it sounds like the Dark Faith is the religion he forsook. Unless you think his account of the missionary was a lie?"

"I don't think he was lying. Not that time."

"Well then," said the abbot, "I don't see how the Red Order and the Dark Faith can be allied. Your uncle used to have a saying . . ."

" 'The Dree are in league with nobody but the devil.' "

"That's it."

"If nobody suspected them," Mannoch prodded, "how did you learn otherwise?"

"Donnach and I found one of their sanctuaries in the hills near our abbey, my lord. It was there that we learned the truth: the Red Order is nothing but a disguise for the Dree of the Dark Faith."

There was an unsettled murmur among the chiefs.

"And you told nobody?"

"We learned too late, my lord. By the time we returned, the Red Order had destroyed Lorudin Abbey." He shuddered at the memory of the slaughter. "On the same day, we learned they had also murdered the local bishop—an ally of our abbot."

"Yet to this point, my brother was still alive?"

"Yes, my lord."

"How then did he die?"

"We had no choice then but to flee. Our plan was to return by ship to Aeld Gowan. But a leader of the Red Order—a monk called Ulwilf—intercepted us on the day we were to depart. He tried to murder me . . ."

"And?"

"And Donnach pushed me out of the way. Ulwilf's blade found Donnach instead." Morumus felt a hot tear running down the side of his face. "There was nothing I could do, my lord. Your brother died in my arms."

When Mannoch spoke again, his own voice trembled with emotion. "And what became of this Ulwilf?"

"I killed him, my lord."

"You!"

These hissed words came not from Mannoch, but from the taller red monk. Morumus turned, and saw the man glaring at him. Hatred burned in the man's dark eyes.

"Have you told him everything?"

This question was from King Heclaid.

"Yes, sire."

"Good. Now translate my words."

Heclaid stood and addressed himself to Mannoch.

"My lord, you have heard the testimony of my brenilad. If you judge him to speak truly, then I beg you to consider and act. The same Red Order that murdered your brother now controls all of southern Aeld Gowan. Mersex and Dyfann are under their sway, and one of their allies has usurped the throne of Nornindaal. They are a threat not only to Lothair, but to all who hold to the True Faith—including many among your own people.

"The legends tell us that once, long ago, three peoples lived in the North of our island: three distinct peoples, yet all united under a single banner for a common cause. They formed a threefold cord to protect their families from the depredations of the Dark Faith, and to preserve their souls by the Truth. What I have to come to propose to this ceilheath is that the time has come for us to do the same again. Those who love the Truth must unite against those who practice the Dark Faith.

"Lothair does not conspire to spend your people's blood on a private feud, my lord. What I am proposing is that the clans of Grendannath, the people of Lothair, and all true Norns join together as brothers for a common purpose. In the providence of God, the time has come for us to once again form the Threefold Cord!"

As his last words echoed through the roundhouse, Heclaid sat down. He motioned for his translator to do the same.

Morumus sank to his stool, and silence fell over the fire-lit hall . . .

But it did not last.

" 'By the mouth of two or three witnesses shall every word be established,' " quoted the tall red monk, stepping forward to the fire's edge to address Mannoch and the seated chiefs. "These Lothairins claim to love and live by Holy Writ. They have hurled many accusations at the Order of the Saving Blood—including serious charges of murder. But where is their second or third witness?" He turned and glared at Morumus.

"It is a fair question," said Mannoch, and many Grendannathi heads bobbed. The chief looked at the Lothairins. "Do you have other proof?"

Heclaid stirred. "You have the testimony of my brenilad. You have the testimony of the fact that we came and volunteered this information. Finally, you have the testimony of the long peace between our peoples. What further proof could I offer, my lord?"

The red monk sneered. "They play with words, my lord. But beneath their evasions is the simple fact that the only witness to the alleged crimes of my order is this brenilad—who has already admitted to killing a man. But I will tell you, my lord, what really happened to your brother."

There was murmuring on the back benches at this.

"It is your turn to speak," Mannoch allowed.

The red monk bowed. "In going to Caeldora, your brother Donnach learned the same truth of which I spoke to this ceilheath earlier: that the New Faith *instructs* the Old Faith, but it does not *replace* it. It is this great truth that my order was established to spread.

"When your brother learned this truth, he realized that the Lothairin missionaries had misled him—and were misleading your people. So he determined to escape from Lorudin Abbey. But the men of Lorudin are cruel and suspicious, and they would not let your brother go free. So Donnach appealed to Ulwilf, a legate of my order.

"To help your brother escape, Ulwilf and other members of my order set a fire in the kitchens of Lorudin Abbey. The ruse worked, and in the ensuing confusion Donnach managed to escape. But before they could get aboard ship, this man"—he stabbed a finger at Morumus—"caught up to them. *He* murdered your brother, my lord. Right before he murdered Ulwilf. It was not this Lothairin who found them. They told *me* everything before they passed."

Morumus was disheartened by the amount of muttering he heard at these words. But Mannoch was not so easily moved.

"And what proof have you of your account?" he demanded.

"Besides my own testimony, my lord, I offer you this." The red monk reached into the folds of his robe and withdrew a small vial. He held it up for the assembled chiefs to see. "This is a special draft mixed by my order. It makes those who drink it tell the truth." He pointed the potion at Morumus. "Let the Lothairin brenilad drink it, my lord. Here, before us all. *Then* let us see what he has to say."

This proposal caused quite a stir among the assembled Grendannathi lords. Morumus gritted his teeth.

Clever.

Mannoch looked at Morumus. "What say you to this, brenilad?"

No doubt the vial contained nomergenna. Under the influence of the Mother's herb, the Dree could make Morumus do or say anything. Their hissing song could freeze his limbs or command his tongue.

It was a trap.

The red monk knew it, too, and he flashed Morumus a wicked smile.

But Morumus returned the smile. "I know your secret, Morduui," he whispered in Vilguran. Then, before the man could reply, he addressed the chiefs in Grendannathi. "If the red monks will consent to be bound and gagged for the duration of my interrogation—and afterward until the draft's influence has passed—then I will consent."

The red monk's smile vanished. "An outrageous demand! We are emissaries of the Archbishop of Mereclestour, and have been given a promise of safe conduct. Such treatment is forbidden!"

"What he means to say, my lord," said Morumus, "is that he cannot make me tell lies if his own mouth is gagged. That's their trick. That draft"—he pointed to the vial—"contains a potent herb. But it has no power unless activated by their incantations. If they cannot speak, their power is broken. This is their secret. The alleged power of the Dark Faith is nothing but an alchemist's trick."

He looked back to the red monk, and whispered again in Vilguran, "I was at Cuuranyth, too."

"You!" The monk's eyes bulged, but he wasn't done yet. He backed away from Morumus and held up his hands.

"My lord, just now this Lothairin has threatened both my life and the life of my translator. He used the Vilguran language so that you would not understand. He mocks your authority, my lord." He spread out his hands to the seated chiefs, and his voice rose.

"Can you not see, my lords, the crooked ways of these Lothairins? They accuse, but bring no proof! They lie about my order to avoid having their own lies detected! They make ridiculous demands, and issue desperate threats in the presence of your lordships. As they did in Caeldora, so they do now in Grendannath!"

"And of course the Lothairins might say the same of you," interjected Mannoch. "Whom are we to believe?"

Once more, the older chiefs seated in the front of the circle nodded.

The red monk inclined his head. When he spoke again, his tone sounded aggrieved.

"Believe your brother's last words, my lord. He urged me to warn you of the Lothairin deception. 'Tell my brother,' he said to me, 'that the New and Old Faiths are sisters, not enemies. Tell him to avenge my death . . .'

"I urge you, my lord, to cancel the safe conduct given to these Lothairins. Renounce your friendship with Lothair. Return to the Old Faith, and declare a blood feud upon those who would emasculate your people!"

Morumus rose. He was shaking with anger at the red monk's lies—especially the claim to have been at Donnach's side when the Grendannathi died. But he addressed his words to Mannoch. "Do you want to know what your brother really said as he was dying?"

He did not wait for a reply. "'Finish the translation, Morumus. Bring the good news to my people, Prince of Roots. I will wait for you in Everlight.' *That's* what he said, my lord. Why would Donnach spend his dying words in this manner, if he did not want the True Faith to replace the Old? Why would Donnach have dedicated his life to translation if there were no need for conversions?"

"Your brother was deceived, my lord!" insisted the red monk. "He was taught to believe in the lie of exclusivity!"

"'I myself am the way, and the truth, and the life. Nobody comes to the Father, unless through me,'" Morumus quoted. "Your brother *was* taught to believe that Aesus demands exclusive faith, my lord, but he was not so feeble-minded as to believe something just because he was told to, as the Red Order would have you believe." He shook his head. "No, my lord. Donnach believed the True Faith is exclusive because Holy Writ declares it." He scrubbed another tear from his cheek. "It was his dying wish to translate those same words into your own tongue, so that you could read them for yourself.

"But whether you believe me on that, my lord, believe me in this: Donnach would have *never* asked for a blood feud. In fact, there was one time, when *I* was supposed to be teaching *him*, that *he* rebuked *me*. And for what? For holding on to a blood feud! He cited the story of Saint Cephan and the Legionary Coranelix. 'Were not the Legionaries the ones who executed the Lord?' he asked me. 'Were they not responsible for his death? And yet, brother, the Lord forgave Coranelix.'"

Morumus heard some jeering from the back benches, but he ignored them. "Your brother never condoned *revenge*. He called for *grace*."

"Grace?" The red monks hissed. "He mocks your loss, my lord! Strike him down! End his filthy lies once and for all!"

But Mannoch ignored them. Nor would he look at Morumus. "We are finished for today."

The abrupt words stunned the whispering hall into silence. Without another look at either of the parties on the far side of the ring, Mannoch jerked his sword free of the floorboards, turned, and stalked out of the firelight.

The moon had risen high in the clear sky before the ceilheath settled down to rest. In the velvet canopy beyond the waxing moon, a dusty host of northern stars looked down on Grenmaur. There, far below, the myriad clans had arranged their tents into long, makeshift streets. These radiated outward from the roundhouse like spokes from a great wheel—a wheel whose subsequent turnings the day's deliberations had left in doubt.

A tall figure stalked the shadows of that wheel. With one hand, he fingered the hilt of his weapon. With his feet, he crept in practiced silence toward his target . . .

Would he find Morumus sleeping?

Morumus lay dreaming in his tent . . .

He was reliving Donnach's murder.

"You still do not see it, Morumus, do you?"

Ulwilf had caught up to Morumus in an unused stable in Naud . . .

"There is one Source of all things—one Mother of all faiths. She whom all other peoples have forgotten, the Dyfanni have protected.

It is she whom my people worshipped as our goddess, and it is her son whom the Church calls Aesus. They are the same."

"It is you who are wrong, Mordruui . . . I have seen your white tree. It is no goddess. I watched it burn."

"You lie!"

"He speaks the truth . . ."

There had been a *crack*, and Morumus's captor had crumpled to the floor . . . with Donnach standing over him.

"Donnach! How—?"

"Morumus, look out!"

Morumus knew he was dreaming, and he wanted to wake up. But he could not . . .

Morumus wheeled, but the red monk had already lunged. He could not evade the blade. But at the last second Morumus was shoved aside and sprawled sideways onto the floor.

"Oh!" Donnach gasped.

Morumus jumped back to his feet, but it was too late. In the dim lamplight he saw the horrible truth. There stood Ulwilf, his blade buried in Donnach's middle.

What happened next Morumus would never forget . . .

The knife from Captain Brann was in his hand. In the next instant, he leapt to the attack. Ulwilf saw it coming, but was unable to pull his own blade free before Morumus was on him. The two of them tumbled to the floor and rolled a few feet, but . . . The hardy steel plunged deep through Ulwilf's red robe . . .

Rising, Morumus rushed back to Donnach, who lay on his back beside the lamp . . .

"You must finish the work." The light in the Grendannathi's eyes was beginning to fade . . . "Finish the translation, Morumus. Bring the good news to my people, Prince of Roots. I will wait for you in Everlight."

Morumus woke to find himself shaking—but not from the cold.

Pushing back his blanket, he stood. The candle lamp had burned low, but just enough light remained to cast a dim illumination on the interior of his spacious tent.

Morumus was alone. Along with the other chiefs, King Heclaid had received lodging in the roundhouse. The men-at-arms, meanwhile, would find billets with the other warriors. For himself, it seemed that the Grendannathi regarded a brenilad as of sufficient rank to warrant privacy.

Morumus was glad. He began to pace back and forth in the empty space near the front of the tent.

What would become of their embassy? Far too many chieftains had seemed ready to side with the Red Order! And Mannoch himself had walked out! What would become of Donnach's people? What would become of his own?

If we fail here, how can we possibly defeat the Red Order?

As he turned matters over, two verses from Holy Writ floated to the forefront of his thoughts . . .

Trust in him in all times, O people; pour out your heart before him. God is a refuge for us . . . In no way be anxious, but in everything by prayer and supplication with thanksgiving let your petitions be made known to God.

Morumus nodded. He shouldn't be obsessing. He should be praying.

"O Lord, will you let these people fall into the hands of the enemy? Will you not vindicate Donnach's—"

His prayer was cut short as strong hands burst through the flap of his tent. One pair clamped over his mouth like irons. Another gripped him by the shoulders and yanked him backwards. A boot found his stomach . . .

Twice.

Gasping for breath, his vision blurred by a blackness darker than the surrounding night, Morumus was too stunned to resist and unable to shout. His assailants stuffed a thick wad of wool into his mouth, then bound his limbs.

Before Morumus realized what was happening, he was a prisoner.

His captors picked him up and began moving down the silent street.

Where are they taking me? Can I escape?

Morumus tried to struggle. But no sooner did he begin than he felt the sharp point of a knife pressed into the soft flesh of his neck. It jabbed him with every step, and he knew that if he made any sudden movements, the knife would puncture his throat.

He looked up at his captor . . .

. . . and saw only the faceless hood of a red monk.

The next minutes passed in shadowed terror. Morumus knew he was in grave danger and tried not to let it show. But a cold panic seeped into him. He was bound hand and foot, he was a prisoner of the Red Order, and nobody had seen him taken.

Worst of all, he had been foolish enough to boast about Cuuranyth.

Oh, they will kill me slowly for that.

There was nothing he could do.

No, that's not true!

He could pray.

And so he did.

Morumus prayed like he had seldom done before. How long this lasted he didn't know. The minutes seemed to stretch into hours, the hours into eternity as the red monks carried him unseen through the dark streets. He began to feel as though he had died already: mute, immobilized, and floating through the night like an untimely corpse being carried to its tomb.

Oh Lord, help me to die well!

After a short while, Morumus became conscious that his captors were moving uphill. It was a steep ascent, and his weight made what would have been an arduous climb under the best of circumstances even more laborious. But he no longer doubted their destination.

The red monks were taking him to the top of Carrad Gren.

To the stone circle.

When they reached the top, the hooded monks propped him into a sitting position against one of the fallen monoliths. Then they stepped back, and a third monk appeared from behind one of the few stones that still stood. Unlike his fellows, this monk's hood was lowered.

"Hello, Morumus."

The tall monk from the roundhouse.

As the Mordruui spoke, Morumus was again struck by his resemblance to Ulwilf.

"My name is Ultharn," said the monk. He drew a knife as he stepped forward—a long, stone knife that seemed to glow silver in the pale moonlight. "You do not know me, I think, but I know you. Do you want to know how?"

And suddenly Morumus knew.

"Ulwilf was my brother."

Morumus could see the hatred in the Mordruui's dark eyes, and he could feel a new wave of panic threatening to engulf him.

Ulwilf's brother!

"You are well-known among the Red Order, did you know that?" Ultharn circled Morumus as he spoke. "The Mother's Hand has given orders concerning you. We are supposed to capture you, not kill you. After Cuuranyth, the Hand wants to feed you to the Mother himself, I think!"

Ultharn shrugged. "But I do not see how we could ever manage to secret you away from this place, do you? Therefore, we must improvise." He motioned to one of his fellows. "Get me the basin."

Morumus watched as the man brought a large, stone basin. *Just like the one in the Muthadannach.*

"We are going to cut your throat, Morumus. We will drain your blood into this basin, and from the basin into a bottle. After that is done, we will cut off your head. Then we will send both bottle and head to the Hand of the Mother. Not exactly what he wanted, I know. But surely he must understand our extremity. Do you think he will understand, Morumus?"

Ultharn gestured to his men, and it began. They placed the basin in a flat place, and then the two monks picked Morumus up. One positioned Morumus's head carefully over the basin's center, while the other lifted his legs up into the air.

"It will help the blood to drain," Ultharn explained.

When all was ready, Ultharn kneeled next to Morumus. He gripped his hair and jerked back his head, then placed the knife on his throat.

Morumus's pulse quickened as the cold edge pressed against his flesh.

I am not going to escape this time.

To his surprise, he found that the thought no longer made him afraid, for the memory of Donnach's last words now sprang fresh to his mind . . .

"I will wait for you in Everlight."

As the words rose up, something changed within Morumus. The acute panic that had filled him only minutes prior seeped away. Donnach too had died by the blade of the Mordruui. Yet Donnach too had trusted Aesus. That simple fact made an eternal difference. Through faith alone, with no contribution but the sheer grace of God, Donnach *would* be waiting for Morumus in Everlight. Very soon, the two friends would be reunited forever in a world without good-byes.

Morumus smiled.

His pulse quickened again, but this time it was not fear that made his blood race.

It was . . .

Anticipation.

"Genna ma'guad, ma'muthad, ma'rophed," Ultharn whispered in his ear. "Do you know what that means, Morumus? 'Genna my goddess, my Mother, my salvation.' I am praising the Mother for delivering you into my hands, even as she delivered that fool Donnach into the hands of my brother. With both of you out of the way, who will prevent the Grendannathi from returning to the Mother's bosom?"

Despite the tension on his neck, Morumus twisted his head. He looked straight into Ultharn's eyes. "God will keep the Grendannathi. Have you never heard the words of Tertullogus? Know you not that the blood of the saints is the seed of the Church?"

"Yes," Ultharn hissed. "But *whose* Church, Morumus. Yours . . . or the Mother's?"

Morumus spat. "There is only Church, Dree—and it belongs to Aesus, not to a tree!"

It was as if he had spit fire—for in the very next instant, a roar exploded in the night.

"Murderers!"

Morumus turned his head to look for its source, and what he saw astonished him. Ultharn had wheeled to face the sound, holding the knife before him to ward off the sudden threat, but it was no good. There was a flash of moonlight, and the knife arm flew sideways—severed at the elbow. Ultharn howled, but not for long . . .

The next flash took off his head.

Ultharn's body was still falling when the two monks dropped Morumus. The Lothairin grunted as he landed and rolled onto his side. The monks turned away and fled.

There was a third flash, followed by a heavy thud and a loud scream.

Still bound, Morumus had to wriggle to find its source.

A red monk lay face down less than ten paces away, a sword quivering in his back.

"Enemies in the camp!"

The voice boomed out into the dark night from the hilltop. Far below in Grenmaur, shouts could be heard as warriors stirred . . .

"Enemies in the camp! Seize the red monks!"

The command was repeated twice more.

Unable to move, Morumus waited for the large Grendannathi—for that was the voice's language—to find him. But when the man kneeled down beside him, Morumus gasped.

"My lord? But how?"

Mannoch mac Toercanth said nothing at first. Instead, he drew a long knife from his belt and sliced through Morumus's bonds. Then he helped him to his feet.

"I could not sleep, Morumus. I was on my way to speak with you when I saw the red monks drag you from your tent. You are unharmed?"

"Yes, thanks to you, my lord." Morumus rubbed his wrists. "But why were you coming to see me?"

"That story you told today at the ceilheath, the one from Holy Writ about Saint Cephan and the Legionary . . ."

"Coranelix."

"Yes." Mannoch nodded. "Until that point, I was not sure you were telling the truth. I did not want to admit it, because I was angry. But after that, I knew."

"How, my lord?"

"My brother once used it on me, Morumus!"

At this, Morumus could not help laughing. Once again, Donnach had saved his life!

"Our clans will join with Lothair and Nornindaal. The details must be negotiated, and I warn you that we will require you to treat us as equal partners! But we will join. The Threefold Cord will be re-formed."

"Praise God, my lord."

"I would like to, Morumus, but I cannot—unless you help me with something."

Morumus looked at the Grendannathi chief. The battle fury had passed, and there was something new in the man's eyes now. Something *different*.

"Anything, my lord."

"You must teach me what it means to trust Aesus as Donnach did."

Lildas frowned as he stepped out of the king's chamber. Two guards flanked the door on the outside. Both heads bobbed their duty at his appearance.

"How is the king, Doctor?" asked the senior of the two men.

"Tired, Sergeant." Lildas arched one eyebrow at the man. "I am going to my chambers to mix his sleeping draft. If anyone besides the queen comes to see His Majesty, you should . . . *dissuade* them. Is that clear?"

The sergeant smiled. "We'll see them off, Doctor, not to worry."

"Good man." Lildas turned and stalked down the corridor.

He had not gone more than a dozen paces from the royal chambers when he saw a liveried servant scurrying toward him. Lildas's frown, which had become habitual of late, deepened into a scowl. He recognized the young man as a footman of Satticus, Aeldred's private secretary.

No good news thence.

He planted himself square in the corridor's center and waited.

At the sight of the doctor, the messenger stopped. "Doctor Lildas?"

"You needn't take another step, lad."

"But—"

Lildas raised a hand. "Whatever news you have for His Majesty can wait, son." He heard the gravel in his voice and saw its effect upon the youngling. "The king is resting," he finished in a tone that was marginally softer—yet no less firm.

"But Doctor, my message is not for the king."

"No?"

"No, sir." The footman shook his head. "My master always brings those messages himself. I was sent to find you."

"Me?"

"Yes, Doctor. My master wishes to consult you."

The physician's heart skipped a beat. In the three weeks since his discovery at the apothecary's shop, Lildas had felt a growing suspicion of Satticus. The private secretary was Aeldred's right hand. If the latter *had* used nightshade to poison his father, then it was almost certain that the former would have assisted him.

If. Almost. Two big uncertainties.

So far, Lildas had made no move. He had hidden the receipts, of course, and he had purchased all the necessary ingredients for his plan. But to this day, he had taken no overt action. Now . . .

Had he waited too long? "About what does the private secretary wish to consult me?" Lildas asked the messenger.

"Sir . . . he asks if you would be pleased to come to him immediately."

Lildas let a pinch of irritation drop into his words. "Young man, I am in the middle of treating an important patient." He punctuated his words with a sharp gesture up the hall behind him. "Unless you convince me that your master's request is more important, I will not interrupt that treatment."

The servant lowered his voice. "It's very important, Doctor. My master has received some disquieting news today."

Lildas felt a stab of suspicion, and he eyed the footman—watching for any hint of deception—as he asked his next question. "What sort of news, son?"

"News from Teru Bridge, Doctor."

Relief flooded through Lildas, and he relaxed his stance. "I see."

"Do you know what is happening there, sir?"

"Yes." Oethur's meeting with the four outlawed lords was supposed to be a close secret. But people of all ranks confided in their physician. Aeldred was no exception.

"You say there is news?"

The messenger nodded. "Disquieting news, Doctor. My master wishes to consult you about whether or not he can bring that information to your . . . *patient*."

Lildas nodded. Now he understood. "I will come."

As he followed the footman, Lildas's frown returned.

If the news was disquieting, it could only mean one thing . . .

The four lords who had refused to coronate Aeldred had sworn to Oethur.

Four lords—four of seven!

If a majority of the lords of Nornindaal had decided for Oethur, then by the inviolable custom of the Norns . . .

Oethur was the lawful king.

The private secretary's study was a wide chamber with a row of tall windows dominating the left-hand wall. Opposite these, a warren of cluttered shelves obscured the room's far end. The wall facing the door cradled a bright crackling hearth, and in the open space at the chamber's center stood a great wooden desk. High piles of papers dotted its dark surface.

It was from the midst of these stacks that Satticus rose as Lildas entered the room.

"Doctor, thank you for coming."

"I am told you wish to consult me, Private Secretary?"

Satticus nodded. "I do. How is the king?"

"More careworn than ever, Secretary. He is still not sleeping well."

"Even with the drafts?"

Lildas nodded. "They seem to be having less effect of late."

"His Majesty feels the weight of recent events." Satticus sighed, and turned to look out the window. "And I'm afraid I've received some most unwelcome news today. News that truly cannot wait."

"News from Teru Bridge?"

The secretary's head snapped round. "How did you know that? Did my servant—?"

"The king told me of the embassy some days ago." The statement was true enough, and Lildas did not wish to betray the footman's candor. "What other news could be so unwelcome that it cannot wait?"

Satticus nodded. "Halbir, Jugeim, Meporu, and Yorth have all sworn to Oethur."

"A grim business."

"That's a very . . . *forensic* way to put it, Doctor."

"I'm a physician, Secretary."

"You are also a member of the king's court."

Lildas could feel the weight of Satticus's gaze. The private secretary was a dangerous man, and Lildas understood all too well what the man was seeking.

He's trying to gauge my loyalties. He wants me to make some pledge of devotion.

But could Lildas give such a pledge?

What does it benefit a man to gain the whole world, yet lose his soul?

The question was timeless, and for years it had fortified the doctor's integrity. Now it forced him to face two other questions . . .

What if Aeldred planned his father's murder?

What about this new development—that a majority of the lords had backed Oethur?

Lildas felt a great inward sighing. He was an old man. His sworn oath, given many years prior, was to the king of Norn-indaal. For decades, this oath had given clear direction to his duty. Never had it encountered such an obvious conflict as now stood before him.

Who was the true king?

Lildas could not answer that question, not until he had his answers. Which meant he must be very careful in his words now . . .

"As you say, Secretary, but my advice to the king is restricted to medicine. In matters pertaining to the government of the realm, he relies on the opinions of others. What say you of this news?"

"I say that *grim* is a great understatement, Doctor. If this news gets out, it could cause enormous damage to the king's authority. The lords who back Oethur are outlaws, and thus no true lords of the realm. But not all will see this. Some might say that ancient custom now gives the crown to Oethur."

"A dangerous line of thinking."

"Quite dangerous. I trust we can rely on your discretion, then?"

Lildas stiffened. "Has my discretion ever been questioned?"

"I intend no offense, Doctor. I mean only to suggest that these tidings must be handled with great care."

"I understand what you are suggesting, Secretary. May I suggest we get about it? You must carry this news to the king. I warn you, he is in a poor state to receive it."

Satticus nodded. "Yet it cannot wait."

"No, I suppose not." Lildas shook his head. As he did so, a realization struck him . . .

This is the perfect opportunity.

"Under the circumstances, Secretary, I think I will prepare a special sleeping draft for the king—a medicine more potent than his normal prescription."

"That sounds wise, Doctor. How long will you need to prepare?"

"How long will it take you to deliver your tidings?"

"Less than half an hour, I suspect."

"I can be ready by then, if I start now. Shall I retreat to my labors, and leave you to your own?"

Satticus nodded. "Make it strong, Doctor."

"It will be strong, Secretary."

Stronger than you imagine.

Lildas returned to the king's door just in time to meet Satticus leaving. He arched an eyebrow at the private secretary, whose face was ashen.

Satticus met his eyes and shook his head. "Worse than I expected, Doctor," he whispered. "I hope your draft will calm him."

"It will, if it is given time to do its work." Lildas looked from the secretary to the soldiers flanking the door. "The king must *not* be disturbed for several hours. This dosing is delicate, and I must administer it in several stages. I will stay with the king, but *no others* should be admitted. Is that clear?"

Satticus nodded to the men-at-arms. "Nobody passes these doors until the doctor leaves or I say otherwise. You understand?"

The sergeant nodded. "Understood, sir."

Satticus looked at Lildas. "Are you satisfied, Doctor?"

"Almost."

"Almost?"

"With respect, I must ask that you too honor this prohibition, Private Secretary. *Nobody* must enter while I am with the king—not even you."

Lildas saw the man's face twitch, but he preempted the protest with a practiced professional stare. "This is a medical necessity, Secretary, and I must insist. I will send word to you when I am finished. You understand?"

Satticus nodded. "As you say, Doctor."

As the private secretary retreated, Lildas stepped over the king's threshold.

Lord, give me strength to do what I must . . .

Aeldred turned from the windows as he entered. There was an unsettling gleam in the king's grey eyes, and his brown hair hung in lank, loose strands about his shoulders. The color in his gaunt, lined face was not the flush of good health.

It was the heat of rage.

"My lord." Lildas bowed. "I have brought you something to help you—"

"*Help* me?" Aeldred's anger was palpable, his voice thin. "Help me! Have you heard the news, Doctor?"

"I have, sire."

"My brother has stolen half my kingdom! No doubt they are marching on Grindangled at this very moment. And yet here you come . . . for what? To persuade me to rest?" His wave was contemptuous. "Away with your medicines, Lildas! Sleep is a luxury I can no longer afford."

"Would you do Oethur's work for him?" Lildas saw Aeldred's eyes bulge at the name whose utterance he had forbidden, but the doctor ignored the king's temper. "If you do not get some solid rest soon, sire, your brother will not have to fight you for your crown."

Aeldred's wrath subsided by a fraction, and Lildas waved him to his bed.

"Undress and lie down, sire."

As the king complied, Lildas set his small case on the nightstand and opened its lid. Inside were three vials. He took the first and added its contents to a glass of wine, stirring the mixture with a small spoon.

"Drink, sire." He handed the cup to Aeldred, who by now lay propped up amidst a small heap of pillows.

"The usual, Lildas?"

"Something stronger."

"Even better."

Lildas watched as the king drained his cup, then he took the goblet and began mixing the second dose. He was just finishing when the king spoke in alarm.

"I cannot move my arms or legs!"

Lildas permitted himself the briefest smile. The first vial had contained a heavy dose of *nerwunaan*. Under its influence, Aeldred would be unable to move for several hours.

"That's the medicine, sire," he soothed. "It will aid your sleep by keeping you from jerking or kicking yourself awake."

Lildas turned and held the second cup to the king's lips.

Aeldred eyed the goblet, eyes narrowed. "And what will that do?"

The second vial had contained *passiferaal*—an obscure but very potent truth serum. During his training at the Physicians Guild in Mereclestour, Lildas had seen passiferaal used to extract confessions from the most stubborn liars in the Tower of Luca.

"It will unburden your mind, sire."

Aeldred drank the mixture with the eagerness of the parched. When the cup was drained, Lildas returned it to the nightstand and drew a chair to the bedside. There he sat down to wait.

After several minutes, the effects of the potion began to appear. As the tensions in his mind relaxed, the lines of Aeldred's face smoothed and his hard-set jaw relaxed. As the barriers of his mental inhibitions crumbled, the grey intensity of the king's eyes softened into guileless honesty and childlike simplicity.

Lildas waited another full minute before speaking. "How do you feel, sire?"

"Wonderful, Doctor. What was it that you gave me?"

"It is called passiferaal, sire."

"Passiferaal." Aeldred smiled as he repeated the word. "It feels like nomergenna."

Lildas frowned. What was nomergenna? But he shelved his curiosity. At present, there were more pressing questions . . .

"Sire, there's something I've been meaning to ask you."

"Of course, Doctor."

Lildas paused. Passiferaal opened a man's mind like a sharp knife in soft flesh, yet extracting truth was like delicate surgery. Cut too deep or too quick, and you ran the risk of causing irreparable damage. The truth *would* come out. The trick was to coax it.

"I think I must resign as your physician."

"What?" Aeldred looked stricken. "You cannot be serious!"

"I think I must, sire. I have failed in my duty. I failed to save your father's life."

"Oh no, no . . . no, Doctor. That was not your fault."

"Of course it was, sire. I failed to determine the illness. I failed to treat it. I failed." Lildas hung his head. "I still don't know what caused your father's death."

"It was nightshade, Doctor."

Lildas looked up, and found Aeldred looking straight at him. There was no hint of deceit in his words, nor any trace of remorse. The admission was frank and nonchalant.

"Nightshade, sire?" Lildas feigned amazement. "But who . . . ?"

"I did it. Satticus helped me."

"But why, sire?"

"I had to."

"You had to?"

"Father was going to change the succession."

This time Lildas's surprise was genuine. "Change the succession? But that hasn't happened for generations."

"I *know.*" Aeldred's complaint was bitter. "It was horribly unjust."

"But why?"

Aeldred looked away, and there was a moment's silence. Lildas had a sinking feeling that he had pushed too fast. But then the king looked back.

"Alfered."

"Your brother? But he has been dead for years, sire. Why would your father—?"

"Because I killed him, Doctor."

Lildas gasped. "You?"

"I had to."

"You *had to?*"

"How could I ever be king, so long as Alfered lived?"

Lildas's ears tingled. He remembered those dark days as if they were yesterday . . . "There was a Lothairin lord murdered about the same time . . ."

"Yes." Aeldred mistook his muttering for a question. "That too was our work. We had hoped to provoke a war between Nornindaal and Lothair."

"*We*, sire? You and Satticus?"

Aeldred shook his head. "Satticus helped. He always *helps.* But the plan originated with Somnadh and me."

"I don't believe I've met Somnadh, sire."

"Not yet, Lildas—but you will! He is the Archbishop of Mereclestour now."

The Archbishop of Mereclestour!

Lildas pushed the information aside, for a new question had arisen. "But why start a war with Lothair, sire? Our countries have ever been at peace."

"The Mother was threatened . . ."

A half hour later, Lildas's hands shook as he prepared the last draft.

He had heard more than enough to convince him of Aeldred's guilt. There was no doubt in his mind that every charge laid by Oethur against his brother was true. Aeldred was indeed "a heathen, a murderer, and a usurper." The depth of the man's depravity, the extent of his betrayal, was staggering.

There was no doubt now where Lildas's loyalties lay. Yet what could he do?

I could kill Aeldred.

But he dismissed the thought almost immediately. To kill even a villain like Aeldred in this condition would not be justice, but assassination.

I am no murderer.

He was a physician, not a warrior. His work was not destructive, but restorative . . .

And preventative.

The idea hit him with a sudden force.

What if I could prove these things? What if all that Aeldred has confessed could be substantiated? Might it end the looming war?

Lildas turned back to Aeldred, the cup of memory-erasing *droelum* in his hand. "This last cup will give you a long, full rest, sire."

And make you forget everything we've discussed.

"Thank you, Lildas. I am very tired."

"If I may, sire, I have just one last question . . ."

Aeldred looked at him, the passiferaal-induced honesty still plain on his face. "Yes, Doctor?"

Lildas forced himself to smile. "I fear you may have been having some fun with me just now."

Aeldred feigned offense. "Never, Doctor!"

"But all these things you have told me . . . some of them are quite astonishing, sire. Can you actually prove any of them, or were you just exercising my gullibility?"

Aeldred smiled. "I will let you read the letters in my black box. Then you will see!"

Lildas's pulse quickened. "Black box?" He looked around the room.

Aeldred laughed. "It's not here, Doctor!"

"Where is it, sire?"

"Satticus has it. But I warn you, Lildas, you may have to fight with him for the key. He doesn't even like to give it to me."

Lildas forced a conspiratorial smile. "Do you know where he keeps it?"

"He wears it on a chain around his neck."

The last light of day died slowly beyond the bars of Urien's window. She watched it go, the orange blazes fading to a dull red, finally swallowed by a purple gloom. It was not until the last rays vanished in the west that she turned away . . .

From the dusk without, to the dusk within.

Despite the relative comforts of her cell, nothing could soothe the desolation in her soul. The fire on the hearth gave no heat, and the food brought to her tasted like ashes. She would rather starve, only she knew that Somnadh would never permit it. If she did not eat, he would come and make her swallow. And so she ate.

Urien did not want to see her brother.

Not now, and perhaps not ever.

Not since last week . . .

Nothing could erase the hideous vision. Seven days had passed since Abbess Nahenna's death. Yet it might have happened yesterday, for Urien could remember every detail: every gruesome implement, every inhuman brutality. Hours of them. Even in her waking hours, Urien heard the screams of agony, saw the flash of blades, and smelled the tang of blood. The memory burned in her waking mind like a livid, throbbing scar.

And then there were the nightmares . . .

Shuddering, Urien crossed the room to a seat before the fire.

Something had broken inside Urien that day. It was as if a great storm had smashed into an unsheltered village along the coast of her homeland. She had seen such a village once—years ago when she was very young, before she was taken away to Caeldora.

There had been nothing left.

No fires. No heat. No life.

Nothing but broken pieces.

Urien felt like that village. She had lost her faith, lost her home, and now she had lost the only family she had ever known. Abbess Nahenna, whose gentle kindness had been like a mother's, was dead. And her brother, wrapped in his scarlet vestments, had become a monster . . .

Like a great red dragon . . . of the Dark Faith.

Urien's life was broken pieces. She had not foreseen the storm, but she had felt its devastation. The lifeless cold was all that remained, the seeping damp bequeathed by the departure of malevolent waves.

She shivered as she stared into the fire . . .

Was there anything left?

Was there ever anything there?

The arrival of Morumus and Donnach that fateful day last autumn in Caeldora had proven precipitate. Yet Urien knew that her undoing commenced long before. It had begun with a little girl swept away by the lies of the Dark Faith. It had festered in years of solitary misery at the Muthadannach. It had moldered in the bloody rituals of the Mother . . .

In truth, Morumus and Donnach had brought Urien the only thing she never had . . .

Hope.

But Donnach was dead, Urras Monastery was destroyed, and Morumus had disappeared. What was left of their hope?

There is still Aesus.

The thought startled Urien. Yet after a slow moment, she shook her head.

It doesn't help unless it's true. And how can I know?

She remembered her conversation with Abbess Nahenna about this very question . . .

"I want to believe, Abbess."

"You do?"

"I do. It's just . . . for years I was convinced that the Old Faith—the Dark Faith—was true. I don't believe that anymore, but I've had to face the fact that for years I was convinced of a lie. For years I served a lie, Abbess—and you cannot imagine the horrible things I've done."

"Aesus's death will pay for them all, my dear."

"I know what your book says. I've read it for myself. I want to believe it."

"Then why do you not?"

"Because I don't know how to know if it's all true. I want it to be true. But for years I wanted the Dark Faith to be true, too—and it's not. What I want makes nothing true. So what does? How can I know that your Aesusian faith is true?"

Tears welled in Urien's eyes as she remembered the abbess's patient answer . . .

"Holy Writ is God's own Word. He breathed it out himself. The authority to believe it comes from itself."

"I still don't see."

"It is God the Spirit who speaks in Holy Writ, Urien. It is God's voice that you hear every single time you read or hear Holy Writ. If you are honest with yourself, you know this is true."

"I'm still not sure . . ."

And Urien still wasn't sure. She had read portions of Holy Writ before leaving Urras, and she had sensed its difference from the myths of Dyfann. But still she had found no solution to her impasse.

How can I know whether or not it's all true?

A log collapsed in the fire, causing a cascade of sparks—and sending a single burning ember tumbling out of the hearth onto the rug before her.

Urien's response was swift. Jumping to her feet, she unwrapped the heavy shawl from her shoulders and bunched it in her fist. In the next moment she was kneeling on the rug, beating the dangerous ember into benign ashes.

Within moments, the danger had passed.

And so had Urien's impasse.

Returning to her seat with a sigh, everything came clear . . .

"It won't be long now, dear . . ."

The abbess had whispered the words through gritted teeth and a sheen of sweat in the moments before she died.

"But before I go, I must tell you . . ."

Nahenna's voice had turned into another scream as Somnadh's torturers did their work, but a moment later it returned, the final flush of life giving her words strength.

"At the first, God made the heavens and the earth . . . And God said, 'Let there be light!' And there was light, Urien—there is light to this day, because God speaks!"

These were the last words of Abbess Nahenna of Urras. After speaking them, she closed her eyes, smiled, and died.

Urien had not understood the significance of the words at the time. Now they bored into her . . .

They were connected to that distant conversation.

And not just connected . . .

They were the answer!

When the log collapsed in the fire, Urien had not hesitated. She had not paused to reflect upon whether she knew the ember would ignite the rug this time, or *how* she had come to such knowledge. The knowledge of what would happen was immediate and intuitive, and she had responded without doubting.

But why?

How was it that she could reliably assume that a glowing ember would ignite a fire? It was a small thing, Urien knew. But it triggered a much bigger question . . .

Why is it that I cannot help but trust that there is a regular order in the world? Where did I get such faith? More than that, from where does such order come?

Urien knew the world's order could not originate in her own authority. If it did, then she should have been able to change it. She could have neutralized the ember with a word.

But I didn't even try—because I knew it wouldn't work!

No. The world worked in certain ways quite independent of whether she wanted it to or not. She herself could not be the explanation.

But if not me . . .

And in that instant, she knew.

"At the first, God made the heavens and the earth."

There was only one reason that embers started fires . . .

Because God made the world!

And yet there was more . . .

And God said, "Let there be light!"

More of that distant conversation with Abbess Nahenna now returned . . .

"It is God the Spirit who speaks in Holy Writ, Urien. It is God's voice that you hear every single time you read or hear Holy Writ. If you are honest with yourself, you know this is true."

"How can you be so sure?"

"Because God made us, and in making us he made us able to recognize his voice—whether in the dim whisper of conscience or the clear words of Holy Writ. His law is written on our hearts and revealed in his Word. We may suppress the former and deny the latter, but we cannot eradicate or silence either. This what makes all people guilty before God. We see his signature not just in the fabric of creation, but upon the very fibers of our being.

All of us know that God is there, and all of us know that he is speaking. Faith is born when we stop denying this truth and entrust ourselves to it."

At long last, Urien understood.

The *order in the world* was only half the answer. The other half was *her own intuitive faith in that order!*

There was one reason why Urien could not help but trust an ember to start a fire . . .

One reason only . . .

That intuitive trust, though inaudible . . .

. . . was itself a *direct communication* from God.

Abbess Nahenna had been right. God had spoken to her already.

The force of the realization smote Urien like a war hammer . . .

He has been speaking to me since the day I was born, and he is speaking to me today.

Not just in the world's perceptible order.

Not just in the whispers of conscience . . .

But also in the words of Holy Writ.

It was no longer a question to be debated . . .

It is a truth to be acknowledged.

Urien wept. Her tears made the flames of the fire cracking before her seem brighter, and through her weeping, she smiled. Now, for the first time, she sensed a glimmer of something . . . *new.*

Her life had fallen to pieces.

But God raises the dead.

"There is light to this day, because God speaks."

Urien would deny his voice no longer. How could she? She would acknowledge the God of Holy Writ as her Creator. And starting from this point, she must further confess that nothing in Holy Writ was impossible for him . . .

Not the incarnation of Aesus.

Not his miracles.

Not the death of Aesus.

Not his bodily resurrection.

Not even his free offer.

That last bit was the hardest to believe. How could *she* be accepted and pardoned, she who had been complicit in the slaughter of innocents?

But if God was the Creator, then grace was grace. And grace, by its very nature, was unmerited. No, it was more than that. Grace was not just *unmerited.* Grace functioned in the face of actual *demerit.* That was what made it so terrifying . . . and so very, very wonderful.

Urien had acknowledged God as her Creator. Therefore she must acknowledge his grace. There was no longer any choice . . .

She must put her trust in that grace.

She must trust in Aesus. She must trust in Aesus alone—however difficult it might be, however little she deserved it, and no matter what the cost.

And so she did.

Sometime later, Urien opened her eyes.

I am made new.

Though she was still a prisoner, Aesus had delivered her from the darkest prison.

"Will he deliver me from my brother?"

As though in reply, Urien heard the sound of a key in her door. She got to her feet and turned in time to see a single figure enter. The man wore the familiar scarlet robes . . .

"What do you want?"

The figure closed the door behind him, locked it, and then turned. Facing Urien, he lowered the cowl of his robe to reveal a face etched not with cruelty, but compassion.

"My name is Yens. Though I am dressed as a red monk, I am no servant of the archbishop. I am a *Lumana*—a Hand of the Moon. Do you know what that means?"

Urien shook her head.

Yens smiled at Urien. "It means I will help you escape."

PART III

THE THREEFOLD CORD

"The Grey Men have cold breath today, my friends!" Chief Mannoch flashed his companions a broad smile.

Riding close behind, next to King Heclaid, Morumus grunted.

"What did he say, Morumus?"

"He said it's cold, sire."

"It will get worse until we clear the pass," Anguth warned.

The four men—the two kings and their brenilads—rode together four abreast up the winding mountain track. Ahead of them loomed the mist-shrouded summit of the *Firaith*. Behind them followed a long column of Grendannathi warriors.

As if to confirm Anguth's words, another gust swirled down out of the heights. It raked the climbing riders, its frigid fingers seeming to pass right through their heavy cloaks. The horses snorted, and their riders shivered.

Morumus huddled deeper into his cloak, and reminded himself to be thankful. *You almost didn't live to feel this cold!* But not only had he survived . . .

They had achieved a great victory.

Ultharn's attempted murder had enraged the Grendannathi. To attack the brenilad of a foreign emissary during a ceilheath was like cutting down a parleyman riding under a flag of truce. It was unthinkable treachery. This treachery, combined with Mannoch's personal support, had resulted in unanimous approval of the Lothairin proposal to re-form the Threefold Cord.

Yet Mannoch had not exaggerated when he told Morumus that his people would demand to be treated as equal partners. By the terms of the treaty ratified by the ceilheath, the Grendannathi agreed to embrace the Aesusian faith and join with Lothair and Oethur against the forces of Aeldred. But this union carried a strong condition in the opposite direction: Oethur and Rhianwyn's first son—the heir of the unified kingdom—must marry a Grendannathi princess, thus sealing in blood what was promised in writing.

I wonder what Oethur will say.

Morumus frowned. But it was not Oethur's reaction that worried him. He knew his friend would see the equity of the arrangement. No. What troubled him was something quite different . . .

How will the Red Order respond?

Despite Mannoch's alarm, one of the red monks had escaped Grenmaur. Nobody knew the direction in which he had fled, nor had the patrols found any trace of a trail.

The escape made Morumus uneasy. Did the red monks have secret allies among the clans, or had they a separate force hidden somewhere beyond Grenmaur? Either seemed possible. Both gave him a sense of foreboding . . .

They will attack. But when? Where? And how?

These were the questions that vexed Morumus as the column climbed toward the fog-furrowed brows of the Grey Men.

They reached the summit about an hour later. Here at the apex, the trail wound through a deep crack in the mountain's flank, a great fissure left by some ancient seismic turmoil. The walls on either side were sheer and unstable, and their slow disintegration had littered the track with chunks of stone—some quite large. As a result, though the pass remained wide enough for the four leading horses to walk abreast, the debris forced them to slow their pace and pick the way forward with care. Meanwhile the wind, hemmed in by the strict geography, grew ever more froward.

Because of the wind's ferocity, most of the men kept their heads down. Whether on horseback or afoot, there seemed little need for any to keep eyes forward. With rock walls on either side, it would be impossible to get lost.

Yet for some reason, when they had traversed about three quarters of the distance, Morumus did look up. Squinting into the wind, he saw something.

Ahead of them, out beyond the far end of the pass, a great bird soared up out of the lower fog. Up and up it rose into the wind-cleared sky at the summit, lifted by the strong currents. When it had cleared the top of the pass, it winged north.

Smart bird, to avoid this wind tunnel.

Morumus followed the bird's flight, shielding his eyes and turning his head as the creature soared overhead and back, along the column of warriors.

That's when he saw the red monk.

The scarlet robe was unmistakable atop the eastern rim of the fissure. The monk was rolling something large toward the brink . . .

Something too round to be a stone . . .

. . . something that smoked as it rolled!

Horror came over Morumus as he realized what the thing must be.

A barrel of nomergenna . . . with a burning fuse!

"Look out!" he yelled at the top of his lungs, gesturing toward the Dree. "Enemy!"

But it was too late.

The barrel tipped over the edge of the ravine and dropped...

Halfway down, it detonated.

The explosion ripped through the narrow pass like dragon fire. A score of warriors below the barrel simply disintegrated, and huge plumes of fire consumed a dozen others in each direction. Men screamed as the firestorm engulfed them.

But the fire was the lesser problem.

The force of the blast tore into the pass itself. There was a deafening chorus of cracks, followed by a hundred cries of rending stone. Wide swaths of the volatile walls erupted, creating a lethal shower of boulders and fragments that cascaded down on the unprotected warriors.

Men died—some bludgeoned by the stone rain; others tumbled beneath waves of rock, never to rise again. The red monk who had wrought the devastation was himself consumed as the cliff beneath him collapsed.

The air turned to coarse dust. It choked the living and coated the dying, and even the fierce wind seemed cowed before the dirty cloud that engulfed the summit.

For several moments, time seemed to slow around Morumus. He saw the fire and felt its heat, though the flames fell short of his flesh. His ears popped at the roar of the avalanche, and his heart lurched as the weight of the mountain began to crash over the column.

Then, with a terrible fury, the storm hit him.

Time returned to normal.

Exactly what happened, Morumus did not know. What he did know was that he was suddenly flying. The force of the explosion had torn him from his mount and hurled him toward a strange crevice that had appeared in the western wall of the pass. He saw the darkness rushing to meet him, and closed his eyes . . .

The first thing Morumus noticed upon waking was the silence.

He was alone, lying on his back, and surrounded by a palpable stillness.

He opened his eyes. As they adjusted to the dim light, he saw that he was in cave of some sort. Overhead, about twice a man's height above where he lay, he saw a stone ceiling. There was something odd about it . . .

Where am I?

The last thing he remembered was being thrown from his horse.

Toward an opening in the wall of the pass.

Had he passed through it? Was he inside the wall?

With some significant trepidation, Morumus tried to stand . . .

. . . and found that he could.

Thank God.

But where was he?

It *was* a cave of some sort—of that there could be no doubt. But the walls, like the ceiling, were somehow *wrong*. His head throbbed, and he frowned as his eyes strained to pierce the dimness.

What is it?

Then he had it.

They're smooth!

The walls and ceiling were not the rough, natural contours of a cave. They had been cut.

The wall before him was the same way, except at one place where a narrow fissure split it from top to bottom.

Morumus studied the crack. Through it came a faint, hazy stream of light. That light, however vague, was the only source of illumination in the small chamber where he now stood.

I must have come in through that . . .

And he gaped.

But it's hardly wider than a man!

Morumus felt a strange tingle on the back of his neck as he realized what this meant.

"The Lord will guard your going out and your coming in . . ." he whispered, bowing his head.

After a moment, he opened his eyes. *What is this place?*

Turning, he saw that the chamber was a long, rectangular space. He could see, too, that the wall through which he had been cast was one of the shorter sides.

But why it is here?

He turned to peer toward the back of the chamber . . .

And his breath caught in his throat.

He knew now what this place was.

It was a tomb.

At the back of the chamber he could just make out the shape of a stone sarcophagus.

But what was that lying atop it?

Despite the meager light, his eyes caught a brief glint of metal . . .

And in the next instant, the memory of his conversation with the king on their journey north came rushing back to him.

"We wanted to find the very tomb of Tuddreal. We wanted the Sword, you see . . ."

"No!" Morumus exclaimed, his excitement building. "It cannot be!"

Now every hair on his body stood on end . . .

"Morumus!"

He heard the shout—he thought he even recognized the voice—but he did not turn. "I'm alive! I'm in here! Quickly, bring torches!"

It took all the discipline Morumus could muster to wait for the others to come.

But if I'm right, then this is too important for me to do alone . . .

When at last torchlight filled the narrow crevice, Morumus smiled.

"Morumus! Thank God you are alive!" It was King Heclaid, followed by Anguth and Mannoch. "So many have died, and the pass has been destroyed—"

"Sire." Morumus trembled as he spoke, and he gestured to the chamber about them. "We have found it, sire. The Tudbara!"

Heclaid gasped. "No . . ."

"What is this place, Morumus?" Mannoch spoke in Grendannathi.

"Follow me." Morumus took the torch proffered by Anguth and led the way to the back of the tomb, then held the light aloft to illuminate the sarcophagus.

But nobody looked at the coffin. All eyes were fixed instead on the object lying atop it.

A sword.

Its blade was a great, glittering length of steel—long enough for a giant. The keen edges running down both sides glinted in the torchlight, appearing quite undiminished by centuries of dormancy. And within the fuller—the beveled groove extending most of the blade's length—some ancient smith had inlaid a line of script in a dark, precious metal.

"'Their sword shall pierce their own heart,'" Heclaid quoted the legendary inscription from the Psalms.

"He can read the inscription?" Anguth could not understand the king's words, but he heard the reverent tone in the Heclaid's voice.

"No, but we know what it says." Morumus translated the verse.

Anguth gasped. "But that means . . . is this what I think it is?"

"The Sword of Tuddreal," confirmed Mannoch.

Melechur.

"You have found it, Morumus," Heclaid whispered. "The Sword of Dathidd."

"No," said Morumus twice—first in Grendannathi, then in Northspeech. "This is indeed the Sword, *Melechur.* But it is no longer the Sword of Tuddreal—or even of Dathidd."

The eyes of all three men fixed on him.

"This is now the Sword of Oethur."

Two lions stared at Stonoric, their gaze fixed and unblinking.

He stood this afternoon in the heart of the Tower of Luca. Before him, the great double doors of the throne room stood closed. Upon those doors Luca Wolfbane, a dozen years earlier, had carved two great lions. Each lion had a name inlaid on a banner beneath its paws . . .

King and Country.

The Duke of Hoccaster did not flinch. Though distasteful to his private sensibilities, he had done his duty and pacified Dyfann. Motivated only by love for his nation and loyalty to his sovereign, he had dealt death and risked lives—including his own.

He had nothing to fear before the scrutiny of these eyes . . .

Or of those waiting beyond the doors.

Without a creak, one of the lions swung inward and a liveried soldier appeared. "Their Majesties will see you now, my lord."

The audience hall of the Tower of Luca was a large square chamber with a high ceiling. Nestled within the greatest fortress in Aeld Gowan, the room itself had no need to impress. If those who passed its threshold were not convinced of Mersian power prior to entering the Tower, then they were incorrigible fools—and chances were they would not leave alive.

Stonoric crossed to the chamber's far end and kneeled on the carpet before the canopied dais. "You have summoned me, sire."

"Your arrival is most welcome to us, Cousin. Please stand."

Stonoric stood on his feet.

Before him, the king and queen sat on their thrones.

King Wodic seemed to have grown since Stonoric had last met him. The change was perceptible, yet not a matter of physical stature so much as a shift of settled authority. Wodic was no longer the lesser son of Luca Wolfbane, and he knew it. He was now the Conqueror of Dyfann and Sovereign of Southern Aeld Gowan.

Stonoric smiled. "You are looking well, sire."

To the king's left, Queen Caileamach was resplendent in a satin gown adorned with a sash of Dyfanni tartan. Stonoric knew it would be improper to make any acknowledgment of the slight bulge in her middle, so he instead he offered her a deep bow.

"It is good to see you, Your Majesty."

To the queen's left, a third chair had been placed at the foot of the dais. On it sat a familiar figure.

"Duke Stonoric." Archbishop Simnor rose from his chair and inclined his head. "It is good to see you again, my lord."

Stonoric returned the gesture. "And you, Your Grace."

"The archbishop has just been telling us of your campaign in Dyfann, Cousin." Wodic nodded toward Simnor.

"A most efficient military operation, Your Majesties," Simnor continued. "No unnecessary slaughter, and his lordship showed considerable respect for the native customs of our people."

Stonoric wondered at those last words. *Has Garallodh informed Simnor of the incident after the final battle?*

But there was no trace of irony in the archbishop's smile. "If his lordship had not already professed a desire to remain settled in Hoccaster, I should have petitioned Your Majesties to grant him a second duchy west of the Gwyllinors. His government would be most welcome in Dyfann."

It was the queen who spoke next.

"Your restraint in securing our kingdom is noted, my lord, and most appreciated. Are you firm in your resolve to remain in Hoccaster?"

Stonoric bowed low. "I am, Your Majesty."

"Stubbornly so, I assure you, my dear," Wodic said with a laugh. "Cousin Stonoric has never been one to journey abroad by choice. He would not even visit Mereclestour, were he not summoned!"

"Is that so, my lord?"

Stonoric inclined his head to the queen. "Our late King Luca once told me that the men who fight best are those who love their homes most, Your Majesty. Hoccaster is my home. I was born there, I have responsibilities there, and I will be content to die there. I desire nothing more."

"An admirable attachment, my lord." There was a wistful edge to the queen's approval. "I will pray you get your wish."

"Yet before you die, cousin," Wodic interjected, "I have further need—"

As he spoke, a sudden look of queasiness came over the queen . . .

Caileamach rose. "My lords, if you will all excuse me . . ."

All three men stood in silence while the queen left the hall in haste.

"She will be all right." Wodic looked at Stonoric as he returned to his seat. "No need to worry."

The duke straightened his frown. "Yes, sire."

Yet in truth, his expression had nothing to do with the queen's condition. Lady Hoccaster had borne several babes, and he was quite familiar with the early sicknesses and their sudden manifestations. No, he had no concern for *that*. Rather, he had scowled because he suspected he knew what the king had been about to say . . . what he was going to say now.

But he was wrong.

"Word has arrived from the North. Aeldred of Nornindaal seeks our aid. It seems his brother has claimed the kingdom for himself. The young pretender has garnered enough support to make it a fight, and is marching toward Grindangled. Archbishop Simnor believes we should reinforce Aeldred. What say you, Cousin?"

For a moment, Stonoric said nothing. This was *not* what he had expected . . .

It is worse.

But could it be averted?

"With respect to the archbishop, sire, I disagree. A war in Nornindaal is no affair of Mersex. Our quarrel in the North is with Heclaid of Lothair, who refuses to surrender his bishop. If there is to be an invasion, it ought to be a limited strike by sea from Marfesbury against Dunross. It would be my honor to lead such an expedition, sire, and I am confident that we could succeed."

Wodic pursed his lips. "What say you to the duke, Archbishop?"

Simnor nodded to Stonoric, then looked at the king. "Duke Stonoric raises a legitimate point: Your Majesty must punish Heclaid's treachery. And furthermore, I have no doubt that the capable duke could execute such a campaign. But"—he raised a finger—"to sack Dunross now would be . . . *inefficient.* Heclaid marches with Oethur the Pretender. What good would it do for us to commit forces to Dunross, only to allow our enemies to take Grindangled—from which they could march down the eastern coast into Mersex itself?"

"The archbishop has a point, Cousin, don't you think? Shouldn't we do whatever is necessary to secure our northern frontier?"

"I agree with your concern entirely, sire." Stonoric inclined his head to the king, then looked at Simnor. "However, I yet disagree with the archbishop. Your Grace assumes that the Norns would invade Mersex. I am not persuaded. Never before have they done thus."

"Surely my lord is forgetting"—Simnor gestured to the king—"the assault on Their Majesties persons, which you yourself so gallantly thwarted! Would you not call that an invasion, my lord?"

"I would not call it a *Nornish* invasion, Your Grace. The evidence we found points us toward Dunross, not Grindangled." Stonoric resisted the urge to scoff at the archbishop's flimsy justification.

He knows as well as I do where the evidence points. What's he playing at?

Then he remembered his conversation with the archbishop as they rode to the invasion of Dyfann . . .

"The union of Dyfann and Mersex will bring many benefits to our peoples. But far more important is the merger of the Old Faith with the New . . . A new golden age will dawn over Aeld Gowan, my Lord Duke—and from here, the light will spread to all the world!"

The duke's irritation flared. *Curse the ambitions of bishops!*

But curses alone could not avert an unnecessary conflict.

Stonoric appealed to Wodic. "Sire, what benefit is there to Mersex in taking sides in this Nornish civil war?"

"A question I myself have asked." Wodic gestured at Simnor. "Tell the duke what Aeldred is prepared to give us, Archbishop."

Simnor smiled. "Beyond his own goodwill, King Aeldred has promised us two things. Firstly, he will place his bishop under the primacy of the See of Mereclestour. And secondly, he will cede to Mersex the city of Toberstan, with all of its surrounding territory."

"You see, Cousin?" Wodic smiled at Stonoric. "We will at last reverse the only setback ever suffered by my father."

Toberstan.

Stonoric remembered it well. King Luca and Archbishop Deorcad had tried to force their will onto the bishops of the Northern Church. The Northmen had refused. Luca had threatened to impose his will by force, but then news had arrived from Hoccaster . . .

The Dyfanni had crossed the Gwyllinors and invaded Mersex.

Neither Stonoric nor Wodic had attended Toberstan. Both the duke and his then-ward had been busy saving Hoccaster. Stonoric shuddered at the recollection. The speed of the surprise attack had set his city in a panic. The tenacity of the tartaned warriors—who attempted an escalade on the city walls and almost prevailed!—had been alarming.

For several harrowing hours, he had feared his home would be lost.

Twenty years gone, yet as fresh as yesterday.

As fresh *and* as terrifying. Stonoric shoved the memories aside. "But sire, what guarantee do we have that Aeldred will keep his word?" The duke looked at Simnor. "Does not even Holy Writ warn us against the pride of a king with his army, Your Grace? Once we secure Aeldred's throne, how do we know he will not reconsider his promises?"

Simnor's expression clouded. "I have received reports from the far north—reports that suggest the Northmen are stirring up the barbarians of Grendannath. I have sent missionaries to attempt to dissuade them, but no word has returned." The archbishop looked from Wodic to Stonoric. "Aeldred's position may be more precarious than even he realizes, my lords. And so may ours. If the clans of Grendannath come south, why should they stop in Grindangled—or even Toberstan?"

The hall fell silent for several moments. At last, Wodic spoke.

"We will march north, Stonoric—you and I together. We will reinforce Aeldred, and once we have dealt with his brother, we will have his help to extract our debt from Dunross. And if the barbarians of Grendannath appear . . . well then, you and I have fought the like before, have we not?"

"Yes, sire." Stonoric hid his disappointment with a bow.

More war.

Yet there was nothing for it now. King and country were his creed—

Even when he did not agree.

The sun was halfway to its zenith as the Lothairin embassy entered Dunross.

The mounted company desired no fanfare as they passed through the gates, yet word of their return could not be suppressed. The officer of the watch had sent a runner up the King's Mile as soon as he'd spotted them, and attentive citizens—along with the usual crop of listless busybodies—had seen him hastening toward the castle. By the time the riders reached the walls, the news was spreading.

King Heclaid and his company had returned from beyond the *Ballaith*.

Alone.

"I'm sorry, sire," said the officer, who came down out of the gatehouse to greet them, "We were given standing orders to send word as soon as—"

The king brushed aside the apology. "There is no need to apologize, Lieutenant."

A short while later, when they reined up in the castle forecourt, they found Haedorn and Rhianwyn waiting.

"Father!" Rhianwyn ran to embrace the king. "Praise Aesus you are safe."

Haedorn and Morumus shook hands.

"You are looking well, brother."

"And you, Haedorn."

The four of them passed indoors to a sitting room, where the forewarned servants had laid an ample spread of refreshments.

"What news from Oethur?" asked the king once they were all settled.

"He met the four lords a fortnight ago. Against my counsel, he surrendered to them without promise of safe conduct."

The king's brows arched. "And?"

Haedorn smiled. "And he succeeded, sire."

Heclaid sighed his relief as Haedorn continued.

"I don't know all the details, only that it had something to do with Bishop Treowin and a missing tongue that turned out not to be missing."

Morumus grinned. *That sounds just like Oethur . . .*

"God be praised," said the king.

"But what of your embassy, Father?" Concern etched Rhianwyn's face and echoed in her voice.

"Yes," agreed Haedorn. "If you will forgive me saying so, sire, we had thought you would return with an army of clansmen!"

"We thought so, too."

For the next several minutes, the king and Morumus related to them the events of the ceilheath and its aftermath—ending with the attack at the mountain pass.

"It was a grim business. The explosion, and the avalanche that followed, killed fifty warriors and trapped the rest on the wrong side of the pass. Mannoch and his servant were with us, but they risked a climb over the debris—most of it quite unstable—to rejoin their men. Their army must now find another path over the mountains."

Haedorn frowned. "Will they arrive in time, sire?"

"Mannoch thinks they will, but I don't know. There is another pass to the east, north of Grindangled. But before they can turn in that direction they will have to travel north, back down out of the mountains. If they reach us, it will be beneath the gates of Grindangled."

"I am sorry to hear it, sire. But I rejoice that your embassy was a success."

"Yes," added Rhianwyn. "Oethur will be delighted."

"The alliance was not forged without conditions." Heclaid shook his head. "But no, we will not speak of such things now. Not when there are better tidings to share." He brightened and turned to Morumus. "Show them."

Morumus retrieved the long bundle he had carried in from the horses, and laid it on the table beside where they sat. He loosened the leather bindings and unwrapped the heavy cloth. Then he gripped the sword and held it up for them to see.

"You see, Lord Haedorn," said the king. "We did not come back quite so empty-handed as you might suppose."

Morumus proffered the sword to his brother, who took and lifted it in a slow arc.

"Perfect balance." He tested the edge with his thumb. "Sharp, too." He looked from Morumus to Heclaid. "What is this weapon?"

"Something out of legend," said the king. "It is Melechur, the great Sword of Dathidd! The lost Blade of Tuddreal!"

Haedorn's eyes went wide. "Where did you . . . how?"

"The explosion that destroyed the summit pass uncovered Tuddreal's Barrow," said Morumus. "I found the Sword inside, lying atop the sarcophagus."

"You're only telling the half of it," said the king. "Your brother was thrown from his horse into the Tudbara, through a crack no wider than this table." He gestured at the board beside them. "It was nothing short of a special providence."

Haedorn handed the sword back to Morumus. "Such a blade is beyond me."

"It is beyond the both of us," Heclaid agreed. "But it is not beyond Oethur. It belonged to the king of the last Threefold Cord. Now it will belong to the king of the new Threefold Cord."

"The Threefold Cord," Rhianwyn whispered, "and the Sword of Tuddreal."

"But if it is to last, we must win." The king's tone turned brisk. "I will take the Sword to Oethur when we combine forces. Is everything on schedule with the muster of Lothair?"

"Yes, sire."

"Good. We leave in three days."

"Will you excuse me, Father?" Rhianwyn stood, and the men hastily followed. "Three days is not much time."

"Not much time for what, my dear?"

"The banners, of course."

"What?"

"Oh Father, they must all be changed. If the Threefold Cord is now re-formed, then the banners of Lothair—which depict the broken pieces of the Cord—must be remade."

Heclaid smiled as the realization dawned. "Of course, my dear. How right you are!"

Rhianwyn turned and hurried toward the doors. As the men stood waiting for her departure, Morumus remembered a conversation he and Oethur had shared on Urras . . .

He pointed to the three arcing curves centered on the orange field of the Lothairin banner. The ends of each arc curved away from the other two. Moreover, each was a different color: red, green, and black.

"According to our history, three ancestral peoples once lived north of the Deasmor. For many generations, they were constantly at war—with each other and with invaders. There was no peace. Then one day, a king arrived from across the sea. With his strong arms and wise spirit, he united all three peoples under his gracious rule. As a symbol of his kingdom he devised a threefold cord. Each arc was a

different color to stand for the different peoples, yet the three were interwoven at the center and connected at their ends to symbolize the unity of the kingdom."

"But on the flag above the boat, the three arcs were not connected."

"No, they were not. Treachery destroyed the great kingdom, and the threefold cord unraveled. But the ancestor of my people, Lothair the Wise, believed that a new king would someday arise who would reunite the peoples of the north. And so, to keep both hope and the memory alive, he placed the three cords—separated at present—on his banner. And yet, if you draw them together from the center"—Morumus paused, picked up a rock, and drew in the dust—"they will connect once again. You see?"

Oethur nodded. "I see it. But it might not need a great king."

"What do you mean?"

"You said your ancestor believed a great king could unite the peoples by drawing them together."

"That's right."

"Yet it strikes me that a sufficient threat might just as easily push all three together from the outside."

Morumus smiled at the recollection. Oethur might have been correct about the threat, yet he felt certain that his friend would prove to be the sort of king who needed no external threat to command the loyalty of his people.

The door had barely closed behind Rhianwyn before a liveried servant rushed into the room, his face pale.

"Sire," said the man, making a low bow. "A ship has arrived."

"A ship?"

"A Trathari ship, sire. They bring ill tidings."

"From where?"

"Urras, sire."

Morumus's hackles stood on end. "From the monastery?"

"What's happened?" demanded the king.

"Sire . . ." The servant's voice shook. "Urras Monastery has been destroyed . . ."

19

Morumus could not believe his ears.

No! It cannot be! Not again . . .

Memories of Lorudin Abbey rose unbidden before his eyes . . .

Oh, no! Lord Aesus, no! Not that! Not again . . . But he forced himself to ask, dreading the reply. "Who?"

The servant shook his head. "I do not know, my lord. But perhaps the survivor—"

"There is a survivor?" demanded Heclaid. "Where is he?"

"He is waiting outside, sire."

"Send him in, man. And bring us some more wine." The king's eyes were red. "I fear we will need it."

The servant vanished, and in his place came a thin monk in a ragged habit. His black tonsure was dirty and unkempt. His blue eyes seemed clouded.

"Landu!" Morumus had not known the other monk well, but Urras Monastery was too small for anybody to remain anonymous. "Thank God you are alive!"

"Morumus?" Landu blinked his eyes. Then he saw the king. "Your Majesty." He made a hasty bow. "It is an honor to meet you, sire. I only wish I bore better news."

"So do I, my son." Heclaid gestured him to a chair. "But please sit down, and tell us what you can."

Haedorn poured the monk a goblet of wine, and Landu began his tale.

"They came in the middle of the night, while the monastery slept. It was the abbot and abbess who raised the alarm. But it was too late. They had already landed . . ."

Morumus could not contain himself. "Who, Landu? *Who* came in the middle of the night?"

The monk frowned. "I'm not sure. I thought they were slavers, for I saw them dragging many brothers and sisters away. And when I found the abbess in the corridor, she said they were indeed sea-raiders . . ."

"But?"

"But now I'm not so sure. You have to understand, it was hard to see anything clearly through the fire and smoke—and with the noise and terror, one's mind can play tricks. Yet I thought I saw other figures in the night . . . men dressed in red."

Morumus growled. "The Red Order."

"I do not know that name, Morumus. What is this Red Order?"

Morumus almost gaped, but caught himself. Landu had not shared in any of the events that had burned the scarlet name across Morumus's mind. Nor had he been party to Abbot Nerias's councils . . .

"I'll tell you later. Keep going."

Landu resumed. "I cannot be sure, you understand. Abbess Nahenna ordered me to flee through a tunnel hidden in the basement of the scriptorium. She said there would be others, but when I got there . . ."

"There were no others."

The monk nodded, his eyes closing. "There were signs of a struggle: smears of blood, and a child's doll torn apart." A rivulet of tears burst down Landu's unshaven cheek as his eyes reopened. "I should have gone back and tried to help."

"You'd have only been slaughtered or taken yourself." Heclaid stood and put a hand on Landu's shoulder. "There was nothing you could do, son. Do not blame yourself."

Landu nodded, but said nothing.

The king looked at Morumus. "You will see to his needs?"

"Yes, sire."

"Good." He gestured to Morumus's brother. "Come, Haedorn. There is nothing more we can do here, but there is much we must do if we are to put a stop the depredations of the Red Order—and their allies."

As the two monks watched the warriors depart in silence, Morumus felt a great sadness descend over him. It felt like a cold rain in winter . . .

"Then everything is lost," he whispered. "Abbot Nerias, Donnach's Volume . . ."

And what of Urien?

"What happened to Urien, Landu?"

The monk flinched. "She was not there."

"I know that. We received word a month ago that she had vanished. Do you have any idea what happened?"

"Yes."

Morumus could sense the hesitation. "Do you know when? Or why?"

Landu licked his lips. "It's a long story, brother. But part of the blame belongs to me."

"Whatever it was saved her life. Tell me, Landu."

Morumus listened as Landu unfolded the tale of the body hidden in the old chapel, and how the realization of a murderer-at-large had set the abbey on edge—and turned the suspicions of many toward Urien. His eyes widened at the news of Feindir's confession and suicide.

"That seems so out of character for him." Morumus shook his head.

"Abbot Nerias said it often: sin is *always* irrational."

"True enough, but if Feindir confessed, why did Urien still flee?"

Landu hesitated. "This is the part which brings me shame, brother. I was in love with her, you see."

Morumus started. *In love?* "Go on. As I've said already, whatever it was saved her life."

"I knew that Urien wanted to leave, but when I heard the news of Feindir's death, I thought she might change her mind. So I went to her chamber to tell her—" He fell silent for a moment. "I know it is forbidden, Morumus, but I did not want her to go!"

"Go on."

"She would not listen. She insisted on leaving. I tried to stop her . . ." His voice was shaking now, and the words tumbled out. "I blocked the door, grabbed her wrist, and told her that I would not let her go unless she agreed to marry me."

Morumus felt a fierce anger rising in his chest, but he forced himself to remain calm.

God meant it for good . . .

"What happened?"

"She hit me with a book—a heavy book, right in my throat." Landu put a hand to the place. "It knocked the wind out of me, and I fell. But as I fell I knocked over Urien's lamp . . ."

"You started a fire?"

"No, thank God. The only thing that burned was a book. But it must have been a special book, because its loss made Urien furious . . . she stepped on my throat until everything went black. When I woke up, she was gone."

For a long moment, Morumus just stared at Landu. The earlier report confirmed everything the monk said. Abbess

Nahenna had found Urien's cell empty, and her translation of the Bone Codex in ashes.

"It was the Bone Codex."

"The Bone Codex? What is that?"

"That's the name of the book you destroyed, Landu. It belonged to the Red Order."

"That's the second time you've mentioned that name. What is the Red Order?"

"They are the Mordruui, Landu. They are the practitioners of the Dark Faith—an ancient, murderous, and very pagan religion. The Dark Faith worships a tree called the Mother, which they believe to be a goddess and the source of all other religions. From this tree they harvest an herb that gives them great powers of deception. But to produce the herb, the tree must be nourished with human blood."

"But why are they called the Red *Order*?"

"Because they now have a foothold in the Church. They are everywhere on the Continent. Even here on our island, they have infiltrated the Church—especially in Mersex."

Landu looked stricken. "They are here?"

"You saw them yourself. They are called the *Red* Order from their scarlet robes."

The monk shuddered. "And Urien . . . was she part of this Order?"

"No." *Not anymore.*

"But then why did she have their book? What was she doing with the Bone Codex?"

"She was translating it for me." Morumus felt heat rising as he thought of the lost translation. "I found the book in Caeldora, and brought it back to Urras. We had hoped that it would tell us the location of the last Mordruui stronghold." He gave Landu a hard look. "Now we'll never know."

"I'm sorry, Morumus! But in this, perhaps, God has helped us."

"What do you mean?"

"Not all of Urien's translation burned."

"It didn't?"

"No." Landu reached into his robe. "I managed to save a page. It was on the bottom, which is why it did not burn. I've kept it with me ever since that day."

Landu handed the leaf of singed parchment to Morumus, who looked at it.

He did not recognize the diagram inked on its surface. There were a number of dark points, scattered seemingly at random across the page. In their midst was a single circle, its perimeter drawn using small, square crosses.

What does it mean?

But as Morumus scrutinized the page, he saw a small line of script near the bottom edge. Its end had been lost to the fire, but the first portion was still barely legible. It was written in Vilguran, in a small clear hand . . .

Urien's translation of the diagram's inscription?

Morumus's eyes widened as he read the words aloud . . .

"The location of the Ring of St—"

"I cannot make anything of those words," Landu said. "They say it's a map, but to what? The ring of some saint? What does that mean?"

"It's a map, all right, but not to a saint's ring."

Landu looked up.

"Part of the inscription is burned, Landu. The letters 'St' don't stand for 'saint.' They are the first two letters of the word *Stars*. The caption reads, 'The location to the Ring of Stars.' "

Morumus felt a surge of hope pierce through his enveloping sadness . . .

"The Ring of Stars?"

"This is the clue we have been seeking, Landu—the location of the Ring of Stars! Praise Aesus, Urien found it!"

"Found what?"
"The map to the Mordruui's last stronghold."
Urien had found the map.
Landu, despite his misdemeanors, had preserved it.
Now all Morumus had to do was decipher it.

Five days had passed since Yens promised to help Urien escape. Five days, and yet the latter was still a prisoner—while the former was nowhere to be seen.

A lot could happen in five days.

Urien heard the key in the lock, and stood to face the door. *Oh Lord, don't let it be Somnadh.*

Nearly a fortnight had passed since Nahenna's death, and Somnadh had not come to see Urien.

Not yet.

Urien feared their next encounter. She had tried to show him the truth, and he struck her. She had refused to return to the Mother, and he murdered the abbess. What would he do when he learned she had become an Aesusian?

It would be ghastly. Worst of all, it would not be done to her. If only her brother would vent his rage on her! But no. Somnadh would never harm the one he intended to become the Queen's Heart. Others would suffer in her place.

Oh Lord, let it not *be Somnadh at the door!*

It was not.

But there were two red monks with their cowls up. One of them turned to lock the door. The other just stared at Urien. She could feel his unseen eyes. It made her skin crawl.

"What do you want, monk?"

The faceless monk never answered, for in that moment the second monk acted.

With a speed that belied long training, he turned from the door and struck his fellow with a double-handed, downward blow to the back of the neck. There was no cry, only a grunt. Then the first monk toppled forward onto the floor.

Urien stood, dumbfounded, while the first monk lowered his cowl.

Yens!

"Hello, Urien." The Lumana flashed her a tight smile. "I bet you thought I had forgotten." He dropped to his knees beside the fallen monk, pulling back the man's cowl and putting a finger to his neck.

"Unconscious, but alive." He looked up at Urien. "Help me."

Together, they completed the task in minutes. When it was finished, the monk lay stripped, bound, and gagged on the floor of Urien's cell.

Yens handed his red robe to Urien.

"You'll need to shift your clothes, if you are to walk out of this place."

Urien took the robe and retreated to her dressing screen on the chamber's far end. But no sooner had she stepped behind it than she heard a gasping moan.

"Is everything okay?"

"Fine."

But when Urien stepped out from behind the screen, she saw that the situation had changed.

Yens had crouched, rolled the unconscious Mordruui onto his stomach . . .

. . . and thrust a dagger up through the base of his skull.

"Oh!" She put a hand to her mouth and took a step back. "Is he . . . ?"

"Dead." Yens voice was flat, professional.

"You just . . ." Urien did not know what to say.

"As my captain said some time ago: mercy is for fools and neutrals, and this man was neither."

Urien could not disagree, yet the cold-bloodedness of the killing still appalled her. "Just like that?"

"Do you think he deserved better?"

"No. It's just . . . you might have offered him a last chance to repent."

Yens got to his feet. "I did. On our way here, I asked him if he ever had any regrets about our work. He said he had none." The Lumana shook his head, and looked straight at Urien. "This man worked . . . *downstairs.* You know what that means, I suspect?"

Urien nodded.

"Let's be going, then."

The escape from the Tower of Luca was a harrowing affair. Every foreign footfall filled Urien with the fear that the corpse had been found, that her escape had been detected. Every time they rounded a corner in the corridor, she feared she would find her brother waiting. And then there were the delays . . .

Twice they were stopped by other red monks—not because of any suspicion, but simply so that their interlocutors could pass the latest news. Had they heard about the king's decision to march north? Did they have any idea why the archbishop would send along so many casks of the precious nomergenna?

Urien held her breath through both exchanges. Yens was fluent in both Mersian and Vilguran, and had grown used to this sort of thing during his long masquerade as a dispatch rider. Besides this, she feared what would happen—or what would be required—if her voice should be recognized as female. For she had no intention of returning to her cell.

Not alive.

I'll not be the cause of any further suffering . . . Come what may, Urien *would* escape the Tower of Luca.

Yet in the end, things did not come to extremities. Despite the loud thumping of her heart, which she felt sure would give them away, Urien and Yens rode out of Mereclestour unmolested. Dispatch riders came and went from the Tower every day. As a result, nobody questioned a pair of red monks on horseback carrying full satchels.

They slipped out of the city just before the gates closed at dusk. They rode west together for several leagues before Yens drew rein. He pushed back his cowl. "Where will you go, Urien?"

"West. I am going to Dyfann. I intend to put an end to the Red Order."

"How will you do that?"

"I don't know yet." Urien had an idea, nothing more. She knew what must be done, but she did not know how to do it.

Not yet.

"And what about you, Yens? Where will you go?"

"I ride south to rejoin the Lumanae. My captain and my ship wait at the coast. We will return to Midgaddan."

Urien nodded. "May the Lord fill your sails and guide your paths."

"And yours, Urien."

"And Yens?"

"Yes?"

"Thank you. You have saved my life—and perhaps the lives of many others."

"I did no such thing, for the Hands of the Moon have no authority to interfere on this island. You escaped quite on your own. Remember that, my lady."

But he bowed and smiled all the same before riding away . . .

"She did *what?*"

Somnadh was on his feet in an instant.

"She has murdered one of our brothers, Archbishop. We found his body in her cell."

Somnadh covered his black eyes with one hand. *Curse it all, Urien! You will rue this lunacy. I swear by the Mother, you will rue it . . . !*

"And where is my sister now?"

The red monk—barely more than a catechumen, and probably forced into this unpleasant duty by his seniors—cowered. "She has escaped, Your Grace."

Somnadh was not a man to lose control often. Even under severe provocation, he usually found that he could keep his head. Urien seemed to be the sole exception. Her impudence had pushed him over the edge not once, but twice. Now it did so for the third time . . .

Howling with wordless rage, he overturned the desk in front of him. There was a terrific crash as candles broke, a dish and goblet clattered, and his inkwell shattered. The papers, which had piled high, now scattered like leaves before a whirlwind.

The messenger leapt back. It was his whimpering that brought Somnadh back.

"Where?" His chest heaved as his wrath subsided. "Where did she go?"

"There is a report, Your Grace. Two red-robed figures on horseback left the city just before nightfall. They were heading west."

West? Why west?

Then he knew.

Father.

The horrible conversation at Banr Cluidan came back to Somnadh in an instant . . .

"What about the hurt you would cause our Father, Urien? In his old age, as he lies moldering in his bed, what would Father say if he

heard your words? . . . Must I tell him now that his beloved daughter has renounced the faith of our ancestors?"

It had been the first time he had ever struck his sister. But the blow had served only to magnify Urien's defiance . . .

"I will tell him myself!"

"You will do no such thing!"

But Urien would try. She had promised as much. And like him, Urien was one to keep her promises . . .

"Oh I will, brother. I will tell him, too, that his son is a coward—a coward who struck his own sister, and then tried to blame her for it!"

It must not happen.

It would not.

"Spread the word to make ready," Somnadh snapped the command. "And summon my secretary. Word must be sent to all of our chapter houses. Every gate must be guarded, every road watched. I depart at dawn."

"Yes, Your Grace." The messenger bobbed his obeisance. "Depart to where?"

"To Banr Cluidan. I will see to this personally."

There would be no more attempts to persuade. No more efforts to secure a willing repentance.

His sister would be captured, and he would carry her himself to the Ring of Stars. There, he would exhume the black stone. There, Urien would drink the Elixir of Knowledge.

He would recapture the Queen's Heart . . .

. . . even if it meant destroying her will.

21

Morumus would have loved to lose himself in the library at Dunross Castle. It was just the sort of place he enjoyed most: a vast chamber of cool shadows and crammed shelves, a sprawling world of leather spines and dusty shafts of light. Though neither as exotic nor as extensive as the bishop's library at Aevor, King Heclaid's library was still a realm of silent treasures.

Yet Morumus had no time for the recluse's luxury today. There was important work to be done.

And it was not going well.

"Set those volumes here," he said to Landu, pointing to an empty space on the long table between them.

The dark-featured monk off-loaded the two awkward, large-folio books with a grunt. Then he looked across the table. Despite their lack of progress, Landu's blue eyes seemed clearer now than they had when he first arrived. Morumus knew why.

A fruitless task is better than a hopeless memory.

"Which one do you want?"

"It doesn't matter." Morumus slid the top book toward his side. "I'll take this one."

Each monk opened his book and began turning the yellowed pages . . .

The two of them had spent the last two days pouring over every volume of maps they could find. The king's library had many such books, yet few of these contained maps of Dyfann. Of what maps they found, few had charted more than a handful of Dyfanni villages.

How will we ever match the pattern if the villages aren't marked?

Morumus believed that the diagram salvaged from Urien's book was meant to be laid over a map of Dyfann. His idea was that each of the dark points scattered on the singed leaf stood for a village. If so, then finding the Ring of Stars was but a matter of finding a map where every point matched a known settlement. Once they discovered the settlement pattern that corresponded to the drawing from the Bone Codex, they would know where to find the stone circle marked at the diagram's center.

It should have been easy.

But the task had proven far from it. The same mapmakers capable of displaying a frightening knowledge of the other countries of Aeld Gowan and Midgaddan demonstrated a frustrating ignorance when it came to the land west of the Gwyllinor Mountains. Compared to other places in the known world, Dyfann was a relative unknown.

Morumus reached the end of his volume well before Landu finished his. He closed the book's broad, leather-bound cover and frowned. *Only a small map . . . and it was too small to have settlements marked.*

To avoid dwelling upon his disappointment, he shifted his gaze across the table. Landu had paused a little over halfway through his volume, and his finger now traced the outline of something at the top right corner of the open page before him. Morumus leaned in. What had captivated the other monk's attention? What he saw surprised him.

Landu was not staring at a collection of marked villages. It was not even a map of Dyfann that occupied his attention. Instead, he was tracing his finger over a chart of the island of Tratharan.

No, it was not even the island . . .

It was the map's compass rose.

To be fair, it was peculiar symbol. It did not have the usual arrows pointing outward—like petals on a rose—to indicate the cardinal directions. Instead, the cartographer had drawn this one to resemble a bard's thick ring. Nothing lay within the circle, and the ring itself was simple. Its only markings were four dark whorls etched in the band at equidistant points.

"What is it?"

"I don't know." Landu's voice seemed pensive. "For some reason, this just strikes me as curious. These marks about the perimeter . . ."

"The cardinal directions." Morumus shrugged. "Trathari bards are notoriously poor, except for a single gold ring which they are forbidden to sell."

Landu shook his head. "It's not the symbol that interests me, but the fact that the marks are at points along the perimeter of the *ring* . . . Morumus, what if the points on our map indicate not *villages*, but points along the Dyfanni *border?*"

Morumus just stared at Landu.

Could he be correct?

Morumus reached down and reopened the volume he had just closed.

There's one way to find out . . .

He found the small, unmarked chart of Dyfann. Then he picked up his tracing of Urien's page and laid it over the chart. He pulled the table lamp close to the book. The map of Dyfann showed faintly through the thin sheet.

Good.

Bending low over the page, Morumus began moving the tracing across the map. He slid and turned the sheet in small increments, hoping to find some precise alignment that would match the Dyfanni coast and make sense of Urien's diagram. It was delicate work, and at first he thought it must end in frustration.

The scattered points did not seem even close to corresponding with the coastline drawn on the map underneath them.

He sighed.

Then he saw his mistake.

He had assumed that the bottom of Urien's page, where she had written the caption, corresponded to cardinal south on the map of Dyfann. That was why none of the points aligned. But when he rotated Urien's caption to the east . . .

"Landu, *look*!"

The alignment was almost perfect. West of the Gwyllinor Mountains, ten prominent vertices defined the Dyfanni coast. Urien's diagram inked a dark point near each of them. There were minor discrepancies, but Morumus could see at a glance that the culprit was nothing more than the slight variation in scale between the two sheets.

The circle made of square crosses overlaid a spot in the country's interior near the northwest coast.

Landu moved around the table, saw the result, and grinned. "Morumus, you found it!"

"*We* found it, Landu. To think of coastline rather than villages was your idea."

"But I would have never thought to turn the map—"

Morumus forestalled further argument with a raised hand. "We will share the credit, how's that? In the meantime, we've got to transpose this location onto a more detailed chart." Morumus looked at the books stacked on the table. "Where's that map you had an hour ago?"

"I put it back." Landu was still smiling as he walked away to fetch the reshelved volume. "But I remember where."

Morumus felt an upward tug at the corners of his own mouth.

They *had* done it.

The Ring of Stars.

It took another hour of careful labor to transpose the location of the Ring from the unmarked to the more detailed map. Morumus and Landu had little experience in cartography, and they made several mistakes in the course of marking angles, measuring relative distances, and multiplying everything for scale. But they were beaming when they brought the results to the king.

They found Haedorn and Heclaid in the latter's private study. The two warriors were going over a stack of troop musters and commissary reports when the two monks entered. The king looked up as the door opened, the lines of irritation plain on his features.

"What is it now?" But the lines faded as he saw the monks. "Ah, Morumus." The king smiled. "Forgive me, my boy. We've had a flood of interruptions this morning."

"Yes, sire." Morumus bowed. "I apologize for the further intrusion, but . . ." He gestured to Landu, who carried a roll of parchment. "We've found it, sire. We've found the Ring of Stars!"

For a moment, both Heclaid and Haedorn said nothing. Standing beside him, Haedorn blinked. "You've . . . found it?"

Morumus looked at Landu. "Show them, brother."

Haedorn made a space on the broad desk, and Landu unrolled the parchment. All four men leaned over the copied map of Dyfann.

"There." Morumus jabbed his finger at a point about twenty leagues from the northwest coast. The location indicated by Urien's chart corresponded to a place where a minor waterway made a slight bulge in its course toward the ocean. None of the available maps had indicated a settlement within a week's journey.

"It's remote," Haedorn observed.

"Yes." Morumus gestured to the contour lines flanking the watercourse. "It appears to be a deep vale of some sort."

"A three days' journey from the coast." The king rubbed his grey-flecked beard. "A small squad of men, traveling light, could make it undetected."

"I will go, sire," said Morumus. "I'm no warrior and I would be of little use to you or to Oethur in the war to the east. But, in this, I believe I might prove adequate."

Heclaid looked at him. "By my honor, Morumus, I have little doubt. But you cannot go alone."

"I will go too, sire." Landu's face was grim. "My own honor demands I make some return to the Mordruui for what they did at Urras."

The king nodded. "You shall have your wish as well, my son. Even so . . ."

"I will go, sire." Haedorn's eyes flashed. "I too have a debt to collect from the Dree."

Heclaid shook his head. "That is impossible, Lord Haedorn. I need you by my side in the eastern campaign."

"You flatter me, sire." Haedorn inclined his head. "But you have many capable thanes—several of whom are far more experienced captains than I. I am not essential to the success of the eastern campaign. But in this"—he gestured to the map—"my presence could prove pivotal. The more men we send, the greater the risk of detection. But if just we three were to go . . ."

The king's face looked stubborn, but so did Haedorn's—and the latter pressed on before the former could respond. "And besides all this, sire, this is a matter of the highest honor for me. For more than ten years, I have allowed my father's murder to go unanswered. Morumus has acted—both in Caeldora and at Cuuranyth—while I have done nothing." Haedorn's eyes burned like green fire. "A man cannot let his little brother bear all the risk and still count himself worthy to be a king's thane. Sire, if I do not go this time . . . then I fear I must surrender my title."

For a full minute, silence descended on the study. A long, searching look passed between Heclaid and Haedorn. Noble blood flowed in both men's veins, and Morumus could sense the tension. The king's authority commanded Haedorn's allegiance. At the same time, a thane's honor demanded his lord's consideration . . .

Beside Morumus, Landu squirmed. *He didn't grow up in the councils of the great.* Morumus said nothing, but he laid a hand on the other monk's arm. The moment was about to pass . . .

The king sighed.

"Very well, Lord Haedorn. I grant you your request. There is a Trathari ship in the harbor. On my orders, they will convey the three of you to the Dyfanni coast. You leave today. Complete your errand, absolve your honor, and rejoin me with all possible haste."

Haedorn inclined his head. "Thank you, sire."

Heclaid acknowledged his thane's duty, then turned to Morumus and Landu.

"May our Lord grant you all a happy hunt. Much depends on your success."

As the two monks bowed, Morumus felt a chill creep up his spine. *If the Dark Faith is to be vanquished,* everything *depends on our success.*

He knew it was true. Despite their success at Cuuranyth, and regardless of the outcome in the east, the Dark Faith would not be overthrown . . .

Unless the Ring of Stars is broken.

But why, all of a sudden, did he sense an inexplicable cold?

Why now?

Was it just the weight of duty? *Or is it a more sinister foreboding?*

What would they find in the land of the Mordruui?

22

Urien heard the noise and increased her pace.

She could not break into an open run, for that would attract attention. *But if I do not move faster . . .*

She would be caught.

A blinding flash filled her vision, followed by an ear-splitting crack. Along the street beside her, she heard windows shaking. Above her, the thick clouds churned . . .

. . . and burst.

Too late!

The rain fell almost as fast as the lightning. Within seconds, the first deceptive patters had swollen into long, sweeping sheets. The water soaked the cobbled streets of Hoccaster, darkening the stones and turning the trickling gutters into frothing torrents of foul sluice.

She was trapped—at least for a few minutes—so Urien took refuge under the broad awning of a fruit-sellers shop. The young girl minding the open bins gave her a wary look, but did not dare object. Seeing the maiden's face, Urien winced.

Nobody questions a red monk.

Retaining the disguise had allowed her four days of unimpeded travel. Riding west across the Mersian midlands from Mereclestour, she had met no interference along the road.

Even the loneliest stretches of road were no danger for a red monk, for no highwayman in his right mind would dare waylay those who wore the scarlet robe.

Yet the ruse disgusted Urien. She was a new woman now, and her fledgling instincts, reborn and redirected, recoiled from *any* association with her former way of life. She knew the disguise was necessary. But it *felt* unclean.

Only for a short while.

Urien was moving west because she had a plan. She had paused in Hoccaster only for the night to rest her horse and resupply her provisions. Tomorrow morning she would depart, striking out of the city west toward the Gwyllinor Mountains. Another day or so and she would be across the mountains, after which—

"Under here!"

The words caught Urien's attention because of the language in which they were spoken . . .

Dyfanni.

She looked round in time to see two other red monks join her beneath the awning.

"Greetings, brother." The shorter of the two monks spoke to her in Vilguran.

"And to both of you," Urien replied in her native Dyfanni.

Both of the newcomers flinched.

"You too are Dyfanni?" asked the taller monk.

"I am."

"We thought we were the only two from the Motherland in this wretched city," said the short monk. "Most of the chapter house are Mersians—or Vendenthi imports!"

The tall monk snorted. "We're not sure which is worse, Brother . . . ?"

"Firin." Urien used the name of her father's deaclaid.

"Well, Brother Firin, we are glad to see you. Have you been in the city long?"

"Not long." Urien could hear something strange in the question. "Why do you ask?"

The shorter monk lowered his voice. "There is news, brother."

"News?"

"A message from Mereclestour," said the taller monk. "From the Hand himself."

Urien's stomach lurched, and her heart clouded as black as the sky above. She knew what the news would be . . .

"The escape."

"That's right!" exclaimed the shorter monk. "But how did you know, Firin? The bird's only just arrived, and we were the only ones in the fowler's tower."

For a moment, Urien was speechless. She had not intended to speak her thoughts aloud . . .

Now she must think quickly! "I have known for several days." That part was true enough.

"How?"

It was a good question.

How can I throw off their suspicions? "Do you think the Hand of the Mother would trust such an important dispatch solely to a bird?" Urien shook her cowled head. "Why do you think I have come so swiftly west?"

The tall monk nodded, then bowed his hooded head. "Forgive us, brother. We did not know you were come from the capital."

Outside the awning, the storm had lessened in its fury. Seeing the lull, a sudden urge to flee filled Urien. But she could not hope to escape unless she knew more . . .

What was Somnadh planning?

She dismissed the monks' apology with a wave. "It is forgotten. We have greater things than petty formalities with which to concern ourselves today. Can I assume your message carries the same instructions as mine?"

"Yes," said the shorter monk. "Every member of the chapter house is to be alerted. The Queen's Heart will be traveling in disguise. Every gate must be watched, every traveler stopped. She is not to be harmed, but held until the Hand himself arrives."

"Exactly the same," Urien confirmed. "Have you informed the chapter?"

"Not yet," said the tall monk. "Truly, the message only just arrived this hour."

Thank you, Aesus.

There was still time to escape.

"See to it immediately, then." She gestured out at the rain, which was now little beyond a heavy drizzle. "I will go and speak to the brothers at the gate."

"Yes, brother."

The three of them left the shelter of the awning and parted ways. The two monks, pulling their hoods down against the rain, headed east. Beyond them, Urien could see the rising spire of the city's new cathedral. The chapter house of the Red Order was in its cloister. She had been there only an hour ago herself.

Urien turned west. She would fetch her mount from the small inn near the western wall, and leave the city before sundown. The horse would be tired, she knew, but she could not risk spending the night in Hoccaster.

Not now. Not with Somnadh coming . . .

"Brother Firin!"

Urien turned back. The taller of the two monks was calling after her.

"Brother, forgive me, but I forgot to ask. Should we expect you at the cloister for dinner, or have you made other arrangements?"

Before Urien could answer, the storm rallied. Another flash of lightning streaked across the sky behind the cathedral spire, followed an instant later by a loud crash. There was a sound of manic pattering as the rain regained its former intensity, and at the same moment a gust of wind howled down the street from the east.

Urien saw the rapacious air whipping at the monks' robes . . .

. . . and then, in an instant of lurching terror, felt it throw back her hood!

For a moment, the two monks, no more than fifty yards distant, gaped.

But only for a moment.

"You!" shouted the taller monk.

Urien fled.

The torrential rains gave the chase an eerie, isolated feeling. The curtains of water moved across the cobbles like inverted waves, sweeping the streets of Hoccaster clean of normal foot traffic. Moreover, the rushing wind made it impossible for Urien to hear the sound of her pursuers.

It felt like something out of a nightmare.

Are they closing the distance?

Urien dared not check her pace by risking a glance.

She just ran.

She was in trouble. Even if she should evade these monks, what then? Could she hope to get to her inn, gather her mount, and escape before they raised the alarm? And if she forswore the horse and went straight to the gates, how far could she get from the city before pursuit overtook her?

Overhead, the sky flashed and the thunder boomed in regular cadence. The sound reminded Urien of drums, the sort used to organizing a marching army . . .

Or signal an imminent execution.

What am I going to do?

Flying down the street like a fallen leaf before the wind, Urien began to pray. There were few actual words. She did not know what to say. Rather, she implored heaven with the inarticulate pleadings of a soul on the brink of panic—and wondered if it was enough. Could such disorganized outpourings actually mount a successful escalade of the gates of Everlight? Would her wordless cries be answered, or dismissed for their impertinence?

Squinting through rain-scrubbed and tear-streaked eyes, Urien saw an alley opening off to her right. But beyond the alley, coming toward her through the howling squall, she saw another cloaked form . . .

Or were there two?

More red monks?

Feeling the noose tightening, Urien gathered a breath and sprinted for the alley. It was a risk, for there was no telling where the narrow passage would lead. It might not lead anywhere. But maybe she could find an unlocked door?

Or a weapon.

Crossing the last yards, Urien wondered what chance she could stand against the two monks. She had fought a red monk in Marfesbury, but it had been Lenu—the little girl she had rescued from the cloister dungeon—who had killed the Mordruui. What could she do by herself against two?

In the end, she never found out.

She reached the mouth of the alley ahead of her pursuers, but as her feet left the cobbled street for the unpaved alley, they plunged into a wide puddle of muck and mud—and slipped. Almost before she realized it, Urien was flying forward. She hit the ground hard, her hands scraping against its rough scree.

Before she could get up, the red monks were there.

"Get her!" The voice of the taller one sounded only moments before the hands of the shorter monk closed on her shoulders. "Get her up."

But Urien was not finished. Feigning resignation for a moment, she regained her breath as the monk hauled her to her feet. But as soon as she was sure her feet were on stable ground, she threw up both arms and wheeled. At the same time she dropped down and rolled back.

It was a complicated maneuver, but it had the desired effect. The red monk had not lost his grip on Urien's red robe, but it did not matter, for Urien had slipped out of the scarlet disguise and now came to her feet clothed in plain peasants' brown.

Again the red monks gaped, and again Urien turned to flee. But she had taken only a few steps before she saw it.

The alley was long and narrow . . .

But its far end was sealed with a tall stone wall.

"There is no escape, my lady." The taller monk motioned to his companion, and the latter tossed aside Urien's red disguise. The discarded robe landed atop a fetid midden, quenching its steaming response to the cold rain. As it settled, the two monks stepped toward Urien with deliberate caution, walking abreast to preclude any attempt she might make at a flanking dash.

Urien backed away, her skin crawling and her eyes scanning side to side for anything she might use as a weapon. The alley was full of refuse and small debris, but she would need something heavy if she was to fend off these monsters—a broken spar, a shattered broom handle, or even a large stone . . .

She had one advantage. Her brother had forbidden his Morduui to harm her. This meant that the two monks must take her alive. She, on the other hand, labored under no such restrictions. Aesus forbade murder, but murder referred to *unlawful* killing . . .

But this is war, and these are the enemy . . .

Then, a moment later, she saw it.

Less than a pace to her left, lying beside a broken barrel, was a knife. Despite the deep shadows of the alley and the dark clouds overhead, its blade caught some stray strand of light and glinted.

There!

But the monks must have seen the blade at the same time as Urien, for all three lunged at the same moment. Urien reached it first, but no sooner had her hand closed around the hilt than the two monks were on her.

"Get off me!" she screamed, flailing and kicking.

The two monks held fast. One of them—she could not tell which—grabbed her wrist and gave it a violent wrench. Her fingers opened, and the knife fell to the ground. Then two hands rolled Urien onto her back, and another pair pinned her wrists to the ground.

She looked up, and saw the taller monk stooping over her.

"There is no escape, my lady. You will not be harmed, but you are coming with us."

Urien glowered, and was about to spit when a new voice sounded.

"Unhand that lady, you villains!"

Urien lifted her head and looked. There, standing silhouetted against the light at the mouth of the alley, were two forms . . .

The two figures she had seen approaching in the storm!

One of them was clearly a man.

The second form was that of a large dog.

"Stop 'em, Bane!"

As the man spoke, the dog leapt toward the red monks. Nearly the size of a wolf, its amber eyes burned and its growl seemed almost as loud as the thunder overhead. A wide muzzle opened to reveal long, yellowed teeth.

The short monk released his grip on Urien's wrists, and both monks—with more than one undignified noise between them—fled to the back of the alley. The large dog followed, slowing its pace to a menacing lope as it saw its quarry trapped. Its hackles stood on end, and it seemed to regard the red monks with a dark, feral relish.

"Hold them, Bane!" Then the man was calling to Urien. "Are you able to stand, my lady?"

"Yes." Urien, still stunned by the man's appearance, got to her feet.

"You'd better come out, then."

Urien obeyed, pausing only long enough to retrieve her disguise from the midden. A few moments later she found herself standing at the alley's mouth, looking at a tall man in a heavy, brown cloak. Like the robes of the red monks, this man's cloak had a raised hood. But more notable still, a thick scarf covered all but the man's eyes. Those eyes, blue as a summer sky, now regarded Urien.

"Did they hurt you, my lady?"

"No." Urien shook her head. "They intended to make me a prisoner, not . . ." There was no need to finish the sentence.

"Good." The man turned his gaze down the alley. "Then I suppose I won't kill them." He sounded disappointed.

Urien's curiosity got the best of her. "Who are you, sir?"

The man looked at her again. "I am a Mersian, miss—a Mersian who does not love the Red Order." His eyes narrowed. "Not all of us do."

"Do you have a name, Mersian, that I might thank you?"

The stranger shook his head. "If I had a name, I would be found and hanged. Your safety is sufficient thanks in itself. You understand?"

Urien nodded. She wasn't sure what to say next. "The mask . . . that is clever."

"Take a page from their own book, eh?"

From the alley's far end came angry voices and loud growls. The man's eyes flicked toward the sounds, then back to Urien.

"Bane's getting impatient, miss. You'd best get home."

"Home is far, sir. How long can you hold them?"

"How long do you need, my lady?"

"An hour?"

The anonymous Mersian looked to the sky, then nodded. "I reckon the storm will continue for at least that long."

"Thank you again. If you had not come, they'd have delivered me to—"

The man forestalled her with a raised hand. "Nameless feet leave lighter tracks, miss. Bane and I will hold these two for an hour. Off you go!"

Urien nodded, backed away, then turned west.

Less than an hour later, a red monk mounted on horseback emerged from the thick tunnel that passed through Hoccaster's western wall. Dark stains smeared the red wool in several places, and there was an unwholesome smell that quick washing had failed to eradicate. But if the sentries flanking the outer gate detected the scent, they affected not to notice. Instead, they offered the rider a small salute—grimacing their respect against the pelting rain.

Urien, her red hood raised, acknowledged them with a nod. Above her, the sky still flashed and boomed. Around her, the rain still fell in thick, blowing sheets.

But she had escaped Hoccaster.

Gathering the reins, she urged her mount down the track leading to the western road. On the rim of the distant horizon, the Gwyllinor Mountains waited like a row of low, dark teeth. Urien shivered—and not just from the soaking cold of the storm.

What would she find beyond those mountains? Would her plan succeed? Could she find the Ring of Stars before Somnadh found her?

God, grant me success . . .

The prayer was brief, for Urien dared not articulate her lingering fear . . .

Instead, she nudged her horse into a trot, hoping that unnamed fears—like nameless feet—left lighter tracks.

Lildas's heart lurched as a sudden gust buffeted the narrow ledge.

It was a dark, uncomfortable night. The sky above Malduorn's Keep gave no appreciable light, for the moon was almost new and thick clouds obscured the stars. A foreboding wind assailed his position, and the wall against which the doctor pressed had a damp, slippery feel. The air was heavy with the promise of a storm.

Lildas took a steadying breath before inching himself further along the thin lip of stone that connected the windowsills of his chambers to those of Satticus, the Private Secretary. He wanted to close his eyes, but that would be foolish. The distance was not far, but the height was tremendous. One misstep, and he would plunge to his death.

Lildas shivered and tightened his grip on the stonework.

This is madness!

He hated heights.

And I am no burglar!

But what choice remained?

Lildas was out of time. Events had overtaken his hopes of waiting for just the right moment. Oethur's army was approaching Grindangled from the west. In less than two days, the true king of Nornindaal and his four lords would lay siege to the city. And Aeldred, backed by the three remaining lords and fortified behind his walls, would not surrender. Why should he? For word had arrived that a large Mersian army was marching north to reinforce him. They would not arrive before Oethur—but they would not be far behind him, either.

The situation was unraveling at a dizzying pace. If Lildas did not secure the proof of Aeldred's treachery before the armies arrived, there would be no hope of preventing catastrophe. Even *with* the proof, his prospects were grim.

Would the three remaining lords change sides now, at this late hour, when they have been promised all the estates and holdings of the four lords who sided with Oethur?

Still . . . it was the only hope. If the remaining lords surrendered Aeldred, then the combined strength of Nornindaal—aided by the Lothairins who marched with Oethur—could repel the Mersian invaders. Grindangled was a strong city, and no foreigner had ever passed its walls unwelcomed. If it were defended by a united—

But the thought died in midstream, for in that moment Lildas's leading foot stepped in a puddle of bird droppings . . .

. . . and slipped.

His awareness heightened by the intensity of his fear, Lildas's reaction was instinctive. Even as his right foot slid into the void, he plunged his fingers into the tight gaps between the wall's stones.

It was erosion that saved Lildas's life. Centuries of weather had assailed the masonry of Malduorn's Keep, and in those years the outer layers of the mortar seams flaked and crumbled. This process had left deep gouges between the stones—channels just wide enough for fingertips.

Though the rough stone scraped both fingernail and flesh, the doctor found his grip. There were a few harrowing moments—a near, terrifying sensation—when it was uncertain whether those grips would hold against the weight of his imbalance. But in the end, his right foot returned to the ledge.

For several minutes, Lildas made no farther advance. He just trembled.

Move.

Pressing on was perhaps the bravest thing Lildas ever did. He came to within a sliver's width of turning back to his own windowsill . . .

But his conscience would not acquiesce.

Move forward.

If he cowered now, many would die. Their blood would be on his hands.

"To him who knows the right thing to do yet does it not, to him it is sin."

His duty, both as an Aesusian and a physician, was clear.

Gathering his breath, Lildas took a step toward Satticus's windows.

His plan required that he reach the private secretary's study unnoticed. It was there that the secretary dined alone at the same time each night, and so it was there that Lildas should find the man unprotected.

And asleep.

Less than an hour earlier, Lildas had visited the kitchens and learned which tray was intended for Satticus. While the scullion went searching for an extra mortise—why else had the doctor come to the kitchens?—Lildas dropped a strong draft of droelum into the private secretary's wine. Then, slipping the scullion a coin for the extraneous mortise, he returned to his chamber.

Dinner came. Lildas's chamber was closest to the servants' stairs, and so he had been served first. After finishing his meal, he waited another quarter hour. Then, when he was sure that Satticus would have had time to eat, he slipped out of his window onto the ledge.

A simple plan. Had it worked?

He was about to find out.

Traversing the remaining distance without incident, he came to the windowsills of Satticus's study. There were lights in the chamber, but he heard no sound. Lildas edged his face past the window until he could see the interior.

Then, despite the dark and the heights, he smiled.

It had worked.

From the windows, he had a clear view of the private secretary's broad desk before the chamber's hearth. On the desk sat a silver tray, upon which spread a half-finished meal. Behind the desk, Satticus slumped in his chair, his motionless form silhouetted against the small fire burning in the hearth behind him.

Asleep.

Lildas retrieved a thin knife from his belt and worked it into the space between the window and its casement. The blade caught the latch, and he lifted. He felt it give, then withdrew the knife and pushed.

The pane swung inward.

With a wordless prayer of thanks, Lildas climbed into the chamber.

It did not take him long to retrieve the key. As Aeldred had said, Satticus wore it on a chain about his neck. And with the private secretary deep in droelum-sleep, the only resistance Lildas encountered in removing the necklace was the weight of the unconscious man's head.

Finding the box, however, proved a greater challenge. The wall opposite the windows was a warren of cluttered shelves. Here Lildas found boxes of various sizes tucked between thick volumes and sheaves of loose papers, but none of them matched Aeldred's description.

There was no black box. Had Aeldred lied?

It seemed unlikely, for the key existed.

Had Satticus perhaps changed the box?

Lildas searched again. This time he tried the key on every box, regardless of color.

Still nothing.

Frustrated, the doctor turned away from the shelves and scanned the rest of the chamber, but Satticus was a man of sparse decoration. There were no other shelves, and nothing stood on the mantle above the hearth. The only other piece of furniture in the study was the desk.

The desk!

Shaking his head at such an oversight, Lildas returned to the desk. Were there any locked drawers?

There were no drawers . . .

. . . but there *was* a small locked door on the bottom left.

Lildas crouched beside the chair where the secretary slept. The firelight from the hearth behind them flickered on the polished walnut surface of the door as he inserted the key. There was a *click* as it turned, and the door swung open on oiled hinges . . .

. . . and a sudden, violent hissing filled his ears!

Lildas had only a fraction of a second to lurch sideways before the serpent struck . . .

The viper, a long tan serpent with dark brown markings, sprung out of its confinement. Missing the doctor by mere inches, it turned with terrifying speed and struck again . . .

This time it did not miss.

Lildas gasped as the serpent's fangs plunged into the fleshy calf of Satticus's unmoving leg. The private secretary, drugged and inert, made no response. As though enraged by this non-response, the snake reared back and struck again.

And again.

Lildas scrambled backward toward the shelves. Satticus had confined the serpent within the locked compartment as a trap to any who might force access. Only one thing could garner such a need for protection.

Aeldred's box.

It had to be.

Satticus's cleverness had proven to be his own undoing. Lildas watched the viper strike the private secretary three more times, each bite injecting lethal venom into the sleeping man's veins. After this, the serpent—its wrath apparently sated—dropped to the floor and slithered toward the warmth of the hearth.

The doctor did not move until the snake coiled itself in an empty corner of the wide fireplace. He never took his eyes off the viper as he backed toward the desk and its open bottom door. But the serpent showed no interest in him, and after a few moments its lidded eyes closed. Only then did Lildas relax and turn his attention back to the desk.

There was a small chest inside the compartment, and as he withdrew it he saw that it was black.

Just as Aeldred said.

Backing away from the desk and hearth, Lildas set the chest on the floor and crouched beside it. He inserted the key into the lock, and was not surprised to find that it fit. He edged the lid open, but he need not have worried.

There was no viper in this box.

But there *were* letters.

Lildas scowled as he scanned the loose sheaves, a dated sequence of correspondence between Aeldred and Somnadh going back more than a dozen years. The communications were candid and comprehensive. They described Aeldred's secret allegiance to the Old Faith. They discussed the joint conspiracy to murder Prince Alfered and Raudorn of Lothair. A letter from Somnadh announced the news of his elevation to Archbishop of Mereclestour. And a copy of a dispatch to Somnadh carried Aeldred's jubilance at his father's murder . . .

The letters discussed everything that Aeldred had confessed to Lildas—and several things that he had not.

The doctor's eyes widened as he read further . . .

Of the capture of the bishops, and the use of Ciolbail's token to frame Lothair . . .

For the attempt to kill Duke Stonoric of Hoccaster, whose hostility to the Red Order and influence over Wodic threatened the union of Mersex and Dyfann they had worked so hard to arrange by . . .

. . . killing the High Chieftain of Dyfann, Princess Caileamach's father . . .

. . . and before that, the former Archbishop of Mereclestour, Deorcad . . .

. . . and before that, the former king of Mersex . . .

. . . Luca Wolfbane.

By the time he finished reading, Lildas's skin was crawling—just as much as if the serpent sleeping on the hearth had coiled itself around him. Aeldred's treachery ran far deeper than he had imagined.

And now I have the proof.

He refolded the letters and tucked them into the inner pocket of his robe, then stood. *Now what?*

The private secretary, still slumped in his chair, had gone very still. Lildas checked him and found that the man was still breathing—but only just, and not for much longer.

Satticus would not wake. Given what Lildas had learned about the man's involvement in Aeldred's schemes, he felt little pity. But he was concerned.

With Satticus dead, Aeldred will want his black box. If he finds it empty, he'll know something is amiss . . .

There was only one solution.

Scooping a sheaf of miscellaneous papers from the secretary's desk, Lildas folded and tucked them into the box. He closed the lid, relocked it, and then placed the key in Satticus's hand. Then, careful not to make any noise that might summon guards, he eased the private secretary out of his chair and laid him sideways on the floor.

Having done this, he stood up, took the locked box, and cast it into the fire.

Let Aeldred think his private secretary was struck while withdrawing the box, which he then dropped into the fire. The ashes of the papers would convince him that all evidence of his duplicity was erased.

Lildas waited until the flames had engulfed the box before walking to the window.

Reaching the casement, he looked back. The viper, aroused by the increased heat, had slithered back out of the fireplace toward the prone form of the private secretary. Lildas saw it rear up, and heard its malevolent hiss—

Turning away, he stepped up through the window. Once outside, he took his knife and latched the pane behind him. Then he began the slow traversal back to his own windowsill.

As he inched through the dark along the damp ledge, Lildas's mind raced.

Properly handled, these letters can not only secure Oethur's throne . . . they can stop all the wars about to engulf Aeld Gowan.

Yet if he tipped his hand too soon, all might be lost . . .

What if the three lords won't change sides?

He would be executed as a traitor, and the rest of the correspondence lost or recaptured. *And Wodic of Mersex will never know that his own archbishop conspired against him.*

And then Lothair would fall, and the Red Order would prevail.

No.

Lildas would not—could not—risk such an eventuality. So if he couldn't risk revealing the information to the three lords in Grindangled, there was only one alternative.

I must get this information to Oethur—or to Wodic of Mersex.

Another sudden wind whipped along the wall, buffeting his balance. In its howl Lildas heard his own unanswered question:

How?

24

The pelter of the rain on the roof of the tent was like the sound of galloping horses.

Inside the large tent, Oethur sat drying himself beside an elevated brazier. For the moment, he was alone. Solitude was a luxury seldom afforded to a king—even one who had yet to win his kingdom.

The storm had come upon them without warning. The combined armies of Oethur and Lothair were now within a half-day's march of Grindangled, and he had hoped to have the city encircled by nightfall. Then, in mid-afternoon, a vast front of froward clouds had churned down out of the Deasmor. Within minutes, the sky changed from pale-grey to pitch-black. The breeze rose from a gentle whisper to a careening howl.

And then it poured.

In the face of such an onslaught, Oethur and Heclaid called a hasty halt and ordered their men to make camp. For the next hour or so, the men-at-arms labored against both wind and rain to erect their tents and light fires. It was slow, soaking work—and Oethur had refused, despite the protestations of his men, to seek respite for himself until the entire army was settled.

Yet at last, it was finished. Dripping with rain, all his men-at-arms got themselves huddled around steaming fires beneath shared shelters. Some of these were little more than canvas tarpaulins stretched between trees. But even the barest break was preferable to direct exposure to such a merciless storm.

It was not until he was satisfied as to the well-being of his men that Oethur retreated to his tent. Now he sat beside his brazier, saturated. It would take his clothes several hours to dry.

But he did not mind.

We will reach Grindangled tomorrow. A half day later than he had intended. *But we will still arrive before the Mersians.*

This was the critical point. An army marched north from Mersex to reinforce Aeldred. If it reached Grindangled before he did, then his campaign was doomed. But he was not worried. The storm that had overtaken them—the same vast squall line whose rearguard yet pounded on his roof—was sweeping east.

The Mersians will be caught.

Which meant Oethur would still reach Grindangled first. According to his scouts, the Mersians were only two days behind them. That was not much time.

But it should be enough.

He had a plan.

"Thank God, there is yet time for it." He took a sip of his wine.

"Time yet for what?"

Oethur almost choked on the wine as his tent flap flew open and a cloaked man stepped suddenly through it. "My lord Heclaid!"

"My apologies for not knocking," said the Lothairin king. "But it's still blowing quite nastily out there—and an apology takes less time than all the niceties."

"I understand completely." Oethur stood. He pulled a second chair close to the brazier, then moved to a small table in the tent's far corner, where he poured Heclaid a glass of wine. But when he turned back, he almost dropped the goblet.

"What is that?"

Heclaid had taken his seat on the proffered chair beside the brazier. But on his lap sat something quite unexpected . . .

A sword?

But it was obvious, even from a first glance, that this was more than a sword. For one thing, its blade was longer than any he had seen—and every inch of the double edge glittered with a keen light. For another, there seemed to be a line of strange symbols inscribed within the fuller . . .

"This, Oethur, is a gift."

"A gift?" Recovering himself, Oethur rejoined the king and offered him the wine. "A gift from whom?"

"Every good thing comes from God, and when I tell you how this one came to be found, you will no doubt agree that its arrival cannot ultimately be attributed to any but him. Yet the Lord makes use of means, and in this case he used Morumus. It was he who found this blade, and he who designated it for you."

Accepting the wine, Heclaid handed Oethur the sword.

Taking the weapon, Oethur was surprised to find that, despite its length, it was not as heavy as he suspected. Yet neither was it a flimsy thing: the blade was solid and wide, with a beveled groove running down its center.

An amazing weapon.

Moreover, there *was* a line of script inlaid within the fuller . . .

"What do these mean?" He gestured to the symbols.

"It is a line from the Psalms. 'Their sword shall pierce their own heart.' "

"A line from the Psalms?" Oethur stared at the strange script, recognizing nothing. "In what language?"

"It's ancient Semric."

Something in Heclaid's tone made the hairs on the back of Oethur's neck stand up.

"Ancient Semric? But not even Morumus can read that tongue . . ."

"He didn't read it, Oethur. I did."

"You, my lord?" Oethur arched an eyebrow at the Lothairin king. "You read Semric?"

"*No*, Oethur. But I know the legend of the Sword. Do you not?"

Oethur shook his head.

"Neither did Morumus." The older man snorted. "Do they teach you nothing in these monasteries?"

By the time Heclaid finished, Oethur's head was spinning.

"The Sword of Dathidd," he whispered, balancing the blade on his lap. "*Melechur*."

"It's not magical, but it is strong. It was forged in the ancient past, using skill long lost to the race of men. Legend says that the blade is unbreakable, and the edge will never dull."

"It may not be magical," Oethur whispered, "but it is a powerful symbol. The Sword of Tuddreal—the Blade that commanded the Threefold Cord."

"Exactly, Oethur. Is it anything but the Lord's good hand that led us to the blade mere days after signing the treaty to reform the ancient alliance?"

"I cannot believe it was coincidence."

"Nor I." Heclaid's eyes flashed as they fixed upon Oethur. "By the hand of God, both Sword and Cord are now in your keeping, my son. Wield them well. When we reach the city tomorrow, you must raise the ancient standard—Rhianwyn has had the banner made in secret—and raise the ancient Sword. Call out your brother to face justice—not just the justice of

Nornindaal, but the justice of all the North. You fight now not just for the vindication of your late father and brother, Oethur, but for the vindication of the True Faith. All the defenders of Grindangled will see and hear that—though Aeldred himself will doubtless remain cowering behind his walls."

"He will not remain in the city, my lord."

"He will not?" The king frowned. "You think he will flee?"

"No, he will never flee. Even if he would, where could he go? Our Grendannathi brothers approach from the north, and his Mersian allies march from the south."

"But if he does not intend to flee, why would he ever leave the city?"

"Because I will demand Nuorn's Justice."

It was midnight, and the Trathari Sea had become a nightmare.

Less than an hour earlier, the men keeping watch over the ship had dozed at their posts. The daylight hours had seen some of the smoothest sailing they had enjoyed this season, and the languid memories of balmy sweetness had lulled the sailors into insensibility. Now everyone aboard was wide awake, wide-eyed, and struggling for his life.

The storm was all around them: a vast, violent darkness that seemed intent on crushing the small vessel. Above them, the moon and stars had vanished behind the impenetrable gloom of the great clouds. Around them, the once-becalmed sea now frothed and reared like a herd of mad horses.

The horizon no longer existed. Heaving waves formed terrible mountains above the mast and riggings, and the entire ship canted dangerously as it surged up the slopes. Then the crest of the mountains would break, releasing an avalanche of water that submerged the deck for long moments before the ship resurfaced. For a few heartbeats after this, there would be a slight lull as the ship sloped down into the next trough.

Then the whole cycle would repeat . . .

Over and over again, the storm battered the small ship. And with every blow, Morumus wondered whether *this* would be the time when he lost his grip and plunged into the sea.

He, Haedorn, and Landu had wrapped their arms and legs into the shrouds of the mainmast's rigging. They came above decks with the rest of the crew when the storm began, intent to help where they could. But as the magnitude of their peril became evident, the three landsmen were told to stand clear—and hang on!

Now, Haedorn pushed his face closer to Morumus's ear. He had to shout in order to be heard. "I don't know if we're going to make it through this time, little brother!"

Morumus turned, but it was too dark for him to make out anything more than a shadowed outline of his brother's features. Still, from what he could see . . . he sensed more resignation than fear.

"I hope you are wrong, Haedorn!" he shouted back above the screaming gale. "We've still got work to do!"

The Ring of Stars.

And they were so close!

That evening, just as the sun was setting, the Trathari captain had pointed to a dark mass on the eastern horizon.

"The coast of Dyfann, lad. And right about the middle is the mouth of that river where you're wanting us to land you . . ."

From the mouth of the river, it would be but a three days' journey inland.

Three days, and their journey would be at an end.

Only now, they might never see it.

O Lord, surely you have not brought us this far . . . only to have us fail?

Another massive wave broke, interrupting his prayer as it sent a cascade of dark water pummeling down upon the three landsmen. Morumus had just enough time to close his eyes and clench his fists before he was submerged beneath the salty water. The descending breaker tore at him with horrible ferocity, and his chest ached with the effort of holding his breath against the crushing force of the water. It seemed forever that he was thus squeezed, and he was sure that this time he *must* succumb . . .

But in the next moment, the water was gone and he was breathing air.

Free again.

But for how long?

The ship had finished its downward journey, and already was beginning to climb the next wave.

"Morumus!"

This time the voice came from his other side. It sounded terrified.

"Morumus, my shrouds have snapped!"

"Landu!" Morumus turned his head toward the other monk. He could see little but a darkened form, but he extended his arm. "Landu, take my arm. I'll pull you to our lines!"

Landu reached for Morumus, and the two men had just clasped hands when there was an ominous cracking overhead. Morumus looked up, and then he felt the tension go out of his shrouds—

Haedorn grabbed him by the shoulders. "The mainmast has snapped, brother! We're going overboard! Cling to me!"

"Grab me, Haedorn!" he yelled over the splintering boom. "And I'll grab Lan—" But before he could finish, something heavy struck him in the side of the head.

And suddenly, Morumus forgot the waves and the wind . . .

Everything went black, and he thought no more of seas, of storms . . .

. . . or of the Ring of Stars.

The city of Grindangled stood on the southern bank of the River Fersk, with Malduorn's Keep built on an island near the mouth of the estuary. A long bridge connected the Keep to the mainland, and great walls protected both castle and city from invaders. Whether by land or by sea, Grindangled seemed impregnable.

Nevertheless, an army now encircled the city. It had appeared at midmorning when the thick fog—made denser by the previous day's deluge—lifted from the river and surrounding lowlands. The city had expected the arrival, but the armed force brought with it something nobody in Grindangled had foreseen. Consequently, many people now crammed onto the walls to behold the unanticipated wonder.

"I thought I ordered the guards to clear those parapets!"

"There are too many, sire," said Lord Corised. "Unless you want to use force?"

"No." Aeldred shook his head and turned away from the window—wishing as he did so that he could shake off the vision he had beheld. "Not on our own people."

Oethur's army marched under an orange banner. Upon that banner, three arcs—one red, one green, and one black—intertwined to form a triangular sigil. That banner had not been raised in Aeld Gowan for centuries, yet almost every spectator recognized its insignia . . .

The Threefold Cord.

While the city yet marveled at the legendary standard, the besiegers had gone to work. As the mists cleared, they formed regular siege lines. Nornish companies occupied the forward positions among these lines, with the Lothairin forces held in reserve and guarding the flanks. As the formations solidified, dozens of long ladders were brought to the front ranks—more than enough to attempt an escalade. And thus everybody in the city, from the lowest guardsman in the ranks to King Aeldred on his throne, expected the besiegers to launch an immediate attack.

Yet the army had not advanced.

Instead, Oethur raised a flag of parley . . .

. . . and sprang his trap.

Flanked by his four lords and the two outlawed bishops, Ciolbail and Treowin, Oethur rode forward. Then he unsheathed a sword . . .

"Behold, the Sword of Tuddreal!" the bishops had declaimed.

The sight of the Sword dazzled the eyes of those standing on the city walls. For despite the hazy light of the damp morning, the long blade glittered with the dawn of a clear morning. The whispering on the parapets turned to gaping silence.

And then, in the hearing of all Grindangled, Oethur shouted a single demand . . .

Nuorn's Justice.

"Curse Oethur!" spat Aeldred, stomping from the window back to where his advisors stood in a knot at the chamber's center. "How dare he employ such treachery—Nuorn's Justice, indeed!"

"Ignore him, sire." Erworn, a priest of the Red Order and Aeldred's private chaplain, shook his hooded head. "There is no need to give this another moment's thought. Our allies from the south will arrive in two days, and then you can crush your brother's impudence!"

"It's not that simple, priest." Lord Geraan, the second of the three lords loyal to Aeldred, shook his head. "Nuorn's Justice is an inviolable custom among our people—and the challenge was made in public, in accordance with the proper forms."

Erworn waved his hand. "You Norns have far too many of these 'inviolable customs.' We live in a new day now. We have a New Faith, and it is time for new ways to replace these tedious old formalities. 'The old has departed; behold, new things have come.' "

"A priest can quote Holy Writ," Geraan growled, "but real people live by custom." He looked at Aeldred. "Sire, by now the entire city will have heard the pretender's demand. Those who weren't on the walls will have caught the news from those who were. If you refuse—"

"I know!" Aeldred waved a hand at Geraan as if to fend off the rest of the man's words. "Believe me, Geraan, I know. Before sunrise tomorrow, I must meet Oethur in open battle."

That was the way of Nuorn's Justice. By ancestral Nornish custom, any Norn denounced by another could demand satisfaction. If the demand was made in public, according to the proper forms, then the denouncer must meet the demander in open battle within one day—or else forfeit his life, property, and title.

Aeldred could not help but grant his brother a grudging respect. It had been a clever move, one he might have employed himself several months ago. If he had made the same demand immediately after Oethur had denounced *him*, then it would have been Oethur who faced a trap. Aeldred and his brother would have met in single combat, and Aeldred had never lost such a duel.

But Aeldred had not possessed such foresight. Instead, he had responded to Oethur's denunciation with one of his own.

And thus he gave his brother the legal power to strip away the advantages of a strongly garrisoned, well-supplied city.

Curse his cleverness! But no matter. I will kill Oethur myself—

A sudden inspiration struck him.

"Nuorn's Justice." He chuckled. "Nuorn's spear and war hammer still hang in my armory. I will take Nuorn's weapons and I will meet Oethur. With Nuorn's own spear I will pin my brother to the earth, and with Nuorn's own hammer I will smash his pretty sword." He smiled, seeing it all in his mind as though the battle were finished. "And when Oethur is dead, we will burn him in the old way—and we will use his fancy flag to light his pyre." He puts his hands together. "Rest easy, my lords. In all our years of training together, my brother was never a match for me in single combat."

"An excellent idea, sire." Erworn's head bobbed with enthusiasm. "It will be a potent display."

"The symbolism is fitting," agreed Corised—and even the grudging Geraan nodded.

"But it is not just Oethur you must meet, sire." This time the speaker was Aberun, the last of his three lords. "The four rebel lords also joined in your brother's demand."

Aeldred nodded. Aberun's reminder was unwelcome . . .

But it was correct.

More than a month prior, several weeks after denouncing Oethur, he had issued a second proclamation. In this he declared Halbir, Jugeim, Meporu, and Yorth to be traitors—thus vacating their titles. It had been a legal maneuver, necessary to secure his crown while maintaining the ancient customs. But now it left Aeldred trapped.

"I know it, my lord. We will meet them all."

"This is foolishness!" hissed Erworn. "Without our Mersian allies, we are outnumbered. Behind the city walls, we can easily hold out until they arrive. But to march out . . . sire, that is madness! If Lord Satticus were still alive, he would say the sa—"

Aeldred wheeled on the chaplain. "But Satticus *isn't* alive!" The private secretary's demise had unsettled all of Malduorn's Keep, and Aeldred shuddered as he remembered the appalling sight of the swollen body and the triumphant serpent. "He is dead—killed by his own cleverness. And I'll not follow his example by dissembling now. My brother has challenged me before all Grindangled. If I refuse to meet him, then I might as well clutch a serpent to my own throat!"

Forced backwards by Aeldred's vehemence, Erworn raised his hands and relented with a cowled bow.

"Very well, sire. What must be, must be. But *if* it must be, then by all means let us employ what power we possess to our advantage."

"What do you mean, priest?" demanded Geraan.

"There is power in the Saving Blood," whispered the red-hooded cleric. "And with its help, victory might yet be won." Erworn turned toward Aeldred. "My brothers and I will need a few hours to prepare, sire, but we can be ready by nightfall."

For a moment Aeldred just stared at the red monk. Then realization dawned . . .

Of course!

He laughed, then turned toward his vassals. "Prepare your men, my lords. We attack at midnight."

The calm rhythm of the crashing surf belied the horror of the Dyfanni shore.

It was the morning after the storm, and all along the pale beach were strewn the leavings of the nocturnal violence. Fragments of the rigging lay splintered in the sand, wrapped about with tangled strands of the torn shrouds. Some of the ship's cargo had washed ashore, too, leaving a trail of broken casks and shattered crates from the tideline to the water's edge. But worse than all this were the bodies—nearly a dozen—that lay broken and crumpled amongst the receding waves. Most of them were sailors. But among these were two men clothed in long robes. The brown wool, made even darker by the seawater, clung to their inert frames . . .

A pair of dark birds landed next to the bodies. One of them cocked its head sideways as if trying to determine whether the prone form was truly dead. The second, emboldened by the lack of response, hopped forward and pecked at an open palm.

The hand twitched.

With an alarmed caw, the second bird leapt clear and took wing.

The first bird remained a moment longer, until a shout from behind it caused it to join its fellow.

"Leave them alone!"

A man staggered toward the two prone forms, waving his arms and growling until the birds had cleared off entirely. His red hair stuck to his face, and he cleared away a sopping strand from his eyes as he knelt between the two men.

"Morumus!" Haedorn coughed as the exclamation forced salt brine up his throat. "Landu!"

The figure on his right gave a slight stir. The man opened his eyes, blinked, then blanched. Realizing what was happening, Haedorn rolled him onto his side. He felt the body heave, then heard the gagging as the man evacuated the sea from his lungs. After this there was a long shudder. Then the figure gasped.

"Help me."

Haedorn helped Landu to a sitting position, then turned to his left where Morumus lay motionless. His eyes stinging with a salt not borne of the ocean, he leaned his head toward his brother's drawn face. Morumus's eyes were shut, his lips blue. Yet as Haedorn turned his ear toward that mouth and listened, he thought he could just make out a faint, uneven sound . . . intermingled with a soft gurgling.

Breath!

Morumus was still breathing, but only just . . . there was a lot of water in his lungs.

There is little time.

With one hand, he pinched Morumus's nose. With his other, he tilted back his chin and opened the jaw. Then he took a deep breath, and leaned forward.

"What are you doing?" Landu sounded bewildered.

"I've seen sailors do this . . ."

Taking another breath, Haedorn leaned down and breathed the fresh air into his brother's mouth. He repeated the process several times, then paused to listen.

The faint sound was still there, but growing fainter . . .

He tried again, then listened again.

Nothing.

Nothing!

"O Lord, no!" Haedorn lifted his eyes to the leaden sky. "Lord, please!"

Gathering more air, he tried for a third time . . .

Breathe.

Inhale.

Breathe.

Inhale . . .

Morumus gave a sudden, wracking gasp . . . then rolled onto his side and retched.

Several moments passed like this before Morumus could sit up. When he did, he seemed disoriented. He looked from Haedorn to Landu, then back again.

"What happened?"

"There was a storm," Haedorn said.

"I remember the storm, but how did we . . . ?"

"How did we get here?" Landu completed the thought, looking around the beach in amazement—and shivering as he saw the bodies. "And the rest of the crew?"

"Drowned." Haedorn frowned. "As to the three of us, I don't remember much of it myself. The mainmast broke, and I lunged for both of you as the ship foundered. There was a piece of the mast floating overhead, and so . . ."

"And so you saved our lives," Landu finished.

"Thank you, brother."

"It was not I." Haedorn shook his head. "I lost you both at the end. When I woke, I found myself quite a distance further down the strand. So don't thank me. Thank God."

He stood then, and gestured along the beach at the many sodden corpses. "We'll bury these men first." He pointed back the way he had come. "But we're not far from the mouth of that river where the Trathari intended to land us all along. We are not defeated."

Morumus heard the echo of their father in his brother's words, saw the familiar fire flashing in Haedorn's green eyes. He turned and looked at Landu—who looked queasy, but nodded.

"We press on."

A few hours later, they were on their way. Haedorn led, Landu followed, and Morumus brought up the rear. Each bore a small pack of supplies scavenged from the flotsam, but none spoke. The journey ahead might be shorter than some, but already it seemed long to them. And all three were weary from burying the Trathari sailors.

At dusk, they reached the river and turned inland. As they turned east, Morumus lifted his eyes to the horizon. He saw low hills covered with old forests . . .

What lay beyond their rims?

To land in Dyfann had proven far more disastrous than he could have imagined. What other unpleasant surprises awaited them in the land of the Mordruui?

PART IV

CREATURES OF FLESH & BLOOD

26

Urien picked her way uphill as quickly as she dared. Years ago, as a little girl, she had climbed this same path through bloody mud to a burned fort. Yet today, both dirt track and ancient fort had vanished. In their place, a paved walk of white stone climbed the ascent to the Cathedral of the Sacred Tree. The only thing that had not changed was the sky. It had been leaden then, and today it was the same expanse of dark slate. But everything else had changed . . .

Urien most of all.

Gone was the little girl so full of naïve hopes, so ready to believe her brother's lies. Gone, too, was the daughter so eager to find her father.

This is not going to be easy.

She had not seen her father since that day long ago, when she had burst into the meeting of the Circle of the Holy Groves. The last time their eyes met, Comnadh had knelt to hug Urien. Then he blessed his daughter and sent her off to be the Mother's Chosen.

Urien shivered. *So many years of horror . . .*

She had returned to Banr Cluidan since then, of course. Less than two months prior, she had walked this very path to confront Somnadh about his involvement with the Dark Faith. But that confrontation had gone horribly wrong, and her brother had refused to let her see their father . . .

"In his old age, as he lies moldering in his bed, what would Father say if he heard your words? To this day, I have concealed from him your treachery to the Mother. Must I tell him now that his beloved daughter has renounced the faith of our ancestors?"

Urien had promised Somnadh that she would tell her father everything herself. She intended to keep that promise. Yet now, as the time approached, she felt her boldness flagging.

What will Father think of me?

Urien had come a long way since their last meeting.

She had not just renounced the Mother.

She had embraced Aesus.

And she knew the difference.

Whatever claims her brother or his monks might make to the contrary, there was an antithetical relationship between the Old Faith and the faith of Aesus. The goddess of the Old Faith demanded life, but the God of Holy Writ *offered* life. The Mother demanded blood for herself, but Aesus gave his blood for others. The Mother sold power, Aesus gave grace.

The difference could not be more pronounced.

The New Faith peddled by the Red Order was nothing but the Old Faith reclothed. And the Old Faith was nothing but the Dark Faith. As a little girl, the Dark Faith had deceived Urien.

It will never do so again.

She reached the crest of the hill. Looming above her, the Cathedral of the Sacred Tree embodied her brother's deceit. It wore the shape of an Aesusian cathedral, yet its stones were white and its windows red—the colors of the Mother consuming life. Worst of all, above its double doors hung the great blasphemy of the Red Order: a great likeness of the

Mother cradling a baby in its lower boughs, while two others branches formed a cross over the crèche.

The cathedral's white wall was like a drawn face, its expression cold. Did it detect an enemy? Despite the weak afternoon light, the scarlet windows seemed to glower down at her as she approached . . .

Like a disapproving father.

Urien paused. Maybe she had not changed as much as she thought. Like that little girl from so long ago, she still craved her father's approval.

She looked toward the sky, feeling as bleak as the clouds. *Is that wrong, Lord?*

After a moment, she shook her head.

There had been no voice, but she had remembered a verse from Holy Writ . . .

"If anyone comes to me and does not hate his father and mother and wife and children and brothers and sisters—yes, and even his life—he cannot be my disciple . . ."

Urien had her answer.

It was not wrong for a daughter to seek her father's approval—unless that approval required compromising her greater loyalty to Aesus.

She sighed. *This is going to be hard.*

But she had to do it—and not just because she felt she must face her father.

He was also her hope to find the Ring of Stars.

The location of the Ring of Stars, the Mother Glen of the Old Faith, was a carefully guarded secret. Urien had made inquiries at the chapter house in Hoccaster. Any member of the Red Order might be permitted to visit the Muthadannach, but only blindfolded, under escort. The knowledge of the actual location belonged only to the Hand and his most trusted lieutenants. Learning this, Urien had thought her plan was at an end.

Then she remembered.

The location of the Mother Glen might be a secret among the Red Order, but it was known to all the members of the Circle of the Holy Groves . . .

. . . including Comnadh, former priest of Banr Cluidan.

Urien resumed walking toward the cathedral.

She found her father's cell on the second floor of the cathedral cloister. For all her brother's other crimes, Somnadh had provided well for his progenitor. A small fire kept the room comfortable, and the covering on the bed looked better than most monks of any order might expect.

Comnadh himself, however, was failing.

Urien remembered her father as a man of strength. Though he had reached five decades before she left for Caeldora, her father had never seemed frail. His cheerful face had possessed some lines, but they seemed to add little age. The image Urien carried with her these many years was that of a man past his prime—but not beyond his vigor.

But more than twenty years had passed since their last meeting, and those years told. The once-brown hair had lost all its color, and now lay in limp tresses on a soft pillow. The flowing white framed a thin, withered face. The knobby nose so distinctive to both Comnadh and Somnadh had not changed, but the same could not be said about the eyes. Once, both father and son had shared the same dark, pensive eyes. Now, Comnadh's eyes were dull and pale.

Yet if Urien's father was now blind, he was not deaf. "Who's there?" he whispered as she entered the chamber.

At first, Urien could not answer. For a long moment, she was too overcome by the visible decline. Words failed, and she could do nothing but weep.

"Is that you, Somnadh?"

The name of her brother arrested Urien's grief. The knowledge of his pursuit was never far from her thoughts. Yet in her grief she had forgotten for a few moments . . .

I do not have much time.

"It is not Somnadh." She came to kneel beside his bed.

The aged head turned toward her voice. "I must apologize, sister. I do not know your voice."

"Father, it's me. Urien."

"Urien? Urien, my daughter?" The thin voice shook, the wrinkled mouth gaped, and tears began forming at the corners of the blind eyes. When he spoke again, Comnadh's whisper was hoarse. "Is it really you, my dear one?"

"Yes, Father." Tears blinded Urien's own vision. "I am here."

"Urien." Her father smiled at the name. "I cannot see you, my daughter."

"I know, Father."

"But I can hear you, dear one. And your voice is as sweet to me as the voice of the Mother herself."

Urien's heart lurched. But she said nothing. *Not yet. Not just yet.*

"When I first asked your brother to send for you, he told me you could not come."

"You asked for me, Father?"

"Yes, dear one."

"Why?" Urien asked the question, but she knew the answer. She had known the answer the moment she entered the chamber.

"I am dying, Urien. Soon—very soon, I sense—I must return to the Mother. There is little time."

Little time.

Even as they brought more tears to Urien's eyes, the words spurred her to speak. "Father, I don't want you to die like this." Her voice faltered. "You are not ready to die."

"Do not be dismayed, dear one. Death is a natural part of life. One day we will meet again in the Mother's embrace."

"No." Urien shook her head, as though thereby she might vanquish all echo of such lies. "No, Father. We will not meet again. Not if you die like this."

The wrinkled brow creased. "My daughter, why do you speak thus?"

Urien took a deep breath.

Now.

"Father, the Mother is not waiting to welcome you."

"Urien, you are upset. I understand. But the Mother is the source of all life, and to her all life must return. In time you will follow."

"No, Father, I will not follow. That's what I'm trying to tell you. I no longer belong to the Mother. I belong to Aesus. When I die, I will go to him."

"Ah, my daughter." Comnadh shut his eyes, and rolled his head back flat. "You speak of the New Faith. Your brother has told me about it. Worshipping the Mother through her son. But underneath, it is all the same."

"Somnadh is right, Father. The New Faith is no different from the Old. But that is not what I mean when I say that I belong to Aesus."

The unseeing eyes reopened. "I do not understand, Urien."

"Father, there's no easy way to say this."

"Urien, I am your father. There is no need to spare me with soft words."

Urien steeled herself. "It is a lie, Father. The Old Faith, the New Faith—all of it. Using Aesus to worship the Mother is no better than worshipping the Mother by herself . . ." She hesitated, knowing the next words carried the real sting. "Because the Mother is no goddess at all. It is just a tree."

When Comnadh spoke again, the frail voice quavered. "Your words unsettle me, my daughter."

"I know, Father. And I have no desire to hurt you—"

"I have but a little time left, Urien . . ." His voice was growing fainter.

"There is still time, Father! Turn to Aesus. He is not like the Mother. He will receive you even now, if you will but trust him—"

The soft voice became suddenly grave. "You misunderstand me, Urien."

"Father?"

"I know what you have done, Urien." Now the tears streamed down Comnadh's face. "I know how you betrayed the Mother in Caeldora."

Urien gasped. "How did you learn—?"

"Your brother."

"You knew? All this time?"

"Yes." Her father turned his head back toward Urien, and though his eyes saw nothing, they seemed to Urien to be boring into her. "Your treachery is great, my daughter. But listen now! This very day I will die. When that happens, you will take my blood to the Mother. She dwells within the Ring of Stars, atop a solitary hill in the Vale of Hol Fywen, the River of All-Life. Offer my blood for your sin. You will be forgiven . . ."

"Father, I cannot."

"You *will*, Urien! I am still your father, and you *will* heed me."

For a long moment, Urien said nothing. But she knew this was it. *This is the test.*

The realization struck her, and she sobbed for a long moment. Not because she was tempted to go back to the Mother, but because she knew—now she *knew*—that she would not.

She *could* not.

I belong to Another.

"No, Father," Urien said at last, shaking her head. "I will not take your blood. I have already been forgiven by the blood of Aesus."

"Urien!" Comnadh wheezed, and as his breaths became agitated rasps, Urien knew they would be his last.

"Father, please! You must not die trusting in the Mother. Turn to Aesus—he is your only hope!"

"No." With the final vestiges of his strength, Comnadh turned his face away from his daughter. "I will not betray the faith of my ancestors."

And with these words, Urien's father breathed his last.

Urien never knew how long she knelt beside that bed . . . moaning, sobbing . . .

Heartbroken.

But when at last she found the strength to stand, she was resolved. *No daughter of Dyfann shall ever need to endure this sort of loss again.*

She would go the Vale of Hol Fywen.

She would find the Mother within the Ring of Stars.

And she would burn the white tree, as she had burned the sapling in Caeldora.

She could not change hearts. But she would break the Dark Faith.

Aesus, give me the strength to see it done!

With a last glance at her father's body, she turned toward the door . . .

. . . and stopped dead.

The door of her father's cell stood barred . . .

. . . by her brother.

Dusk descended over the Vale of Hol Fywen. To the west, the long horizon was a blazing tapestry of deep oranges and textured reds. The vestigial sunlight settled slowly, and as it faded, stars began to emerge above the cloudless eastern skyline. These were a vast host, but they gathered by ones and twos: distant diamonds blinking themselves awake amidst the deepening gloom.

It was a glorious evening.

Haedorn, Landu, and Morumus made camp near the top of a waterfall. They had spent most of the afternoon scaling the rugged heights that flanked it—hours of climbing through a permeating mist, clinging desperately to damp holds while their feet inched along slick ledges. It had been harrowing work. Yet by the grace of God, the three men had survived. Now they intended to glean some return for their labor. For their bivouac they selected a strip of turf about a hundred yards from the forest edge. There, under the lee of a rocky knoll overlooking the brink, they would rest until dawn—and let the crashing roar of the falling water lull them to sleep.

It would be a pleasant night.

Morumus sang as he carried the bundle of sticks back toward the camp. For the first time in weeks, his heart felt almost cheerful. It was not just the rich vista that buoyed his spirit . . .

We are almost there.

More than anything else, it was this thought that made Morumus sing. From its beginning on that black night in the Mathway Vale, his private war against the Dark Faith had spanned almost half his life. Now at last, on this burgeoning night high in the Vale of Hol Fywen, the end was in sight. God willing, they would reach the Ring of Stars tomorrow.

Tomorrow.

By this time tomorrow, he would finish the war.

The Dree had won most of the early battles. They had murdered his father and Oethur's brother. They had slaughtered Abbot Grahem, stabbed Bishop Anathadus, and butchered the brothers of Lorudin Abbey. They had slain Donnach, sacrificed children, and subverted nations.

For all this, the enemy had suffered but few losses. Ulwilf had died, and Urien escaped. The Mother in Caeldora had burned. Cuuranyth was overthrown.

Yet the Ring of Stars still stood.

And even now, the armies of Mersex marched to reinforce Aeldred in Grindangled. The future of Aeld Gowan stood poised on the edge of a sword. Each stroke and counterstroke caused a precarious lurch. Yet so far, neither side had landed a killing blow.

In the next few days, all that would change.

Oethur's army would attack Grindangled. Morumus did not doubt his friend's courage or the valor of his men, but the Norns had built the walls of their city thick. Garrisoned by the combined forces of three lords and Aeldred's royal guards, the tops of those walls would bristle with steel. Oethur's resolve had not flagged, but he had confessed to Morumus his doubts . . .

"If I cannot goad Aeldred to come out, the assault might fail. And even if I do lure him out . . . I might fail."

"What do you mean?"

"We sparred often as kids, Morumus."

"So? What has that got to do with anything?"

"Aeldred is a fiend in battle. The weapon does not matter. He excels with them all. I never beat him. Ever."

"You'll win this time, Oethur."

"I know I must—but I do not know if I will. If all else fails, I will sacrifice myself to destroy him. If that should happen, promise me you will protect Rhianwyn . . ."

Morumus frowned at the grim recollection. It had been an unsettling conversation, and he did not like to think of it. Yet what if Oethur was correct?

What if the assault on Grindangled failed?

He shook his head. Either way, there was nothing he could do . . .

Not in Nornindaal.

But in Dyfann, he would act. Tomorrow, God willing, they would reach the Ring of Stars. And when they did, Morumus himself would lay mortal fire to the roots of Genna.

The last Mother of the Dree would burn.

Tomorrow . . .

The Dark Faith would lose everything.

It was almost dark when Morumus returned to the camp.

The gathered firewood he carried was of three sorts. The first was an assemblage of thin twigs. These would be sliced and snapped for kindling. The second was a collection of more substantial branches. These would form the fire's base. Finally there were a handful of long, thick limbs. These they would feed to the flames by inches, providing for steady light and warmth throughout the cool hours of the night. Overall, it was a most adequate supply of wood—if a bit awkward to hold together, and more than a bit bulky to transport.

Perhaps it was the preoccupation with hefting his burden that caused Morumus to miss the first signs of trouble. Or perhaps it was simply the fading light. Either way, he did not perceive the danger until it was too late.

He left the edge of the forest and had crossed halfway to the camp before he realized what was happening. Then his foot caught on the edge of a moss-concealed rock, and he stumbled. He almost lost both his balance and his bundle. It was only after he recovered the former and rearranged the latter that he saw his brother at the very edge of the falls. Haedorn was standing with his back to the camp, looking out over the dusk-draped country to the west. Meanwhile, the sound of his movements concealed by the roar of the water, Landu stepped toward Haedorn . . .

With a raised knife!

"Haedorn! Behind you!" Morumus did not understand what was happening, but a knife in the back needed no interpretation.

The sudden shout caught both men off-guard. Landu's head wheeled toward the sound. For the briefest moment, the dark monk flashed Morumus a look of fierce triumph. Then, with lethal speed, he turned back to his attack. Meanwhile, Haedorn too was turning . . .

But too slowly!

Morumus's heart lurched. Had the sound of the water muffled his warning?

"Watch out! He's got a knife!"

It was a long, dull-looking weapon, but sharpened stone could kill just as surely as honed steel. And at such close range, how could it fail?

The blade fell.

At the last possible instant, Haedorn sensed the danger. With the speed of a trained warrior, he took a short step backward—

The blade struck empty space . . .

But so had Haedorn's foot!

Haedorn had been standing at the very edge of the falls. When the warning came, he had turned in place, but when he saw the falling blade, his instinct had sent him back . . .

Over the brink.

"Haedorn!" Morumus's yell seemed to make time slow, but it could not turn time back.

For a moment, Haedorn's arms wheeled as he tried to regain his balance, but it was no good. In the last instant, the two sons of Raudorn Red-Fist locked eyes. Morumus saw surprise in his brother's expression. Surprise, and something else besides . . .

Affection.

Good-bye, Morumus.

And then he fell.

Haedorn, Lord of Aban-Tur, Warden of the Upper Mathway, vanished into the void.

"No!"

Morumus heard the forlorn anguish in his voice. *This cannot be happening!* He had lost his father to an ambush in the dark . . .

And now his brother, too?

"Haedorn!" He began to weep. "Oh my brother, no!" He turned streaming eyes to the star-speckled sky. "Lord! Sweet Aesus, no!"

But heaven did not answer.

The only response came from Landu. "I don't expect either will answer, Morumus." The false monk still held the stone knife and spread his hands with a sardonic grin. "They never do!"

"Landu." Morumus spat the name like a curse. He felt his eyes go dry. *I will weep later. After . . .*

He threw his bundle to the ground. The sticks clattered as they tumbled onto the grass, and he waited till they settled before reaching down to lift the longest, thickest branch. The makeshift stave was as long as his height, thick as his fist, and more or less straight. He hefted it with both hands, testing the weight and balance.

This will do . . .

With a savage growl, he stepped toward Landu.

Landu raised his knife. "You are a fool, Morumus."

The two men began circling on the turf.

"I was foolish to trust you."

"Yes, you were. You all were!" The man's laughter was harsh. "But it's not so surprising, I suppose." Landu made a dismissive gesture with his knife. "What can one expect, from a faith that emphasizes *humility* and *trust?*"

Morumus saw his opportunity. In his exaggeration, the betrayer had lifted his guard. Morumus sprang forward, thrusting with the stave at Landu's unguarded middle.

It almost worked.

But Landu was quick as a cat. With a vicious hiss, he leapt sideways. The knife came back down and batted away the blow. "You are too slow, Morumus." He stepped away and raised the blade as the circling resumed. "You might as well surrender, before you get any more of your friends killed."

Morumus flinched, and Landu barked another laugh. "You realize it at last, don't you? All of these deaths are your fault. Your brother's, your uncle's . . ."

His uncle?

Uncle Nerias?

"It was *you*!" The realization felt like a blow to Morumus's stomach. "*You* betrayed Urras Monastery!"

"Of course it was me. Did you really believe that story about sea-raiders?"

Morumus answered with another lunge.

Again Landu skipped away with a mocking grin. "Of course you believed it. Because the alternative was too terrible to contemplate." Landu screwed up his features in mock horror. "How could anybody ever betray the *True* Faith?"

"Why?"

"Why what?"

Morumus spat. "Why did you betray so many innocent people?"

Landu's eyes widened. "Me?" He shook his head. "No, no, Morumus. I told you already: *I* did not betray them. *You* did."

"I did nothing of the sort!"

"You did *exactly* that! You burned the Mother Glen in Caeldora, then you blew up Cuuranyth. Did you really think you could escape? Did you honestly expect that *any* who sheltered you would escape? The Dree do not forget, Morumus! The Mother is not so forgiving as your precious Aesus! She is a real goddess, Morumus—and a real goddess demands reparations!"

Morumus scowled. "So it was you all along?"

"Of course."

"Everything on Urras?"

"Yes."

"The attempt on Oethur? The so-called 'suicide' of Feindir?"

"Yes, yes." Landu snorted with impatience.

It all made sense. Obvious sense.

How could I have failed to see it?

"And the map that lead us here?"

"Fabricated. The real Bone Codex was burned to ashes."

Of course.

The memory of how Landu had 'discovered' the clue to deciphering the map came back to Morumus with galling vivacity . . .

"Morumus, what if the points on our map indicate not villages, *but points along the Dyfanni* border?"

He shook his head, appalled by the totality of his blindness . . .

It had been far too easy. Too simple by half!

I should have seen it.

"And the Ring of Stars? Is it anywhere near us?"

This time Landu's smile was triumphant. "That is the best part, Morumus! We actually *are* less than a day's journey from the Ring. The map was fabricated, yes—but it was fabricated to lead you here!"

I've walked into a trap. And worse, I brought Haedorn!

The thought of his brother—his *late* brother—filled Morumus with anguish. *Is there anybody I love on whom I've* not *brought harm?*

And then he remembered.

Urien!

Every other thought scattered. Morumus felt his heart quicken, and his fingers tightened on his staff. "And what of Urien, Landu?"

The question caught Landu off guard. "Urien?"

"Yes, Urien." Morumus feared to ask the next question, but he knew he must. "Did she really flee, or did you murder her, too?"

Landu's lip twisted into an ugly curl. "Everything I told you of *her* was all too true." He spat. "She got the better of me once, but never again. I will have her yet—and I will teach her respect!"

"You will not touch her!" With a sudden fury that surprised even himself, Morumus flew at Landu. He no longer worried about dodging the stone blade. He no longer regarded his own life. One thought—and one thought only—rebounded in his mind:

I must protect Urien from this monster!

The ferocity of the attack threw Landu off-balance. The dark monk could do nothing but leap backward, and before he could recover Morumus's stave came crashing down on his knife hand. The blade tumbled from his hand, and Morumus brought the staff back to launch a killing blow at the betrayer's head—

But before he could swing, Landu responded. He clutched at the stave and kicked Morumus in the stomach. The blow landed hard, but Morumus did not release his grip.

Both men tumbled onto the turf, grappling for control of the weapon.

For several minutes they rolled back and forth beside the roaring falls, the staff held between them. To release the staff was to lose the fight, and so they kicked, spat, and even bit at one another . . . the brawl becoming more ruthless as both men became more desperate.

Landu was adder-quick, but Morumus was determined. He had failed Nerias and Haedorn. But he must not fail Oethur. And he would not fail Urien. He must defeat this dark monk, and then he must vanquish the Dark Faith . . .

But in the end, Morumus lost.

He did not know how it happened. He fought with all his might. He gave the struggle every ounce of strength he possessed. Yet at some point the fight ceased . . .

. . . with Morumus on his back, pinned to the ground by the heavy staff. And Landu sat atop him, holding the stave across his throat.

The false monk's chest heaved, his face bled, and his eyes promised murder, but as his breathing stabilized, his expression changed. "It's a pity I cannot kill you, Morumus," he growled through gritted teeth and a split lip. "Believe me, I would like to—especially after this." He shook his head. "But I have my orders."

Morumus barely heard him.

I've lost.

Landu spat blood into Morumus's face, then pressed down on the staff.

Hard.

Morumus tried to struggle, but desolation had swallowed his strength. *I have failed.*

It was unthinkable, but the dark monk had triumphed . . .

The Dark Faith had won.

The night closed in, and the stars above him vanished.

The battle began at midnight . . .

. . . with confusion.

The army of the Threefold Cord thought itself prepared for assault from any direction. Despite the late hour, sentries kept a keen watch on the wall of Grindangled—ready to sound the alarm if the great gates so much as creaked. Likewise, a double ring of pickets encircled the camp's entire perimeter, each point of both lines double-manned so that every inch of the surrounding terrain remained under night-acclimated eyes. The precautions would make a surprise attack impossible.

And yet there was one direction from which no assault was expected . . .

A direction for which there could be no real defense . . .

The bells of Grindangled Great Church had just finished striking twelve. The ethereal echoes yet resounded through the city.

Then a sequence of new sounds began.

At first, the noises seemed disjointed. The squeal of cartwheels, the snapping of rope, the groaning of timbers . . . what did they mean? Then there followed an unmistakable series of swooping notes . . .

Whoosh . . . whoosh . . . whoosh!

From behind the walls of Grindangled, small fires leapt into the night. One after another, burning points catapulted over the battlements. They soared up into the dark—bright candles against the obsidian canopy of the sky. Each followed the same arcing trajectory.

At first, the threat appeared uncertain. The sentries of Oethur's army lifted their heads to watch the hurtled torches, and as they did so, many men arched their eyebrows. What damage could such tiny projectiles hope to inflict? Were they perhaps nothing more than a diversion—an elaborate ruse intended to distract from the real attack?

Then the fires began dropping into the front ranks of the besiegers' lines.

Too late did the army of the Threefold Cord realize its peril. Aeldred's catapults were not flinging distraction at his enemies. They were dealing death.

The tiny lights were not torches . . .

They were fuses.

The bombs began exploding. The ferocious blasts killed many men instantly. Many others who did not die found themselves staggering and disoriented: ears ringing, eyes stinging, and lungs filling with noxious fumes.

Thick clouds of smoke blossomed in the wake of every detonation. As more missiles fell, the clouds multiplied. As they multiplied, they joined. Soon, the city lay wreathed in a band of glowing, unnatural fog.

As the fog rose against the walls, the great gates of Grindangled opened. The smoke obscured sight, of course, but it could not hide the sound of the massive hinges. Nor, a few moments later, could it contain the sibilant chants that seemed magnified in the murk.

And it was then that men began to scream.

The attack had begun.

Atop the gatehouse, Aeldred listened as the gates creaked open. Then he watched the first lines of skirmishers—a company of mounted red monks—ride forth through the breach. Their scarlet robes sank into the all-enfolding fog, and for a moment there was silence.

Genna ma'guad, ma'muthad, ma'rophed.

He had barely finished the prayer when the Dark Song began rising below him. It permeated the mist like a great uncoiling serpent. As it spread, there came confused shouts among the besiegers, whose front ranks, already choking with the smoke, found themselves paralyzed.

The viper swelled with venom, and the music rose to a crescendo.

Then the Dark Song broke . . .

And the Red Order struck.

The sound of the killing filled Aeldred's head and thrilled his heart. The screams of the dying formed a perfect complement to the chanting of the Dree, and in the first cries of death he heard the prelude to a great symphony.

The Doom of Oethur.

He smiled. It was a fitting title for what would transpire tonight: the last throes of an impotent faith, the first great victory of the Mother's renaissance.

Aeldred turned from the parapet. "It is time to make history, my lords."

The lords Aberun, Corised, and Geraan followed their sovereign.

The four leaders descended to their army. Men jammed the street beyond the gatehouse. Every soldier stood ready for battle: his weapon sharpened, his tunic belted, and a scarlet handkerchief covering his nose and mouth. All eyes turned as the four leaders emerged from the tower, and at the sight of Aeldred the usual pandemic whispering paused, then—

"It's him!"

"The Red King!"

Aeldred's smile broadened and he looked down at his armor. His hauberk was painted bright scarlet, and just this afternoon he had ordered it polished to a shimmer. Now, in the flickering illumination of the torchlit street, he himself looked like a living flame.

The Red King.

He had heard it before, and thought it most fitting.

He climbed into his saddle, and the three lords followed suit. Then all four wheeled their mounts to face the soldiers, and Aeldred stood in his stirrups.

"Our enemies have done us a great favor!" He swept his eyes from left to right across the faces of his men-at-arms. "They have gathered before our gates to be killed. The power of the Saving Blood has gone forth already to speed our arms and vindicate our cause. And now, I will show you a marvel."

He motioned to a burly sergeant waiting by the gatehouse entrance. The sergeant, seeing his signal, ducked into the door. He reappeared a moment later, holding two weapons. In his left hand, the man held a heavy war hammer. In his right, he grasped an ornate spear. These he carried to Aeldred.

The Red King received the weapons and held them aloft. "Behold, the weapons of our ancestor Nuorn!"

A great cheer went up from the ranks.

"Tonight, we return to the Old Way of the Norns! Tonight, we shall scythe the fields clean of these western pretenders—and when they are gone, you shall have both their lands and their women. Show no mercy!"

Men-at-arms shouted their approval.

"The Old Way!"

"The way of power!"

"Yes!" Aeldred beamed, his heart swelling with the shouts of his men. "The Old Way is the way of power—the way of strength!"

"The way of strength!"

"And I myself shall lead you in this way." Aeldred sat down in his saddle, turned his horse, and spurred toward the open gates. As he went, he called back over his shoulder. "Follow me, my countrymen! Follow the Red King!"

Coarse laughter punctuated the cheers.

"Forward, boys! Follow the Red King!"

Neither Oethur nor Heclaid had gone to their tents this night. Despite the length of the march, despite the fatigue of organizing the siege, neither was able to sleep. Both had made extensive rounds through the camp and along its perimeter, encouraging their men and checking the pickets. Yet even after all that, when they met again near the camp's center both continued to feel the same, inexplicable restlessness.

Now, as fire and death began raining from the sky, both understood why.

"Nomergenna."

Heclaid said it first. He had experienced the explosive power of the dark herb firsthand in the high pass of the Ballaith. But Oethur needed no identification. He recalled the account of Colba, the little boy from the ruined village of Dorslaan. And he had heard Morumus recount the fall of Cuuranyth . . .

But there was more.

He remembered, too, what Gaebroth had reported to Heclaid's council about the way nomergenna worked: *"The herb is the source of their power. Without it, the dark song cannot command you. But once you breathe or drink it . . ."*

Oethur stared toward the city. To protect themselves from attack on a moonless night, Grindangled's defenders had ignited great bales of pitch-soaked straw. Tossed down from the top of the wall, these maintained a steady illumination along the city perimeter. But now, rising against the light, Oethur saw a fog bank forming. Everywhere a cask exploded, the smoke blossomed and spread. As the clouds grew and merged, they obscured his view of the city—and of the front ranks of his army.

Oethur heard the telltale signs of the gates opening . . .

"My lord!" He gestured toward the city.

Heclaid frowned at the fog. "What the devil—?"

"Close enough," Oethur agreed.

Screams rising from the mist-shrouded front confirmed his suspicions. "The attack is coming now, my lord—and the Dree are leading it!"

29

Aeldred's horse stormed through his enemy's lines. Nuorn's war hammer felt light in his hand, and he swung the ancient weapon like a dragoon saber. It sang as it sliced through the air, then cracked like lightning as it smashed life from his foes.

The Red King laughed. Banished were the nightmares that had haunted him these past weeks. Forgotten was the troubling death of his private secretary. The specter of doubt and fear of defeat had fled from his mind.

For now Aeldred was riding into battle . . .

. . . and he was winning!

The front ranks of Oethur's army were in full flight. The sudden carnage of the explosions, followed by the horror of the Dark Song, had plunged them into a mad panic. Those who had not died in the fog were leaving everything behind to escape it. Unmanned and unprotected, they made easy targets. Those who did not die under his hammer fell to the sabers of the Mordruui who rode close behind him. Those who survived the Dree faced his infantry. Very few evaded the infantry. But those who did—those handfuls who managed to return to Oethur's line—carried an infection as lethal as the plague:

Fear.

Aeldred could see the panic spreading through Oethur's army. Men jerked from sleep by the roar of the explosions and the piercing screams, saw gibbering comrades fleeing past them in the dark. For most, this proved too much.

And just like that, the impregnable siege was collapsing.

The grand army of Lothairins and rebel Norns was disintegrating.

The prospect of such complete victory overwhelmed Aeldred, and the battle lust swallowed him. He stood in his stirrups. *"Genna ma'guad!"*

He waved the hammer above him. *"Genna ma'muthad!"*

Behind him, the Mordruui dragoons took up the chant: *"Genna ma'rophed!"*

He would win a great victory this night. He would rout the army of the so-called Threefold Cord. And in the morning, he would write to Somnadh . . .

The Red King to the Scarlet Bishop.

It was a dream made real.

Oethur watched the nightmare unfold. Reining in his stamping horse, he turned to Heclaid. "We must rally the men, or all will be lost!"

The king of Lothair turned in his saddle and flexed his shoulders, a great raven preparing to take wing. His dark eyes glittered in the light of distant flames. "The men are fleeing in two directions. I'll ride west, through the camp."

"And I'll go south." They had but minutes to avoid utter defeat. "Follow me!" Oethur ordered the wide-eyed page, who served as his bannerman.

Without waiting to see if the man obeyed, he spurred his horse into action. Just south of the center of the camp, well within their perimeter, there was a low hill. If he could reach that hill before his men-at-arms, he might have a chance . . .

A thunder of hooves sounded to either side of him.

"Sire!" came two voices on top of each other.

Oethur glanced left and right to see Lords Halbir and Jugeim.

"My lords!" He pointed south. "We make for that rise. Rally the men to me there!"

"Yes, sire!"

The two lords peeled away, turning back to bark orders at their men-at-arms.

A few moments later, Oethur and his page reached the small hill.

"Plant the banner, son, and unhood your lantern. Hang it from the flagstaff, so that all can see."

"Yes, sire." The lad's voice quavered, but he obeyed.

Oethur turned his horse and drew *Melechur* from it scabbard. Then he stood in his stirrups and bellowed, "Men of Lothair! True Norns! All is not lost! To me! To Tuddreal's Sword!"

He lifted the sword high. "To the Threefold Cord!"

The sound of Oethur's cry stung Aeldred's mind like a nail scraped across slate.

He had continued his relentless charge into the retreating ranks. The praise of the Mother was as ceaseless on his lips as the life-shattering blows of the hammer on his foes. But his brother's ringing voice shattered this rhythm, and Aeldred wheeled his mount in a towering rage.

He saw the hill, less than a quarter-league distant. He saw the orange banner, lit by a single lantern. And there, lifted skyward next to the banner, was a long glittering blade. With a growl, he spurred his horse to a gallop.

Behind him, the mounted Mordruui drew rein—and one called a warning.

"Sire, no—the enemy is regrouping there! They are too many. We must wait!"

Aeldred ignored the coward. He would finish this now. *"Oethur!"*

The men of the besieging armies were answering Oethur's call, and gathering in strength to the small hill. Just moments ago, Lord Jugeim had rejoined Oethur beside the banner of the Threefold Cord.

Oethur nodded at the grizzled man. "Welcome back, my lord."

"Sire. It appears the rally is working."

Oethur smiled.

Then he heard the challenge. His smile faded, his pulse quickened, and his eyes scanned north . . .

There!

A lone rider galloped straight at his position. As the horse stomped through the ruined camp, the light from a dozen still-burning campfires reflected off polished scarlet armor.

Jugeim peered into the darkness. "Who is that?"

"Aeldred."

"Alone?" Incredulity thickened Jugeim's brogue, and he tugged at his reins. "The fool! Wait here, sire. The lads and I will fetch his head for you in a quick minute . . ."

Oethur almost let him go. It would be so easy. Aeldred was riding alone toward several hundred armed men. His brother was a good fighter—the best Oethur had ever seen—but even Aeldred was not *that* good.

It would be a simple thing for Oethur's men to overwhelm the lone horseman. A pike for the horse, then half a dozen spears for the rider. Aeldred could be dispatched without any risk. Without any loss of life.

And he deserves an ignominious end!

It was all true. Aeldred was a faithless heretic and a heartless murderer . . .

Then why not?

Oethur shook his head. He knew the answer. *Because I am afraid to face him alone.*

A crown won without courage could not be borne.

Courage.

Courage was not the absence of fear.

It was pressing on despite one's fear.

It must be me.

Oethur laid a hand on Jugeim's arm. "No, my lord."

"Sire?"

"You wait here. Organize the counterattack. I will face Aeldred alone."

"Sire, that's madness."

"No, my lord. That's an order. Aeldred is mine. Do not interfere!"

Oethur did not wait for a reply.

The sons of Ulfered met for the last time amidst a ring of burning tents.

Neither man spoke as they came together.

There was nothing left to say.

Both knew the terms of combat. There could be no reconciliation, and there would be no quarter. Both knew that at least one of them must die—and each intended it would be the other.

Aeldred had seen Oethur coming, and dismounted.

Drawing rein, Oethur did the same.

Aeldred's shield was a scarlet circle, painted with an image of the Mother. Oethur's was a triangle of burnt orange, etched with the sigil of the Threefold Cord.

On the ground between them, Aeldred had tossed his ornate spear.

Which of them would take it up? Whose banner would fly over the fields of Nornindaal—and the future of Aeld Gowan?

Aeldred's weapon was the ancient war hammer of Nuorn. Oethur's, the legendary Sword of Dathidd.

Which would prevail?

Oethur did not know. Fear tangled with determination in his mind, and as they began circling he could articulate but one simple prayer: *Vindicate your cause, Lord Aesus!*

And then it began.

For Oethur, time seemed to slow . . .

Aeldred came at him first. Oethur saw the attack begin, yet was unprepared for its speed. The war hammer came arcing down toward his head, and he did not have time for a complete sidestep. There was no choice but to try to deflect.

The hammer struck Oethur's shield. Its thunderous crash opened a wide crack at the edge of the orange wood. Yet it was not a direct hit, and the shield held together.

As the hammer recoiled, Oethur lunged. Aeldred swung his shield to turn the point—but he swung too soon, turning his shoulder straight into the tip!

The Sword pierced Aeldred's hauberk as though the steel were linen.

Aeldred gasped, yet before Oethur could drive the blade deep, his brother twisted back and aimed another crushing blow at Oethur's head. Again, Oethur had no time to dodge. He raised his shield . . .

The hammer met the shield full on . . .

And splintered it!

Both men reeled backward. Oethur's forearm was numb, so he saw more than felt the shield fragments slide to the earth. Then Aeldred came at him again. A look of triumph glimmered in the Red King's eyes . . .

Without his shield, Aeldred would expect Oethur to fall back, to attempt to dodge the downward stroke.

But what if, instead of falling back, Oethur sprang forward?

He would pass under the hammer . . .

And Aeldred would be exposed!

It was a slim chance. It was his only chance.

Aeldred brought Nuorn's war hammer back, then forward—and Oethur leapt forward.

It almost worked.

At the last second, Aeldred saw him coming. The hammer still fell, but Aeldred twisted his body away.

Oethur's sword slid past his brother's chest, but Aeldred's hammer slammed into his brother's unprotected shield shoulder.

The blow threw Oethur sideways, and he fell . . .

Onto the injured shoulder!

Pain seared through him.

I must get back to my feet! Ignoring the pain, he pushed himself up with his good, sword arm. He turned . . .

. . . and saw the hammer coming down!

Oethur knew it was his death blow. Nevertheless, he raised his sword . . .

The Sword.

No blade could turn away the direct blow of a war hammer . . .

But the Sword of Dathidd was no ordinary blade. Most of the legends surrounding it were spurious. But there was one that was true . . .

The legend of its *making*.

The Sword *was* forged in the ancient world, by skills long lost to the race of men. Thus, its edge *would* never dull . . .

Nor break.

Never.

As the Sword came between him and the hammer, Oethur thought he saw the Semric script glowing in its fuller.

And then the two weapons met.

The space between Oethur and Aeldred exploded. Sparks flew, releasing a sound like the fall of lightning. Nuorn's war hammer, swung with full force, rebounded . . .

While Oethur, holding Dathidd's Sword, stood his ground.

Aeldred's eyes widened . . .

The Red King teetered backward . . .

And Oethur saw his opening. He lunged. And this time . . .

He did not miss.

Parting the hauberk like fire through flax, the Sword plunged deep into Aeldred's heart.

The Red King gasped, and the great hammer slipped from his fingers.

Oethur twisted the Sword and withdrew it. As the long blade came free, his brother lurched forward. For a moment, their eyes met—

But the light had already departed from Aeldred's grey eyes.

The body collapsed to the turf, one hand still clutching the shield bearing the Mother's image. But that image was now marred by a wide fissure.

Oethur gaped.

The scarlet disc had splintered down the center!

Yet he had never struck Aeldred's shield . . . *But then how?*

Oethur's startled thoughts became an awed prayer. *God be praised. Thank you, Lord Aesus.*

Stepping away from the lifeless form of the Red King, Oethur looked back to the hillside. There, in the light of a single lantern, a smart orange banner snapped triumphantly. Its three interwoven arcs—red, green, and black—danced on the night air as though buoyed by an invisible sea.

The battle was finished.

The Threefold Cord had prevailed.

Heclaid rushed to meet Oethur as he staggered back toward the banner on the hill.

"My lord, are you injured?"

"Yes, but I'll live. My brother is—"

"Dead."

"Did you see—?"

"Everyone saw it, son. The cry has gone out. Aeldred's forces are in rout."

"They are fleeing?" He tried to straighten, and the effort almost toppled him. *I have never felt so weary . . .*

But there was no time for rest.

Not yet!

Oethur shook himself into alertness. "Then we must cut them off before they reenter the city! And we must get ourselves and our wounded behind the walls! The Mersians arrive tomorrow. They won't retreat just because we hold the city. They outnumber us nearly two to one, and they won't pity any of our injured as they set their siege!"

"Your lords are seeing to all of it as we speak."

Oethur's father-in-law laid a hand on his shoulder, then withdrew it as Oethur winced. "Be at ease, Oethur. And let me be the first to give you joy of your victory"—his face broke into a victorious smile—

"And of your kingdom, Your Majesty."

30

A dense fog filled Morumus's mind as he opened his eyes, and for a moment he thought he was dreaming.

He was lying on his back beneath the boughs of a great white tree. Torches crackled near his head and feet, but he did not need their light. The tree itself seemed to pulse with a pale, preternatural iridescence.

No. He was not dreaming.

He had reached the Ring of Stars, and the tree above him was Genna—the Mother. The real Mother of the Mordruui . . .

And the last Mother of the Dark Faith.

But how am I here? Then he remembered and began struggling to get free—only to realize that he could not move.

He was strapped to a stone table, and his bonds were unyielding.

"It is no good trying to escape."

The voice was cold, cruel—and close. A face appeared above him, its features unremarkable save one . . .

The eyes.

The eyes staring down at him were pure black—bottomless pits of malevolence.

"I assure you, Morumus, you are never going to leave this place."

The use of his name surprised Morumus, but he knew he had seen this face before . . .

When?

And then he had it.

In the Audience Hall of the imperial palace in Versaden . . . At the Great Session of the Court of Saint Cephan!

It had been nearly a year ago, but the strange eyes had struck Morumus even then . . .

. . . as Simnor, Bishop of Darunen in Vendenthia, strode forward for consecration . . .

. . . as the new Archbishop of Mereclestour.

As the memory of that day stirred to life, another image flashed before Morumus . . .

The tattoo!

As the new archbishop seated himself that day in Versaden, Morumus caught a glimpse of the man's left hand. On the back of Simnor's wrist, he saw the mark of the Mordruui—though at the time he had not yet known its significance.

"I remember you, too, Simnor. Should I address you as archbishop?"

The black eyes did not blink.

"Archbishop is too formal, and Simnor is too Vilguran. Here, in my true country, I am known as Somnadh." He gestured to the boughs above them. "And *here*, within the Ring of Stars, I am the Mother's Hand."

Morumus glowered. "In my country, you are known as Dree. The name means 'night-adder.' Do you know why we use that term?"

"Because you are narrow-minded?"

"Because *you* are cowards!"

Somnadh was unmoved. "You are a tedious example of a tiresome faith, Morumus. Your kind have not changed since Addinu. Always the Mother extends her hand, and always you slap it away. Always you reject enlightenment—too frightened to learn the truth, too timid to embrace the deity without or within. So be it! If you will be useless to the Mother's purposes in life, then your blood will nourish her in death."

"Deity within? Power?" Morumus made no effort to conceal his contempt. "If the Mother is so all-powerful, why do her servants have to skulk about at night? If you Mordruui are gods, then why do you die just as easily as others? And why do your idols burn like firewood?" He spat. "All your power is counterfeit, Somnadh. Your goddess is nothing but a tree—and you Dree are nothing but creatures of flesh and blood."

Dark fire flashed in Somnadh's eyes, but only for a moment. Then he laughed—a long, scornful laugh. "Only a fool mocks what he cannot grasp, Morumus. How you ever persuaded my sister to follow your foolishness I cannot imagine. But now I will show you both how wrong you are."

Somnadh looked away. "Ungag her!"

Morumus heard a noise nearby and turned his head. He hissed as he saw the form of Landu stooping over another stone table—a table on which a second figure was bound between two torches.

Who . . . ?

Then, as the betrayer stepped back, Morumus's heart almost stopped. "Urien?"

"Morumus!"

His name exploded from her mouth, and their eyes met. Morumus saw fear mingled with relief. And something else . . .

Something different.

"Urien, what—how did you—?"

But Somnadh stepped between them and turned to Urien. "Do you yet persist in your rebellion, sister? I warn you for the last time: renounce Aesus . . . or face the consequences."

Morumus was not sure which revelation surprised him more.

That Urien was Somnadh's sister . . .

Or that she had turned to Aesus!

"I would not recant for Father." Urien's voice wavered, and Morumus saw tears glinting in the torchlight. "And I will not recant for you. I belong to Aesus now, and there is nothing you can do to change that!"

"Nothing?" Anger flared in Somnadh's voice. "We shall see, sister!" His head wheeled toward Morumus. "And you, Morumus. Do you still question the Mother's power?"

"There is no power *to* question, Dree. Cuuranyth is gone. And without the herb, you are impotent."

Somnadh returned a thin smile. "Some herb yet remains, Morumus. Enough to show you both how wrong you are!" He called back over his shoulder. "Bring the draft!"

A moment later, Landu appeared carrying a stone chalice.

Somnadh took the cup, then held it aloft. "This is the Elixir of Knowledge." He bowed his head in genuflection toward the white tree. "It will turn my sister's heart back to the Mother."

"I will *never*—" Urien growled.

"You *will*, sister! For once you have drunk the Elixir, you will have no will but what I command! That is the price of your rebellion! And that is the power of the Mother! Serve her willingly, or lose your will! Worship her freely, or lose your freedom!"

Somnadh stepped back, and handed the cup to Landu. "See that she drinks *all* of it." He turned to Morumus. "And now *you* will see the Mother's power, monk!"

But Morumus paid no heed to Somnadh. His eyes were again locked with Urien's.

"Whatever happens, Morumus"—her eyes were wide—"whatever this poison makes me say, know that my heart is true to Aesus!"

"Don't be afraid, Urien." Was he trying to reassure her—or himself? "Our Lord Aesus—*our* Lord, Urien—said, 'I give to them life everlasting, that they may certainly never perish—and none shall pluck them out of my hand.' "

Landu stepped between them and he forced Urien's head back.

"Leave her alone, you!" Morumus strained to escape his bonds—he must protect Urien!—but he strove against stone. "I said, *leave* her! I will drink the cup!"

Landu ignored him.

"Please, Landu," Urien's eyes glistened as the chalice drew nearer. "Please do not do this . . ."

The cup lifted toward Urien's lips.

"Landu, no! If ever you cared for me—if ever your pledge of love was sincere!"

Somnadh had been looking away from his sister's agony, gazing up at the Mother. But Urien's last words made him flinch, and his head wheeled. "What did you just say?"

Morumus heard the danger in Somnadh's voice, and knew, when Landu gave Urien no chance to reply, that he'd heard it as well.

Landu poured the contents of the chalice down Urien's throat. She tried to spit it out, but Landu held a hand over her mouth. Then he pinched her nose shut, and she had no choice . . .

Urien swallowed the Elixir of Knowledge.

The dark monk stepped away . . .

And the potion began its work.

Urien began to shake. Her eyes widened, then rolled back into her head. The cords on her neck popped, and she gasped for air. Then she began to scream, and Morumus saw her back arching beneath her bonds.

"Urien, hang on!" He blinked tears from his eyes as he watched the poison attack her, and he could not help but remember the death of Lady Isowene at Oethur's wedding. "Do not succumb!"

Urien's eyes returned, and her head turned toward Morumus. "Help me!"

"Fight it, Urien! Remember Aesus! Remember who he is, and what he—"

But Morumus's words vanished in a sudden rush of wind. It began high above them, as a light whisper of crimson leaves at the top of the white tree. But then the whisper became a stirring, and the stirring grew to a fierce whirlwind that gathered strength as it descended through the ivory boughs. By the time it reached the bottom, its roar swallowed every possibility of spoken words.

Morumus tried to shout over the storm, but it was too loud.

The torches guttered, then went dark. As their light vanished, Morumus saw Urien's eyes roll back again. He saw her head turning away from him once more . . .

Oh Lord, help her! Sweet Aesus, rescue your daughter!

The preternatural wind howled for a minute longer . . .

Then all was still.

Somnadh stepped forward, holding a shielded lamp. He handed it to Landu. "Relight the torches."

Then, while his minion worked, Somnadh stooped to peer into his sister's eyes.

"Urien," he whispered, and kissed her on the forehead. "Urien, have you returned?"

Urien blinked. "Somnadh?" She sounded surprised. "Is that really you, my brother?"

"Yes, dear one. It is I."

"I cannot move, Somnadh. Why am I tied?"

Somnadh straightened, and he gestured at Landu. "Unbind her."

Landu cut the bonds, and Urien sat up.

"How do you feel?" asked Somnadh.

There was a pause.

"Different." Urien's voice sounded hesitant at first. Then, abruptly, she laughed. "Much different."

Morumus had seen the strange light in her eyes, and yet he had hoped. But now he heard the unwholesome tone in her voice, and he could not bear it.

He turned his head away and wept.

"Hold open the monk's eyes, Landu."

Morumus felt the fingers on his eyelids, but he did not resist. *Why bother?*

He was beaten.

Landu place his lantern at the foot of the table, then leered down. The pale glow illuminated several ugly lumps from their altercation. "I will enjoy watching you die, Morumus," he whispered.

Morumus tried to look past him, tried to think of a world beyond the Ring of Star. A world without failure—without the Dark Faith.

Everlight.

"But now they long for a better country, that is, a heavenly one . . ."

"Pick up the knife, sister." Somnadh's voice was hard. "Kill him."

Morumus heard the scraping of stone as Urien took the ritual knife. Soon, he would be reunited with Haedorn, and their father—and Donnach.

But all of them died heroes. What am I?

He sighed.

"Therefore God is not ashamed of them, to be called their God . . ."

Urien's soft footfalls drew nearer on the stone cobbles.

"For he has prepared for them a city."

Morumus tried to close his eyes as Urien raised the stone knife over him, but Landu would not let him. In fact, the dark monk was so preoccupied with maximizing Morumus's misery that he did not realize his own doom. With a wicked smile, Urien twisted her wrist on the downward stroke, and the knife's trajectory changed.

Its long blade plunged into Landu's chest.

Morumus gaped.

Landu's blue eyes widened. He lurched backward and opened his mouth. But he could form no words—only a pinkish froth and a rasping croak.

Landu clutched at the knife, but already clouds gathered in his eyes.

Urien spat at him, then shoved. The knife came away wet, its length glistening in the torchlight. For a few last seconds, Landu clutched at Morumus's table . . .

Then he crumpled to the ground.

Morumus heard the thump as his body hit the stones. Then he heard clapping.

"Well done, sister."

Somnadh's praise was fulsome as he came to join Urien. "Now tell me, dear one, did you actually love Landu?"

Urien shook her head with no little vehemence. "No."

"Then why did you speak to him of love?"

"It was *his* love, not mine. He tried to force me to marry him."

"But the Heart of Genna may belong to no man. She belongs to the Mother."

"Yes, brother."

Somnadh turned his soulless eyes on Morumus. "You see, monk? My sister has returned. She is beyond your reach now—forever."

For a long moment, Morumus said nothing. What was there to say? He did not want to believe it, and it wrenched his heart to make the concession . . .

But the Elixir had done its dark work.

Urien was gone . . .

Unmade.

"Greater is he who is in you . . ."

The words of Holy Writ startled Morumus, for they rose unbidden in his thoughts . . .

"Greater is he who is in you, than he who is in the world."

For a moment, he did not understand. Then the force of the words struck home . . .

And hope revived.

Morumus looked at Somnadh. "No." He invested the single word with as much defiance as he could muster. "Urien is not lost."

"She is lost to *you*!"

"No." Morumus felt his confidence grow. "You have drugged her. Nothing more."

"Nothing more?"

"The nomergenna gives you control, but it is you, not her. Your words, not hers. Your Dark Faith, not hers."

"We shall see." He turned to Urien and made a slicing gesture. "Cut his throat, sister."

Morumus gulped as Urien lifted the knife. "I don't doubt you can make her kill me, Somnadh." He flinched as he felt the stone blade on his skin. "But that proves nothing."

"You are a fool, Morumus. And now you will die."

"Ask her to renounce Aesus."

Somnadh laid a hand on his sister's wrist. "What did you say?"

"You heard me. Ask her—if you dare." Morumus's spirit trembled as he spoke the words, for he knew they were a risk.

But what other hope remained?

If Urien renounced Aesus, then Somnadh was correct: she truly *was* gone. But if she refused . . .

Oh Lord, let her refuse!

"Ask her." Morumus insisted. "A sharp knife and a swift hand prove nothing. But 'out of the fullness of the heart speaks the mouth.'"

There was a long pause . . .

Did a specter of doubt flicker across the visage of the Scarlet Bishop?

"Very well." Somnadh's hand covered his sister's, and the knife's edge lifted.

"You wish him to live, brother?"

"Only for a moment, dear one." Somnadh's voice was all supplicating softness. "Sister, I want you to do something else before we kill this monk."

"Anything."

The supplication hardened into a demand. "I want you to renounce Aesus."

Renounce Aesus.

The command reverberated through Urien's thoughts. "Brother?"

At his word, she had killed Landu without hesitation. Indeed, even now she felt an overpowering eagerness to obey . . .

It was impossible to doubt, unthinkable to refuse.

But yet she remained silent.

Somnadh's eyes bored into her. They were vast, bottomless pools of authority. Urien wilted under their gaze.

"I said, renounce Aesus."

Renounce Aesus.

Again, the imperative resounded through her mind like the echoes of an immense, tolling bell. The call was inescapable, the compulsion inexorable.

Her pulse quickened, and sweat formed on her brow. *I must obey.* Urien opened her mouth to speak, but her breath caught.

No.

The countersuggestion was tiny, almost unnoticeable against the tingling of her spine and the prickling heat all over her skin. But it was persistent.

No.

"Urien." Somnadh's voice stiffened. "Look at me, dear one."

Urien looked, but she did not see her brother . . .

She saw Abbess Nahenna.

She saw the abbess as she had appeared just before her death: agonized and eyeless, stretched upon the rack in a Merecles-tour dungeon. The last pains had seized Nahenna, and she had whispered to Urien through gritted teeth, *"It won't be long now, dear . . .*

" . . . there is light to this day, because God speaks."

The vision shifted, and Urien knelt beside her father's deathbed in Banr Cluidan. Comnadh's blind eyes bored into her.

"Offer my blood for your sin. You will be forgiven . . ."

"Father, I cannot . . ."

"You will, Urien! I am still your father, and you will heed me!"

The vision shifted again. Now at last she was back within the Ring of Stars—back beneath the boughs of Genna. Now again she saw Somnadh, heard the anger in his voice.

"Renounce Aesus, Urien! I *command* it!"

Urien shivered one last time . . .

And then she spoke.

"No."

Urien whispered the one word, then she looked up.

Morumus saw the change, and his heart leapt.

But if Urien's face was again clear, Somnadh's was the opposite. His brow furrowed, his cheeks trembled, and his eyes narrowed to obsidian slits. "Do as I say, Urien! You must obey me! The Elixir has bound your will to mine!"

Urien shook her head. "For a time, that was true. But it is true no longer."

"It is true still!" Somnadh growled. Then his voice shifted... becoming less guttural, and more sibilant. And as it changed, it grew—swelling until its writhing malice rebounded off the Ring's standing stones.

The Dark Song!

Then, from the midst of the shadow's anthem, the serpent spoke: "Raise the knife, Urien." Somnadh jabbed a finger at Morumus. "Cut his throat!"

Urien raised the hand holding the knife, and Morumus's heart slipped . . .

But he need not have worried.

Urien tossed the knife away.

The Song reared with such palpable malice that even the torchlight seemed to dim.

"Pick it up!"

"No, Somnadh—I will *not*!"

The clear force of Urien's words snapped the Song, and Somnadh reeled backward as though struck. While he staggered, his sister scooped up the lamp at Morumus's feet.

"I remember who I am now—and what I came to do!" As she had done in Caeldora, Urien hurled the lamp at the base of Genna. As it had done in Caeldora, the glass reservoir shattered on impact. Oil splashed everywhere, and a moment later it ignited.

And then, as she had done in Caeldora, the Mother took fire.

"No!" Somnadh had recovered his feet and now dashed toward the tree. *"Mother!"*

But it was too late.

Flames engulfed Genna, spreading with incredible speed. The ivory boughs blackened, then crackled as the Mother's skin split open. The scarlet leaves flared like immolated hands as the fire found them, then disintegrated into incandescent chaff. The fruit they guarded—the precious clusters of nomergenna herb—exploded as they fell, raining a cascade of burning embers down upon the roots.

A frantic Somnadh flung himself at the fire, heedless of the danger to himself. He tore the scarlet robe from his body and used it to beat at the flames.

"Genna ma'muthad! Do not leave me, Mother!"

Bound fast to his table, Morumus could do little but watch. But watch he did, for his eyes beheld a great wonder . . .

The Pyre of Genna.

Morumus had read the tapestries in Cuuranyth. He knew what the Dree believed about the white tree—that it was the sapling of the Tree from Adinnu. He did not believe the myth, but he recognized its force, and he had witnessed the power of nomergenna.

But now there will be no more nomergenna.

For as the last Genna died, so the final clusters of her herb vanished from the face of the earth. As the white tree burned, the compulsive power of the Dark Faith dissolved into a glowering column of ash and smoke—then faded into the night.

At last, it was finished. *Finished!*

Morumus watched the Mother burn . . . and wept for joy.

"Morumus!" Urien was at his side. She had recovered the stone knife.

"Urien! Praise God!"

"Yes," she hissed, "but later! We must get away from here. My brother has wardens on the Vale of Hol Fywen, and by now they will have seen the fire. We must be away before they arrive!"

Aided by the knife's keen edge and driven by urgency, Urien sawed through Morumus's bonds in half a minute. Less than another half a minute after that, she had tossed the knife away for the second time—and the two of them were running together, through the fiery fallout, toward the perimeter of the Ring.

"Where do we go once we're out?" Morumus asked.

"Not back the way I came. How did you get here?"

"Shipwreck."

"Ship—!"

But Urien never finished the word. Something struck the back of her head, and she fell sideways into Morumus. The two of them toppled hard onto the stone, where Urien lay unmoving.

"Urien!" Gasping for breath, Morumus rolled over . . .

And found Somnadh.

The Scarlet Bishop kneeled over him, silhouetted against the flaming rain of the Mother's ruin. His robe was singed and smeared, and in one hand he brandished a makeshift cudgel of charred white wood. In the other, he held Urien's discarded knife.

Somnadh tossed the cudgel away, but he pressed the point of the blade into the soft flesh of Morumus's throat. Then he leaned closed, and Morumus could see the madness in his black eyes as he screamed into Morumus's face.

"Did you think you would escape? Did you? *Did* you?" The thin face contorted into a mask of pure hatred. "You die now, Morumus! You die right now!!"

Somnadh's lips curled back. "I have him, Mother! The desecrator will not escape!" He twisted his head to look back toward the smoldering tree.

"You see, Mother? I have—"

But then a most unexpected thing happened.

Whoosh!

Morumus heard the noise, saw a flash of steel, felt a spray of blood . . .

Then he gaped.

Somnadh's head had left his shoulders.

Morumus did not see where it landed, for now a new wonder consumed his attention. "Haedorn! You're *alive*!"

"Morumus, thank God!"

"But how?"

"I swim." The green eyes flashed with concern. "Are you hurt?"

"I'm fine, but Urien . . ."

Haedorn checked her. "She's alive. I can carry her, but we need to move . . . there are patrols approaching!"

They exchanged no more words for the next several hours. The Dree-wardens had indeed sighted the blaze, and it was all Haedorn and Morumus could do to evade them while carrying Urien to safety. It was a long, harrowing night. But in the end, they escaped the Vale of Hol Fywen.

At dawn, when they at last found cover enough to rest, Morumus closed his eyes with a smile.

Haedorn was alive.

Urien was reborn.

And the Ring of the Stars, with the last Mother of the Dark Faith and the Scarlet Bishop of the Red Order, was destroyed.

God be praised!

It was finished.

32

Oethur had slain Aeldred.

He had confronted both his brother and his fear, and prevailed. Now he faced a far more complicated battle.

Nine men sat assembled at the Table of Parley. A few of the faces were as dark as the table's walnut boards—but even the eldest among them had been children when the worn surface was first polished. The round table had stood in the Great Hall of Malduorn's Keep since the days of Malduorn himself.

The men at the table represented the various belligerents in the battle for Grindangled. King Heclaid and Bishop Ciolbail sat for the Lothairins, while Bishop Treowin and Oethur himself represented the Norns. Mannoch mac Toercanth, whose army had arrived at dawn, sat beside Anguth—his brenilad and translator. The Mersians, whose much greater army had also arrived at dawn, were represented by no less than King Wodic himself and Duke Stonoric of Hoccaster.

Last at the table was Doctor Lildas, court physician to Oethur's family. Oethur studied the man. Though Nornish by blood, at this table he represented no army. Quite the contrary.

He represents the only hope for peace.

Oethur gestured to Lildas. "Show them the evidence, Doctor."

As the doctor untied his thick parcel, Oethur turned to the Mersians. "My lords, what we present to you here is a sequence of correspondence—letters written by or addressed to my late brother. The doctor found them among the papers of Satticus, late private secretary to the usurper. It is a long series—dating back more than ten years—and some of these letters will be less interesting to you than others. However, some of it is *most* significant to explaining the origin of our present conflict."

"As you say, sire." Duke Stonoric seemed a bluff man, but Oethur detected a serious intelligence behind his eyes. "But how do we know these letters are authentic?"

"A fair question, my lord, but you will recognize one of the correspondents. May I assume that one or both of you has seen the handwriting of the Archbishop of Mereclestour?"

Wodic's eyes widened. "Archbishop Simnor? He is named in these letters?"

"Not only named, my lord. His hand penned several of the most interesting." Oethur looked at Lildas. "Do you have them to hand, Doctor?"

"Yes, sire."

Lildas slid a small portion of his tall pile toward the Mersians, and Wodic lifted the first letter on the stack. "This is indeed the archbishop's hand. Now let us see what he writes . . ."

Oethur took a sip of his wine and settled back into his chair. He watched as Wodic's eyes scanned the parchment and saw the face of the young Mersian monarch—hardly older than himself, he guessed—redden. By the time Wodic passed the sheet to the duke, his hand shook.

Stonoric read the letter, his eyes narrowing and his features growing hard. When he finished, he looked at his king. "You are certain this was written by the archbishop, sire—that it cannot be a forgery?"

Wodic nodded. "It bears both his hand and his style. The former might be faked . . . but the latter? It is his, Stonoric."

The duke scowled, but said nothing.

"The next letter will be of particular interest to you, my Lord Duke," said Lildas. Then he addressed himself to Wodic. "And the one below that to your Majesty."

The two men read, then exchanged their letters. After this, there was a long pause.

As the Mersians considered, Oethur prayed . . .

Lord, please grant them—and us—the humility to resolve this in peace.

Lildas had met Oethur first thing that morning, the precious pile of correspondence clutched in his hands. Standing atop the Keep, watching the Grendannathi and Mersian forces drawing near to the city, Oethur wanted to dismiss the old doctor. He had been sure that whatever paperwork the doctor wanted to discuss was of lesser import than the movements of the two approaching armies.

He had been wrong.

And thus it was that, well before the armies met, the call for parley had gone out.

Now it all came down to this. Lildas had just handed Stonoric the letter showing that Aeldred and Simnor had orchestrated the assassination attempt—not on the king and queen, but on Stonoric himself. And the doctor had directed Wodic to an older letter—the one proving that Aeldred and Simnor had murdered Caileamach's father, the previous Archbishop of Mereclestour . . .

. . . and even Luca Wolfbane.

How will Wodic respond?

Wodic lay the letter on the table. "It seems, my lords, that we have come a long way chasing the wrong bishop." His upper lip was stiff as he nodded to Ciolbail. "Please accept my apologies, Your Grace."

"Gladly, sire."

Wodic turned to Oethur. "And you, my lord."

It had worked.

Oethur felt like the River Fersk during spring thaw. Relief rushed through him, erasing several weeks' tension in a swift, sweeping flood. In its wake he felt . . .

Peace.

Praise Aesus, we will have peace!

Inclining his head, he smiled. "For the sake of peace, much can be pardoned. My brother's treachery ran deeper than anybody could have known."

Wodic inclined his head. "As did that of my archbishop."

Lildas made a small noise. "On that note, sire, you may wish to consult the final letter before you."

Wodic read the letter, then handed it to Stonoric. The duke read the first few lines, then shook his head and put the parchment down. "I do not need to read this. Previous conversations with the archbishop convinced me some time ago that his beliefs were less than orthodox—not that such matters rest heavy with me." But then he cast a slight sideways glance at Wodic, and his tone grew far graver. "And I have suspected for even longer that the Order of the Saving Blood was a subversive threat."

Wodic met his duke's gaze with the slightest gesture of acknowledgment. Then he turned back to the assembled representatives. "It seems we have much work to do in our own land. Outlawing the Red Order is easy. Exterminating its influence will be more difficult." His face hardened. "On top of this, it seems I have an archbishop to . . . *replace*."

Oethur drew a breath, and offered a silent prayer of thanks. He had hoped for this opportunity. "My lord Wodic, perhaps there is one thing yet on which we might consult. It seems that all our common troubles share a single root: the spiritual bifurcation of this island."

"It appears so," Wodic allowed.

"In the papers of my late brother, I found the terms he offered for your assistance."

Wodic bristled. "I have already made my apology—"

Oethur held up a hand. "I know, and they have been accepted without reserve. But what if we"—here his gesture encompassed all the men of the North—"were to offer you the same terms, with a few additions, in order to establish a more lasting peace between our peoples?"

"What do you mean?"

"What if I were to cede you Toberstan *and* we agreed to submit our bishops to the Primate of Aeld Gowan—not in matters internal to the Church in the North, but as our representative at the Court of Saint Cephan?"

"What are your additional terms?"

"Our terms are but two. First, that you move the Chair of Saint Aucantia from Mereclestour to Toberstan. By separating the archbishopric from your own capital, you demonstrate that the new archbishop will indeed be Primate for *all* Aeld Gowan. Second, that you agree to submit all future nominations for that Chair for the consent of the Northern bishops. If the nomination cannot secure the approval of at least one bishop from the North, then it will be withdrawn."

Wodic's mouth opened and shut several times before he managed the words. "That is indeed a generous offer. These are your only terms?"

Oethur met his gaze. "These are the only terms, my lord. The North does not want a mere truce, but a lasting peace built on the only true source of such peace: spiritual unity in the faith and worship of our Lord."

Wodic looked to Stonoric. "What think you, cousin?"

Stonoric shrugged. "If we chase out all the red priests from Mersex and Dyfann, there will be a lot of vacancies to fill." He looked at Oethur. "Perhaps you could help supply our need?"

Bishop Treowin leaned forward. "That could be tricky, my lord. There are many points of significant difference between the Church in the North and in Mersex—to say nothing of the ill bog which the Red Order has passed off as our holy religion in Dyfann. Your own words make the point: the Church in the North has *bishops* or *rectors*, not *priests*."

Stonoric snorted, but Wodic spoke before his duke could reply. "Then it seems I will have to direct my new archbishop to convene an assembly."

Ciolbail arched an eyebrow. "An assembly, sire?"

"To draft a new confession of faith and canons of order for the united Church. If there is to be a lasting spiritual peace, then the Church of Aeld Gowan must have serious terms of uniformity."

Ciolbail nodded. "An excellent idea, sire. Like the councils of the ancient Church."

"I'm glad you approve, Your Grace—because I would like you to head the assembly."

All the men of the North gaped.

"Me, sire?" Ciolbail blinked. "You brought an army to arrest me, and now you want me to . . . ?"

"Yes, I want you to be the new Archbishop of Toberstan." Wodic's smile was thin. "A united Church will be most difficult to accept among the North . . . but not, perhaps, as difficult if the first primate is from Lothair. Besides, what better way to show the reconciliation between our nations than to appoint the erstwhile foe to a position of honor?"

From the edge of his chair, Oethur nodded. *God be praised.* "You have made a good proposal better, my lord," he said, then looked around the table. "Do we all agree to these terms?"

They did.

As the assembly stood, Stonoric turned to his lord. "Your father was a mighty king, sire. Yet in years to come, I believe that history will record that the greatest accomplishment of Mersex was won not by Luca Wolfbane, but by his son: Wodic the Wise."

From his own place across the table, Oethur smiled. Now, it was truly finished.

The strife had ended in Aeld Gowan.

The Red Order was doomed.

And the Threefold Cord, though newly forged . . .

Had not quickly torn.

EPILOGUE

Urien returned to the island of Urras on the day of the summer solstice.

She had come to stay.

After the translation of Bishop Ciolbail to the archbishopric of Toberstan, King Heclaid appointed Gaebroth—brother of the late Abbot Graham—to replace him. The new Bishop of Dunross wasted no time. His first order took nobody by surprise.

Urras Monastery would be rebuilt.

It was his second order that proved far more startling—at least to some: Morumus and Urien would lead the expedition.

Not just as brother and sister in Aesus . . .

But as abbot and abbess.

Husband and wife.

The arranged marriage surprised both of them.

At a practical level, it made good sense. Both Morumus and Urien understood what it meant to be haunted by dark shadows of the past. Both had lost family to the Dark Faith—and both were committed to seeing its baleful presence eradicated forever.

Final defeat of the Dark Faith was yet to come. True, they had won an irrevocable victory at the Ring of Stars, but finishing the war required something more. Destroying idols rooted in the ground was one thing—and was hard enough—but expelling idols planted in the heart was another thing entirely. That required a power supernatural.

A power found only in Holy Writ.

And so Abbot Morumus and Abbess Urien would rebuild Urras. Under their supervision, the monastery would become a center for the translation and dissemination of Holy Writ—with especial focus on the lands and languages of Dyfann and Grendannath.

Hand in hand, they would fight the good fight.

And yet there was more to marriage than practical co-belligerence. According to Holy Writ, marriage was a picture of the union that existed between Aesus and the Church. As such, it required willing surrender, sacrificial leadership, and radical commitment. These were difficult things, yet Holy Writ promised that those who pursued them in faith—and faithfulness—would find in marriage a deep stability and abiding satisfaction.

Having been married for only a month, Morumus and Urien knew little of such things. They knew even less of what the future would hold. They were only just beginning to know each other!

Yet they had vowed their commitment . . .

. . . and already they were learning to enjoy it.

Urien squeezed Morumus's hand as they wandered through the ruins, and felt him return the gesture. Tomorrow, other brothers and sisters would begin to arrive on the island. But for today, they had Urras to themselves.

She smiled.

Love might prove difficult . . .

. . . but it was also thrilling.

As it so often did on Urras, the rain came upon them without warning. One minute the sky was clear. The next, it opened to pour out great waves of water that pelted their faces and soaked their habits.

"We should get to shelter," Morumus said.

"Where?" The monastery had been burned to the ground.

"There."

Urien followed his finger with her eyes. Morumus was pointing away from the most recent abbey ruins . . .

Toward the ruins of the old monastery, where one building yet retained its roof.

The old chapel.

Urien shuddered. *The place where I found the murdered soldier.* But then another thought struck her, and she forgot about the dead man.

The place where I left Donnach's Volume—

Donnach's Volume!

The book was an unfinished, diglot copy of Holy Writ. The completed half of it was in Vilguran. The incomplete half was in Grendannathi. It was the legacy of Donnach mac Toercanth, and the dying man had entrusted its completion to Morumus—who had assumed it was lost when Urras was burned.

But it did not burn in the monastery . . . because it was not in *the monastery!*

Urien had forgotten until this moment. She began to run. "Come on, Morumus!"

It was not a short distance to the ruins of the old chapel, and as Urien ran the rain met her in long, drenching sheets. The sodden turf squished beneath her toes. But she did not mind. The day was warm, the grass was soft, and the water felt clean . . .

Clean.

Urien laughed, and stretched out her hands to soak up the rain. Her heart sang.

And why not?

The Dark Faith had dominated her life for so long . . .

But in Aesus, I am clean!

A short time later, within the dry shelter of the old chapel, Urien found Donnach's Volume just where she had left it. As she withdrew the treasured book from its high, recessed niche, so too the sound of the rain outside seemed to recede.

"It survived." Morumus closed his eyes. His fingers trembled as he extended his hands.

But Urien made no immediate move. "Several months ago, you asked me to keep this safe for you."

"I remember."

"But I didn't just keep it. I read it."

He smiled. "I hoped you would."

"Did you?" Urien looked down at Donnach's Volume, and it was several moments before she could speak. "This book changed me, Morumus."

"I am so very glad."

The new abbess of Urras looked up into her husband's eyes. "Me too."

And as they embraced—the book nestled safely between them—Urien wept. Her eyes burned, but the tears did not hurt. They healed. For the fire had come, but it had not consumed.

It had cleansed.

The darkness had been deep, but now it had lost all hold on her.

Because in Aesus, I am free . . .

Forever.

Somnadh proved it, and the proof had been his undoing.

For it is a rule worth remembering as long as one lives:

Dark power may bewitch the senses . . .

But it cannot change, chain, or reclaim . . .

A heart set truly free.

FINIS

GLOSSARY

New Terms First Occurring in *The Threefold Cord*

Anguth: a Grendannathi clansman; *brenilad* to Mannoch mac Toercanth

Ballaith: "Strong Walls"; the mountains between Lothair and Grendannath

Brenilad: "King's Echo" in Grendannathi; a clan chief's spokesman

Carrad Gren: a steep hill east of Grenmaur, crowned with a ruined stone circle

Ceilheath: an official gathering of all the major Grendannathi clans

Dathidd: ancient king of the Semric people, as recorded in Holy Writ

Firaith: "Grey Men"; another name for the *Ballaith*

Foorsbaan: an herb used to produce the memory-erasing tincture of *droelum*

Garallodh: a Dyfanni clan chief who assisted in the defeat of Dyfanni rebels

Glachmor: the leading clan of the Grendannathi, of whom Mannoch is chief

Grenmaur: "Mouth of Grendannath"; the place where the ceilheath meets

Hol Fywen: Dyfanni for "River of All-Life"; a river in Dyfann

Isowene: an attendant and friend of Princess Rhianwyn of Lothair

Mannoch: brother of Donnach (deceased), son of Toercanth (deceased); chief of Clan Glachmor of the Grendannathi

Melechur: "the Sword of the King" which Dathidd took from a slain giant

Nebbs: an apothecary in the city of Grindangled

Nerwunaan: an herb used by physicians to immobilize their patients

Olmhori: an Old Lothairin word meaning "giants" or "giant men"

Passiferaal: an herb with strong psychotropic properties

Table of Parley: a great, round table used by the kings of Nornindaal

Tarwu: a Dyfanni battle god who appears as a three-horned bull

Tertullogus: a father of the ancient Church

Threefold Cord: a symbol in which three arcs are intertwined and joined to form a single, three-pointed unity representing the union of the three of the North; associated with Tuddreal in Lothairin legend

Tudbara: "Tuddreal's Barrow" another name for the *Ballaith*

Tuddreal: the legendary king who united the North under the Threefold Cord

Valerisaan: an herb used by physicians to produce sleeping drafts

Yustaan: legendary giant who fought Tuddreal in single combat

Jeremiah W. Montgomery is the pastor of Resurrection Presbyterian Church (OPC) in State College, Pennsylvania. He has been an engineer, an essayist, and a pipemaker. He and his wife have four sons who love to read and a little girl who cannot wait to begin.

Also in the Dark Harvest Trilogy

The ancient Dark Faith was destroyed long ago. Or so they thought . . .

Morumus was but a boy when the murderous shadow of the Dark Faith fell upon his family. Now a devout monk, Morumus has been given the task of his life: translate Holy Writ into the language of those who practice the Dark Faith. His translation could be a great, sweeping sword, used to break its power. But as Morumus and two fellow monks begin the task, dark currents drag them toward a dangerous conspiracy. Shadows from his past appear—in his sleep, on a lonely road, even on the cover of an old book. Coincidence? Or something more sinister? Can Morumus find the secret to vanquish the Dark Faith? Or will he lose everything—even his life?

They said the Dark Faith was dead. They were wrong.

Hidden behind the holy robes of the Red Order, the shadow of the Dark Faith has returned. As it spreads with political cunning and preternatural power, war threatens to engulf the nations of Aeld Gowan. Meanwhile, Morumus and Oethur have narrowly escaped the Red Order and found refuge at Urras Monastery. With them is Urien, a young woman rescued from the clutches of the Mother. She alone can read the Bone Codex, an ancient book holding dark secrets. But even as she struggles to unlock the haunting text, the Red Order sets in motion plans to eliminate her protectors and to reclaim her . . .

More Fantasy Literature from P&R

CHRISTY
AWARD
FINALIST

Forged to kill and wielded to survive, the blade has bound them all . . .

It was foretold after Malek's first fall that twice more he would bring war, and that the last time, the very waters of the sea would obey him and fight for him. If this be so, then I cannot imagine how Sulare will escape his wrath . . .

"A staggering accomplishment. The vibrancy and scope of L. B. Graham's world-building deserves highest praise. Add in well-rounded and memorable characters, thematic richness, and high adventure, and you have an unbeatable formula for success. Ranks right up there with Tolkein and Lawhead as among the best Christian novels of the fantastic ever written."
—***Jan P. Dennis,*** discoverer of Frank Peretti, Stephen R. Lawhead, and Ted Dekker

ALSO IN THE BINDING OF THE BLADE SERIES:

Bringer of Storms
Shadow in the Deep
Father of Dragons
All My Holy Mountain

Historical Fiction from P&R

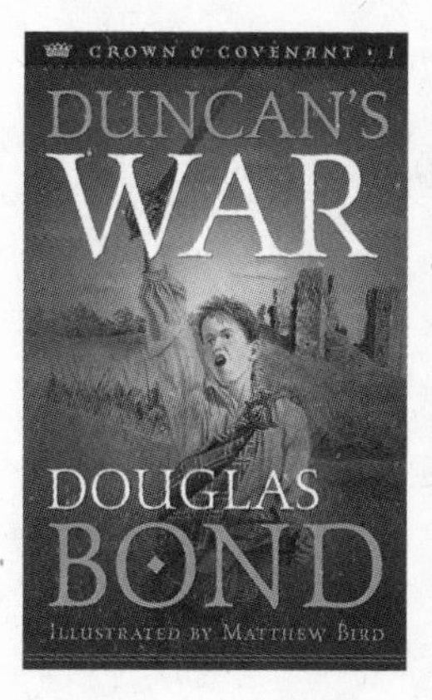

The Crown & Covenant series follows the lives of the M'Kethe family as they endure persecution in 17th-century Scotland, and later flee to colonial America. Douglas Bond weaves together fictional characters with historical figures from Scottish Covenanting history.

"Intrigue. Suspense. High-stakes drama. . . . Educates and inspires us to look back at heroes of the faith in awe and forward to the return of the King in joy."

—***R. C. Sproul Jr.,*** director, Highlands Study Center

"Douglas Bond has introduced a new generation to the heroics of the Scottish Covenanters, and he has done it in a delightful way. A gripping tale full of action, purpose, principle, and character."

—***Ligon Duncan,*** senior minister, First Presbyterian Church, Jackson, Mississippi